'Beautifully written … irresistible intensity and pace.'
BRID CONROY, *MAYO NEWS*

'Capacious, voluble, urgent, readable, translated heroically, and sparklingly.' JULIAN EVANS, *THE TELEGRAPH*

'*My Soul Twin* has an undeniable power and strong ideas … an affecting work examining love, guilt, and overcoming trauma through a couple's touching need to heal their broken childhood.' *THE HERALD*

'Intricately crafted and addictive … An extraordinary, dramatic, and compelling read … The ambitious, vivid, and unflinching translation from the original German by Ruth Martin and Charlotte Collins is in itself a work of art, and deserves to win every translation prize going.' *BOOKBLAST*

'Demonstrates a technical mastery, impressively sustained … more than a family saga: it is an ode, a lamentation, a monument — to Georgia, its people, its past, and future.' BRYAN KARETNYK, *TLS*

'A beautifully written, complex love story … the modern twists and complexities are so interesting and told with forthright energy and compassion.' ADELE PARKS, *PLATINUM MAGAZINE*

'Engrossing … Haratischvili has created a fascinating cast whose lives illuminate some of the greatest events of the 20th century.' DECLAN O'DRISCOLL, *THE IRISH TIMES*

'*My Soul Twin* is full of life and energy, authentic, and to the point.' *DIE WELT*

'A sprawling family saga, to be savoured for its grandeur, scope, and scale … Interwoven with love, loss, triumph, and tragedy are the uncanny impacts of a family recipe for divine hot chocolate, which just might carry a curse … Enthralling and satisfying.' MAUREEN EPPEN, *GOOD READING*

'Truly absorbing, it feels like a dozen little books contained in one.' REBECCA VARCOE, *FRANKIE MAGAZINE*

'An unforgettable, rich, and textured piece of literature.' GEORGIA BROUGH, READINGS

JUJA

NINO HARATISCHVILI was born in Georgia in 1983, and is an award-winning novelist, playwright, and theatre director. At home in two different worlds, each with their own language, she has been writing in both German and Georgian since the age of twelve. In 2010, her debut novel *Juja* was nominated for the German Book Prize, as was *Die Katze und der General* in 2018. Her third novel, *The Eighth Life*, has been translated into many languages and is an international bestseller. It won the Anna Seghers Prize, the Lessing Prize Stipend, and the Bertolt Brecht Prize, and was longlisted for the International Booker Prize in 2020. She lives in Berlin.

RUTH MARTIN studied English literature before gaining a PhD in German. She has been translating fiction and nonfiction books since 2010, by authors ranging from Joseph Roth and Hannah Arendt to Volker Weidermann and Shida Bazyar. She has taught translation at the University of Kent and the Bristol Translates summer school, and is a former co-chair of the Society of Authors Translators Association.

JUJA

NINO HARATISCHVILI

Translated by
Ruth Martin

SCRIBE
Seriously good books

Scribe Publications
18–20 Edward St, Brunswick, Victoria 3056, Australia
2 John St, Clerkenwell, London, WC1N 2ES, United Kingdom
3754 Pleasant Ave, Suite 100, Minneapolis, Minnesota 55409, USA

First published in German as *Juja* by Verbrecher Verlag Berlin in 2010
Published in the United Kingdom and Australia and New Zealand by Scribe 2023
Published in the United States by Scribe 2024

Excerpt from *Melodien* revised edition by Helmut Krausser © 2014 DuMont
Buchverlag, Cologne

'To have your heart I cannot slake my lust' by Ricarda Huch translated by
Timothy Adès, reproduced by permission of Timothy Andès

Typeset in Fournier by the publishers

Printed and bound in the UK by CPI Group (UK) Ltd, Croydon CR0 4YY

Scribe is committed to the sustainable use of natural resources and the use
of paper products made responsibly from those resources.

978 1 922585 07 3 (Australian edition)
978 1 914484 01 8 (UK edition)
978 1 957363 67 7 (US edition)
978 1 761385 35 3 (ebook)

Catalogue records for this book are available from the
National Library of Australia and the British Library.

The translation of this work was supported by a grant from the Goethe-Institut
which is funded by the German Ministry of Foreign Affairs.

scribepublications.com.au
scribepublications.co.uk
scribepublications.com

Fixed, complete, we can understand ourselves
Helmut Krausser, *Melodies*

★

Juja / A song

I want nothing, Juja.
I am dried out,
Like a parched puddle.
And in my heart
It's empty
It's cold.
And the factory chimneys smoke,
And you kiss me on the lips,
But the rain they forecast —
Where is it now?
Today, another drunken evening,
But it seems easier to me this way.
And even the stars shine brighter:
Ro-mance!
And we dissolve each other, Juja,
Like acid, or something worse.
And we have to bear the pain
Together:
The glassy pain …
And on the river, the old boats again
So much older than me,
But even so each one lands
Somewhere
Somewhere
Somewhere … it lands.
Zemfira, 'Juja', on the *Vendetta* album

PART 1

1. ICE AGE / BOOK 1 (1953)

I was an EMBRYO and knew everything. I was pushed out into life and forgot my knowledge. I was fucked into life. My knowledge was taken from me. I want revenge.

I was much. I knew the eight sides of the moon. I embraced all the dead in Hades. I wore all faces.

I walk and walk and grow and this is my murder. Every step is torture: never peace, never silence, never I. I was an EMBRYO and knew everything, and then I was devoured, by the bleeding sexual organ and by all the screaming. I forgot my knowledge.

All the trees caught fire as I walked on, all houses collapsed, and all eyes darkened. Nothing touched me. The nomad land became my bed.

Then I turned to dust and was raped, on the meadow, all living things buried beneath me.

Then I walked through all the waters of the world, flew over all church spires and altars, screaming as I went. No one heard me. I became mute. A mute speck of dust.

The world crashed in and I was buried beneath it. I want to be an EMBRYO again, growing in blood and Omniscient.

I wanted to go home. But there was an earthquake: a violent shock ran through the earth and then it disgorged me.

I wanted to talk to God, who had been there when I was fucked into life. But he didn't come, and so I said: Now nothing will break the monotony; I will sow madness so that I may then go into Hades, to my Achilles. I will take him away from all women and then I will fall asleep in his dead arms and turn to ice myself.

And in 13,090,090,300 years I will thaw. And my happiness will come.

This I decided, and I crossed the desert, which looked like an empty skull. And I crawled onwards with my scorpions; I caressed them and, at night, in the loneliness of the night, I roasted and devoured them. Their poison made me strong and I walked on. I wrote letters to Achilles in the sand. I forged a path, for the two of us.

But I loved so that I might know how entirely senseless love was.

And so I spoke to my lizards and snakes: 'I cannot be your Eve. She died because she did not want to keep the man's rib inside her. She went away and became an ascetic and lived for 999 years in the realm of silence, and her husband raped the trees, and from his seed yet more sons were made … He went mad and when the sons began to fight one another, he killed himself. He missed his Eve. So terribly sad.' And my snakes nodded and wept with me.

'And what became of Eve?' asked the red lizard with the old skin and whorish life.

'Oh, she lived in seclusion, weeping at night because she was alone, and then she came back and saw her dead husband and her many sons that she had never birthed, and they all took her as their wife, and she wept and asked God: 'Why do you accuse me of sin, when you made me the only woman and knew my sons would mount me? She wept and wept and, in the end, she hanged herself with her own hair.'

The lizard, who was beginning to love me, soothed my brow and sobbed quietly.

Later, she told me she had prostituted herself and sinned and had loved a city tortoise all her life. But he had been overbred by humans and paid her no attention and then she had said No to everyone and had gone away and been living like this ever since, in this silence. I embraced her and drank the milk of the trees and became beautiful.

The sand made love to me every night, I had become so beautiful.

I never saw my lizard again; she had brought me to the water and waved to me and I had been almost moved. I did not know what to do next and fell into a dream of a dream and woke alone. That was terrible. Then Ophelia came to me and kissed my breasts and said: 'Get thee to a nunnery, get thee to a nunnery!'

I said all I wanted was to pass into Nothing, but first Everything had to happen. She said Nothing did not exist and I chased her away.

Then I flew over the waters, I bribed the wind, exposed myself, sold myself, and at last he signed my pact and took me with him. I told him how I had once been an EMBRYO and he looked at me with sombre eyes and said: A great pity that you are now a PERSON.

My new nomad land, where he set me down, was quiet and dark. There was a palace in the distance and I walked to it. I wanted to eat and bathe. But the palace was empty and dismal, and spiders and old men lived there. They let me in, not speaking a word to me, and gave me some broth. I drank and did not speak and missed my lizard, whom I called Danaida.

The men said they were there because they were criminals. I caressed their aged skin and it disgusted me, but I felt sorry for them. I said that maybe I could forgive them and that they were free. They laughed at me and spat upon me and called me a blasphemer; regret was the only thing keeping them alive, they said. And so I flew out in the night, onto the road that led nowhere, and screamed and screamed so loud that the whole palace went up in flames and I was happy. For a few seconds, I was happy.

I walked on and came to the people. To the cities and the monsters who made the cities their home. Came to the dogs, who loitered hungrily and licked my feet when I whispered words of love to them. I came to the people ...

Ophelia went on whispering to me, mocking me: 'You are mistaken ...'

★

She strode along the rue de la Grande-Chaumière. She had short, no, long hair, dark brown and brittle. She was wearing a man's coat and was pale, very pale. Yes, that's how she must have been. Bitten lips and small, sharp teeth. She was thin and her nipples were rubbed raw and hurt when she walked. She strode along with a canvas bag on her shoulder, her wide, watery eyes staring obstinately ahead. Her fingernails were pink and chewed. Her nose pointed and reddened; maybe she had a cold and couldn't sleep. Yes, that must have been it.

She stopped in front of a shop window, where a mannequin in a wedding dress was standing. She looked at the mannequin, looked her in the eye, and wanted to strangle her. Then she saw her own reflection and struck her face against the window, but the glass was stronger than she was, nothing happened to it, and her nose began to bleed.

An old lady on the other side of the window let out a little cry and she ran away. She wiped the blood on her sleeve, smeared it down her chin, and then let it be.

She was seventeen. She had just discovered Eros, who sometimes visited her in her room and played chess with her, never saying a word. He was tiny and blond, warm and pink, and she liked him.

Suddenly, she burst out laughing. Her eyes, grey and empty, laughed too. Yes, her eyes … They must have been grey and very clear and somehow dead, beautiful and ugly all at once. Yes, they must have been.

She stopped for a minute; she had been walking quickly and now she paused. Looked in her bag and found some tobacco, rolled a cigarette, and searched for matches. Didn't find any, and asked a girl who was passing if she had one. The girl looked rather surprised, then considered the request, and said: 'Just a moment.' She rummaged in her small, green handbag and pulled out a box of matches. There was an advertisement on the box for a hotel somewhere in Provence.

'Have you been on holiday?'

'Excuse me?'

'These matches!'

The girl was pretty. She wondered whether the girl had been away with a lover, or still went on holiday with her parents. She seemed to have money.

'Oh — yes, but it was a long time ago …'

She kept the game going. It was fun. One day, this girl would become a beautiful lady with a lapdog and a garage with an automatic door.

'I've never been to Provence. Is it pretty?'

'Yes, very.'

The girl seemed confused, but not hostile, which meant curious, which meant there was an opportunity here. People like her were most susceptible to a direct attack.

'The Crèmerie is close by, it's a nice café. Would you buy me a cup of coffee and a piece of cake? If you do, I'll tell you a wonderful story.'

The young woman stared at her, quite taken aback. Only now did she appear to notice the blood.

'I … I have to go … My brother …'

'Oh, come on, you don't have a brother. I'll tell you a wonderful story. I'm just hungry.'

'I don't know … What do you want?'

'I've just told you. That's it, nothing more.'

'I can give you some money, and …'

'No, I don't want money. Just coffee and cake.'

'I …'

'Come with me.'

The girl really did follow her.

She tried to wipe away the dried blood. 'I walked into a window just now. Didn't see it was there,' she explained, with a laugh.

The girl gave her a baffled smile. They went into the Crèmerie and sat down at a table by the window. The waiter recognised her and was about to say something when she gave him a look. He noticed the other girl and kept his mouth shut.

She ordered some coffee and a slice of walnut gâteau. The girl studied the menu sheepishly.

'I can recommend a hot chocolate and the croissant with the peach filling, they're heavenly.'

The girl ordered what she recommended. The girl stayed silent, trying not to look at her, then she took out a cigarette case from the green bag and placed a long cigarette between her apricot-painted lips.

She struck the match on the side of the box, felt the flame on her fingertip for a moment, enjoyed the scent, and finally lit the girl's cigarette.

'My name's Saré. What's yours?'

'Fanny.'

'Thank you for the coffee and cake.'

'Yes …'

'Now I'm going to tell you a story.'

She began to talk about Niobe. About her seven children and her fame and wealth and pride, and how she failed to make sacrifices to the gods, which angered Leto, who visited disaster on her family and had her sons killed by Apollo and Artemis, and how Niobe remained proud, and how Leto destroyed her husband and daughters in front of her, at which Niobe froze in pain and begged for mercy, and how she finally turned to stone, a rock that never ceased weeping. Fanny listened, spellbound. Of course.

'You didn't know that story, did you?'

'No. No, I didn't know it.'

'And so she stands there, on a mountain, the stone queen, and nothing can bring her back to life.'

'It's sad.'

'Yes, in a way.'

'I have to go.'

'I'll come out with you. I'm full.'

'Why are you doing this?'

'What?'

'I mean. All this … first the story, and …'

Fanny stared at her, at her ravaged, fiery eyes. This girl liked her. And she knew it. They left the café together.

'Did you go to Provence with your lover?'

'Excuse me?'

'Your holiday?'

'Um … he's my fiancé.'

Fanny had lovely blue eyes and a rosebud mouth. This girl should have had poems written to her. She sensed that the girl's fiancé had made a mess of things: Fanny's eyes had stopped shining when she said the word 'fiancé'.

'You've got some blood under your nose.'

'Get rid of it. Please.'

Fanny was a little taller than she was; she leaned down, took a handkerchief, white and embroidered, out of her coat pocket, and tried to wipe the blood away, but it was dry, solid and centuries-old.

'You'll have to wet the handkerchief with your spit.'

She brought her face close to Fanny's and waited. The girl's eyes were wary. But then she pressed her lips to the girl's lips — and Fanny, surprised and frightened, impulsively put out her tongue and licked off the blood — then she turned and walked quickly away, shocked at what she had done.

She walked along the rue de la Grande-Chaumière, stopping when she reached the window where the mannequin stood. She threw herself against the glass, but nothing happened. She swung her bag against it, but still nothing happened.

'Damn you! I hate you, you lifeless piece of shit!' she screamed, and then ... then the mannequin died and the whole street fell silent, while the desert secretly sang Haydn Lieder. Soon, she would be able to go back ...

And the dream of a dream awoke and caressed her ankles and licked her temples, and she knew one day it would be over ...

Now she had initiated another woman, and she felt good. She walked on ...

2. BROTHER (1967)

Mother: Will you have some tea, chéri?

Brother: No, thank you, Mother.

Mother: But Patrice, you really must try this cake. Madeleine brought it especially for you.

Brother: Maybe later. Thank you, Madeleine. That's awfully nice of you.

Madeleine: Well, you're going away soon. We'll miss you very much, Patrice, but we're so proud of you. You know that!

Mother: Yes, it's extraordinary, isn't it? His story was printed in a magazine and a journalist from the local paper came round, too, asking me questions about him. It's so exciting!

Madeleine: God has blessed you, Patrice. You should be proud of yourself. There's a great future waiting for you in Paris.

Brother: I'm just doing a bit of writing, that's all, and you're making such a sensation out of it.

Mother: But Patrice, it isn't just a bit of writing! Your novellas are wonderful. Such class — and I'm not the only one who thinks so. They're real gems. You shouldn't talk like that.

Madeleine (finding the subject uncomfortable): And what are you going to study?

Brother: French literature and language.

Madeleine: Truly marvellous. My Jean wants to go to Lyon. He's been offered a job there, in a bank, did I tell you?

Mother: Really? How wonderful.

Madeleine: He's very pleased. He means to work his way up to branch manager. He might come back and manage a bank here, one day.

Mother: Of course, chérie.

His sisters arrive home. Giggling can be heard from the hallway. He wants to go and smoke a cigarette upstairs, on the balcony. But the torture continues. There is still an endless sea to swim through.

Anne-Marie and Simone come in. The dress Simone has on is silly, he thinks. It doesn't suit her at all. And it's still much too cold out for a dress like that. But Mone is more bearable than Anne, so he thinks — even if Anne is better looking and has better prospects, as Mother says. Luckily, he can go on dreaming about that cigarette.

Madeleine: Ah, girls — just look at you. You've grown so pretty. How old are you now, Simone?

Simone: Nineteen, Aunt Madeleine.

Madeleine is a fat cow. He hates her and he wants to strangle and butcher her and bury her deep in the ground and never see her again or hear her or …

Brother: You look silly in that dress, Mone.

Simone: Leave me alone.

Mother: Patrice, must you always be so rude to your sisters?

Madeleine: Ah, that's his age, chérie, my Jean was just the same with his little sister. But he's very good to her now.

Mother: Well, I hope so, I do hope so. Go and get changed, and wash your hands, there's cake. So kind of Aunt Madeleine …

Anne squashes herself in beside him on the sofa. She is slim and blonde and has bigger tits than her older sister and secretly puts on red lipstick when she leaves the house. He knows Anne hates him. She hates him because of what he saw, that night in November, and he knows it. It doesn't matter. He won't tell on her, but a little blackmail now and again — that feels good.

Madeleine: I meant to say: I read the story, and I found it amazingly mature for someone of your age. Jean read it and he liked it, too.

Brother (thinks): Shut your trap, you old cunt, I hate you, you make me sick …

Madeleine (oblivious to what he is thinking): I was very moved by the part where the knight gets wounded. How do you come up with such things — honestly, it's quite incredible.

Mother: Yes, that's what we're all wondering, too, though he's been fascinated by the Middle Ages since he first started school. Do you remember, Patrice, when you had to write that essay? About Roland — you did so like him.

Brother: Hmm.

Simone comes back into the sitting room. She really has washed her hands. She takes a plate and gets one for her sister, too. When Mother dies, Simone will take over her role — that much is already clear. Clear as day.

Simone: This is excellent. Did you bake it yourself, Aunt Madeleine?

Madeleine: Yes. I always do.

Simone: It's really splendid. You'll have to give me the recipe.

Madeleine (laughing like a hyena, he thinks): Gladly, gladly, dear Monie.

How he hates that name — Monie, Monie, it's the kind of name you'd give to a hamster.

Brother: Right, if you ladies will excuse me, I'm going upstairs.

Mother (with what he thinks is a silly laugh): Oh, stay with us a while longer, chéri. We've seen so little of you since you started writing.

Madeleine: Ah, well that's what happens when you have an artist in the family.

Mother: Hahaha.

Pause, stasis. Anne starts eating, licking her forefinger from time to time as she eats, which makes him feel sick. She is always doing things that make him sick. At least Mone is someone you can still have a conversation with. Pause, pause, pause.

Brother thinks about *her*. It's a good job no one can know what he's thinking. Then he goes upstairs. Down below, the same old sounds; Mone is eating that fucking cake now as well. Madeleine looks like a demented old giraffe. Tired, confused, her neck too long. He's sure they're still talking about him and his 'great future'.

He's looking forward to Paris, but he doesn't know how he'll get started there. Still, anything's better than being here. He stands on the balcony, smoking. A crushed packet of Gitanes in his trouser pocket. Soon it will be completely dark. He can almost hear the clacking of the typewriter already. It's only at night that he writes the things he really wants to write. Words that mean something, great and dark and hot and threatening. And then he can love himself.

This fucking town, always so dead and so indifferent; this pond and these idiots, these fucking idiots, these 'proud citizens', and the Sunday services at the cathedral, where the fat cats get to sit at the front. He and his family sit in the middle; he thinks the back row would be better, at least that would be something. Just being fucking average all the time is something he can't bear. The wall clock is ticking in the room; a framed picture of him and his family sits on the dresser, and then one of his father, on the far left.

He was seven when his father died. He doesn't think about him very often, has even stopped hoping he was different from the rest of them; he wasn't, and Patrice accepts that now. Mother thinks he writes because Father died and he's traumatised. He looks at the doily under the photo. It's disgusting, this urge to tidy everything into neat little boxes ...

He smokes, and the sky turns violet, and for a moment he can feel the air. He can feel the imminent arrival of summer, when he can leave. He senses a lot of things like this; he doesn't know exactly where to begin — but no matter, at least there will be a beginning.

The smoke rises up, and it's pleasantly warm. So peaceful. The sound of voices reaches him from a long way off, and they're almost idyllic, as if they didn't belong to the people he knows ... the people he doesn't want to know. Sometimes, he thinks, everything is all right. In comparison to the last few years, these past six months have actually been all right. Almost pleasant, in fact, and he knows this is thanks to the nights he spends writing.

It's thanks to *her!* She will be there, in a city that has barely any associations for him, except a trip, once, with Mother and Anne. (Mone was ill. Poor Mone. Stupid Mone.) And that was an age ago now. Nor does he have any particular interest in the city. It's somewhere he can read in peace and attend lecture courses. That's all.

Footsteps. He sees Anne's blonde mane and then her foolish grin.

Anne: Can I have one?

Brother: If she comes up, I'm not going to take it off you, you'll get caught. And I don't care.

Anne: I'll just throw the butt away.

Her brother shrugs and gives her a cigarette, and she takes a box of matches from the pocket of the shirt she is wearing against her bare skin. He knows that she refuses to wear a bra; Mother is constantly telling her off for it.

Brother: Has that stupid cow gone yet?

Anne: Ugh, no. She drives me crazy.

Brother: Mone looked really silly today. It's not nearly warm enough for that dress.

Anne: What business is it of yours? You have to have an opinion on everything. Why should you? That's not a question, by the way.

Brother: Why are you always so disgusting?

Anne: Oh, Brother! I don't understand you. I really don't. You don't even have any friends, it's sick!

Brother: Shut up!

Anne: No, and you're never in love with anyone, either … I mean …

Brother: Anne, shut up, don't start on this again, it's annoying.

They smoke in silence. Their silence swallows up everything and everyone in this house. They will end up as nothing but skeletons, eaten away by silence. He doesn't want to hear anything. He wants to enjoy the freedom he has bought and extorted, and suffocate on that, rather than on anything else.

Anne: Patrice, take me with you, to Paris. I hate them all, you *know* that, take me with you … Even just a few more weeks here is going to kill me.

He is angry with her: why does she always have to come out with these stupid things? Then a sudden flashback to that November afternoon, when he arrived home and her bedroom door was ajar and she was kneeling on the floor by her bed. And there sat that guy from the school hockey team, empty-headed and made of muscle: his eyes were closed and he was groaning as she sucked his penis. Patrice stared at the two of them, then he ran and ran and couldn't hold back the tears … She'd heard his footsteps. Now he can't help but think about it again.

It's a good job he's leaving soon.

She knows he's thinking about it. He's also thinking about all the guns in Father's room, which Mother cleans and cleans. Everything remains as it was before he was dead, before the phone call that told them he was dead. The person who told them was a blonde named Claudine, from the insurance company. He'd died in her bed. Mother looks after all his guns as if they could bring him back to life.

Anne has large eyes, watery and sometimes beautiful, he thinks. The sky is dark now. Madeleine gets into her car; he can't see her. Anne presses herself against the wall. The cigarettes glow in the darkness; they're already onto their second, and neither of them is speaking.

Mone lets out a laugh downstairs. Mother is sure to be cross that the two of them haven't said goodbye to Madeleine. Anne seems pensive. He hates her all the same and he can't bear the stupid way she talks and the stupid way she laughs and cries and the stupid way she eats, smacking her lips and licking her fingers and enjoying it so much. Anne is someone you can't feel any sympathy for.

The sky grows calm and expressionless and the light above the front door goes on shining after Mother has closed the door. She turns the key twice in the lock. He thinks about the roaring sound he will have in his ears as he types. Everything will be all right.

Anne: Patrice, take me with you …

Brother: Stop it. Finish school, and then you can leave, too.

Anne: Can't I go to school there?

Brother: No, you need to go to school here. Anyway, Mother would never allow it.

Anne: Don't — please, please. I'll die here!

Brother: No, you won't. You've got friends here, haven't you?

Anne: I'm sorry about before, I didn't mean it.

Brother: Either way, you can't come.

Anne: But …

Brother: Please go away, I need to write.

She shoots him a brief, puzzled look. He is content; she is offended. She seems very anxious. He sees her silhouette, hears her tapping the toe of her patent leather shoe on the floor, tap, tap, before she turns and stubs her cigarette out on the wall. She stops then, and whispers …

Anne: I hate you all.

She leaves. He goes on standing there. It has suddenly turned cold, so cold he wants to go inside, but the darkness is whispering something. He listens but he can't hear it, he's never been able to. Why did she have to say a stupid thing like that again and spoil his mood? Mother calls his name from downstairs. He could cry. Everything will be all right, won't it? The sky merely shrugs.

3. APIDAPI (2004)

It's spring in Amsterdam, and of course everyone is very, very happy, and of course she is sitting around thinking about nothing, with the hole in her belly getting bigger and bigger. And everything is foggy and she has no motivation: she forces herself to think about all the important things she has to do, but in hindsight they're entirely insignificant and trivial, and all this just because she's female, and this is precisely what she hates about herself. The most prosaic story, silly and uninteresting and unspectacular ... Though not to her. How she envies all these people, grinning and tipsy, riding their bicycles and arranging to meet people and wearing thin clothes because they're never cold. They have nights out and own a dog and water their plants and they always know what's happening in the world and they're always smiling and they have the latest haircuts. And all that nonsense.

In the mornings she goes to the Academy, takes the old lift up to her office, sits there preparing things, typing, goes to the staff kitchen, has a cigarette, walks back to her office wondering why she came in so early, and then, when she's killed an hour and a half, goes down to the lecture theatre, and talks and talks.

Last summer she went to Canada, to a rural retreat with a spa and all the bells and whistles, very luxurious, flew first class, but it didn't do any good. Oh well. Is this a midlife crisis? How ridiculous everything can be, she thinks, and at lunchtime she goes out for an espresso because she's slept badly again.

Is she lonely, her sister asked her recently; her sister who rides a bike, has two children and a farm in Belgium, listens to soul music, and always talks very passionately about politics. She said nothing at first, then: 'No, just a bit gloomy …' or something like that. She fell silent, waiting for her sister to hang up, but she didn't, and never will, because she's nice, nice, super nice. Her sister said she should come to Belgium, two weeks in the countryside: children and ponies and barbecues and table tennis. She could go out and have some fun there, too, there are loads of nice people around. Then her sister said: 'I think this is partly the separation, you know, things could have been different if you hadn't insisted on getting a divorce, and why on earth …' Blah blah blah. 'You weren't like this before, Laura, really you weren't.' But finally, she does say: 'We miss you a lot.' 'We' is her, the children, the dog, and her husband, the Belgian, whom Laura can't stand. And that's how the conversation ended.

Last Wednesday, Jeremy phoned — the *lover*, Laura had called him, using the English word, during the two years he spent in her bed, an eternity ago, when she herself was still nice. He asked how she was and said that surely, now she had her second doctorate and had written this 'great' monograph that 'everyone' was talking about — now, surely, she should be feeling 'great'. She didn't listen; she was wondering how she could have spent two years sleeping with him, thinking he was special. Sure, she might have been young and nice back then, but still, how could this be? Jeremy, the English *lover*, the man every woman wanted! She had actually been proud that he'd stayed loyal to her and not gone off with someone else … How embarrassing. The whole thing was embarrassing.

He'd always called her 'Lore-a', saying her name the English way, and she had thought it beautiful, not sexy, but beautiful. 'Pure', she'd called it, and now she found that just as ridiculous as her second doctorate, as her whole existence. Was it possible to escape the cliché?

In the evenings now there were books and her notepads and a few phone calls, short and polite; there were pubs for dinner and drinks, invitations to events and wonderful parties, and she declined them; and sometimes she watered her plants, when it was getting late. Then came the nights, sleepless, restless; then came the disgust, and the rest was silence.

She'd also grown tired of having to research everything at all costs, having to find out every last detail, and she'd given up on it. She just wanted to own a nice flat and not have to do anything else. Somehow, the pressure had gone. Separation? Jeremy had asked about that, too, and what was she supposed to say — well, you know, it wasn't too bad.

She had liked being with her husband, really liked it. Had got married at thirty-one, when they'd known each other three years.

What should she have told him?

'I plunged down, into the wellspring of all worldly love. I was jealous and detested him; it was very intense and incredibly dignified, and for his sake I even learned to love that pain and became the most womanish of all little women. I even picked his son up from nursery — in fact that was where I'd got to know him romantically, when I was collecting my niece, my nice sister's little girl, and he was collecting his son — and he was good-looking and I was just planning a research trip and then I saw him. The next day, I went to collect my niece again, can't remember why, and he thought she was my daughter; that left an impression on me. For the first time in my life I liked the idea of being a mother, and I considered having a bit of a fling with him, sure — because, he *was* good-looking.

'I mean, before that, I used to love spending the night with someone, in an apartment, and then drinking coffee and maybe repeating that a few times and then going our separate ways; him satisfied, me satisfied, and everything nice and clear, yes, clarity was good, but you know ... I mean ... Then he spoke to me and that day he didn't have the car and I drove him and his son home — who wasn't cute, by the way, at least not to me — and he thanked me and asked if I wanted to go out for dinner with him, yes, just like that. I'd assumed he was married and he must also have thought that my little girl, my niece that is, had a father, but I said: "Yes, why not?" And thus began the most romantic story of all time ... He was divorced, I was single; and from the restaurant we went back to mine — he thought my flat was "tasteful". We drank wine, ate prunes from the Asian grocer on the corner, I always buy those, I really like them, and then ... then it was crazy, it was heaven on earth, and he was so charming with his broken nose and those full lips and the way he walked around the flat barefoot and the way he kissed my neck, and, and, and ...

'It turned into a long relationship, almost two years, on and off, once a month or twice a week, depending. Sometimes I would read and he would watch me or ask factual questions, and I talked and talked, and he told me he was a doctor and I always thought he was lying, but he really was a doctor ...

'I loved him, I wanted to have hundreds of children with him, I was even prepared to get fat for him and his children. I loved his chest hair and hated the way he wouldn't make a sound when he orgasmed and loved the melancholy in his eyes, you know ... And then at some point things stopped being quite so fantastic.

'One day he left and didn't come back and I howled, but it was okay. I went to Belgium, had a nice time with nice friends and my nice sister — she had moved by then. I forgot him, and then I bumped into him at the cinema, and he just said: "Laura ..." and I had to go and sob in the toilets, and it was exactly seven months since I'd last seen him and then he put an arm around me. That evening we went to his place and fucked all night ... It was good, really good ...

'And in the morning he asked if I thought we should get married, and I stammered: "I need to go, I need to go, I have to get to the Academy!" And that evening I ran back there and said: "Yes, yes, absolutely." Somehow, somehow it would work.'

She could have said all of this, to her English lover or her sister or whoever, but it wouldn't have done any good. And sometimes, she thought about what a terrible sight it was when a dead baby was pulled out of your body; everything else was tolerable, you could just think about the poor children in Africa, about Weltschmerz and poverty or the prostitutes in Thailand — honestly, she wasn't being sarcastic, you could relativise everything — but that sight, on that hot July evening at the hospital, it had been so bad, so terrible, frightening, heart-breaking, and her blood had smelled ominous and she'd been frightened and wanted to hold the baby anyway and look at him and even give him a name: David. Yes, she could have talked about all of it.

Her husband and herself and the stillborn baby and her life in general and, well ...

Four months ago she had been awarded her second doctorate, had dyed her hair darker for the first time, bought a new car, and stuck APIDAPI on the bumper. It was some kind of advertising sticker, pink lettering, very kitschy, but she found the sound of those letters so funny that she stuck them on her car. They made the car look less smart, and everyone thought she had mellowed ...

She was sure everyone must be calling her APIDAPI now, especially the students, and the boys would be forced to abandon their perverse erotic fantasies, in bed at night in their halls of residence, thinking of her, because the name was so silly, unless they had paedophilic tendencies.

How funny.

And she had driven around in her APIDAPI (as the car was now also called) and once she had even signed out some archive files as APIDAPI. And when she was awarded the Royal Academy Prize (best research paper, thank you, thank you, Doctor van den Ende), she had even thought about getting up and giving a speech of thanks to APIDAPI, so everyone would rack their brains trying to figure out what she meant, but then she hadn't dared.

APIDAPI soon became another self, a best friend, something inside her, a favourite teddy, a patient puppy at her side. She cleaned the sticker on the car regularly and found it incredibly comical.

She loved her job; she was a good lecturer, a good art historian, with a gift for languages ...

Oh, Jeremy, you *lover* you, I can't tell you anything, we say nothing to one another and that's how we live. I research and research and you fuck and fuck your way through life (I mean, we all do a bit, don't take that the wrong way) but please leave me in peace. That's what she had thought after the difficult phone call, and she'd allowed herself a grappa. So it went, so it went.

4. ICE AGE / BOOK 1 (1953)

I will speak no more. I am just a clump of dust, heavier than a rock ...

Tonight, little Eros will come to me, I will play chess with him and then time will stand still ... and nothing, nothing will surround us. The room, too, will become boundless and soundless and still. 'We are lost,' Ophelia said to me in the night, 'nothing and no one is coming to save us ...'

Loneliness surrounds my temples. I am calm, I say to myself, but I'm lying.

I ask nothing more; I think of my lizards, I think of my dead friends, detached from the truth, lost in nothingness. I envy them; I have survived, just because I was human. But I, too, am learning to stand still.

I am the bare bones, the scaffold of my SELF. I am just a small, walking ball of hate. I walk and do not know where to, my path is round, as round as a ball, never ending. As I walk, I am bleeding to death, but no one sees the trail of blood in the black earth.

I would like to go away, back into the desert. How have I ended up here, when I was an EMBRYO, and knew everything? I begin to grow pregnant with silence.

I do not know the YOU, for I carry both within me, you and I; I have a thousand sexes within me, I deny the facts.

★

You are lonely. What would happen if she admitted that to herself? No, she mustn't, not yet. She needs to keep serving her mighty gods. Believing in all she wants to believe in. That is important.

She has rented a small room in a building on the rue Bonaparte, the attic floor, where the rent is low. The caretaker, a grizzled old man, is no good for anything. And the concierge is an alcoholic and half-blind from drink.

But she doesn't yet know where to begin. She so longs to duel with death. Perhaps that would be a beginning.

She left home. A small village, not too far from Paris, but far enough. A mother and two sisters. Not a great many worldly possessions, but enough. There was no father, he'd gone 'missing in action' during the war.

She'd only ever been able to talk to ghosts anyway; people bored her. There were problems at her girls' school, St Rita's, where they said she was 'impertinent'. She left at fifteen. The woman who had birthed her, whom she did not call Mother, wanted to send her to a boarding school, but she ran away from the village in the night, without leaving a note.

There was a painter in the parish whose ambitions had come to nothing; he taught children, and she liked him. He had a slight limp. She liked that, too. He told her she had an 'artistic soul'. He proved to be a fool, as well.

She stole some money and left. The woman who had birthed her would spend a while looking for her, but she had other things to worry about, and at that time so many people were looking for their husbands, wives, and children that her case was far from unusual.

She undresses. The room is cold. No heating. No money for heat. Money is so ugly. She needed a place to be alone. Her chamber. To pay for her chamber, she used to sometimes sleep with men from the bar on the corner where she occasionally went for a beer. She cut the thigh of one man with a razor; he stank so horribly and tried to make her do things she didn't want to do. He swore and cursed at her and she ran away, and since then, she hasn't been back to the bar.

She undresses. A small mirror on the wall, to the left. Nothing else. The emptiness is important. She has long hair, yes, she must have long hair. Small breasts, knees that have grown a little too large, her skin pale and cold. The queen of the Arctic. Singing a mournful love song, she climbs into the bathtub (a battered old thing that the man from the greengrocer's helped her carry up here; she showed him her breasts in return), which stands in the middle of the room. Lukewarm water. Cold feet, nails cut very short. How pale she is. Her stomach is hard and flat. Not a beautiful woman, but she has a hurricane inside her. Smashing all beauty with her will. Beauty is so futile and so foul-smelling.

She climbs into the water, leans her head back. She stretches her legs and dangles them over the edges of the tub. Lilies climb up out of the water. The water becomes sand, burying her; she laughs and moves back and forth. Her pubic hair forms a dark patch in the crystal water. She returns to Babylon. She laughs and laughs, and then someone bangs on the ceiling. Go to hell, all of you!

Snakes grow from her hair; monsters do her bidding in all things. Soon it will be night. She lies in the bathtub, drives her hunger away. Her long, shapeless arm becomes an army. Her army, protecting her.

5. WOMAN (2004)

Lynn will be home soon. Make some food. It's so difficult to get up from this couch, to move, to do something. Quickly hide the Scotch bottle.

Everyone says she has problems. She doesn't. Not anymore. Her problems are dead. There are some hot dogs in the fridge, which she can just sling in the oven to warm through.

She was a beautiful woman; tall, a bit lean, perhaps, but a lot of men fancied her. At one time.

The television is on. A fat man is talking some nonsense about a species of armadillo that's going extinct. She doesn't give a shit.

A BATHTUB NOW, START A BLOODBATH NOW ...

That would be good, but not this fat guy on the screen, wearing dungarees for God's sake, and these hot dogs. Wait, why? What's she doing with them? Nothing ... Oh yes, Lynn. She'll be home soon.

GO OUT INTO THE STEPPE AND HOWL LIKE A LONELY, GREY WOLF ... How *can* a person be so empty?

Oh, Francesca, stop it, her son would say: her son, forever five years old, who will never grow any taller. Hot dogs wave bye-bye, the same thing she had to do as a child, when her grandparents were leaving, bless their souls. She didn't like her grandma; Grandpa was okay.

Is the Scotch away? Yes, hidden behind the washing machine, Lynn never looks back there. Lynn, Lynn ... It's her birthday in two weeks, how terrible ... she keeps getting older, while her son stays five forever. Oh well, darling, that's life — say the hot dogs.

Sobering, these walls, this kitchen, this floor with its oh-so-familiar stains. Soon it will be evening, it will be cool, the cars will stop cursing, and she can listen to some music, maybe, or go for a drink at Milly's. Or maybe she can convince Lynn to go to the open-air cinema with her.

'Mum?'

'Yes, Lynny?'

'I'm baaaack!'

'All right, I'm heating up some hot dogs and there's a bit of salad left. Are you hungry?'

'Not really, Mum.'

The voice is distant, she's gone straight upstairs. Great. The hot dogs are browning in the oven. Luckily. She would have liked to see if Lynn had come back from school wearing make-up. But she'll be down soon anyway, and then she'll be able to tell if she's just washed her face or not. Good girl, Lynn.

ALL THE SAD LOVE SONGS AND SUNSETS AND THE DROPPED T-SHIRTS IN EMPTY CAR PARKS; PINK AND BLUE WITH AMERICAN FLAGS ON THEM OR WITH WRITING THAT SAYS 'LOVE' OR 'PEACE' AND ALL THE WORDS THAT HAVE BECOME MEANINGLESS. THAT'S HOW THE WORLD TASTES WHEN YOU'VE JUMPED OFF THE CAROUSEL, WITH THE HORSE STILL GOING FULL TILT …

'I'm having an iced tea — want one?'

Here's Lynn. And of course she was wearing make-up; her face is freshly washed. Must have been caked in it. Silly girl, she would like to say, but she won't. Lynn is wearing a long shirt and an old pair of linen trousers. She bears a certain resemblance to her mum, but not a striking one. Better that way. Lynn there at the table, pretending not to worry again.

'Everything all right, Mum?'

'Yes, sure.'

'Have you been …'

'No, I haven't had a drink. Do you fancy the cinema this evening?'

'Nah, Mum, not tonight, I've already made plans with some friends, there's a party on. You're not upset, are you?'

'No, it's fine.'

'Good. Want some iced tea?'

'No thanks.'

'Are you watching the TV?'

'No, not really.'

'I'll switch it off, then. It's doing my head in.'

'All right. How was school?'

'Okay.'

'Uh huh.'

'Why don't you go out — call Jen, or something … It would do you good.'

'Lynn?'

'Yes, Mum?'

'I … I …'

'What, Mum?'

I CAN'T GO ON. ALL I WANT IS TO EXPLODE INTO A THOUSAND LITTLE PIECES AND BE ABLE TO FLY. I'D BE WEIGHTLESS … IT HURTS, LYNN, YOU'VE GROWN SO BEAUTIFUL. YOU'VE FORGOTTEN ALL OF IT, AND I CAN'T. LYNN, MY DARLING, I JUST CAN'T. AND SOMETIMES I THINK I COULD STOP BREATHING AND NOTHING WOULD BE ANY DIFFERENT, AS IF I NEVER EXISTED, YOU KNOW? NEVER, NEVER, AS IF I NEVER EXISTED. LYNNIE, I'M AT THE END OF MY TETHER …

'Huh?'

'You were about to say something.'

'Oh, right. It wasn't that important, I've forgotten now.'

'Is everything okay, Mum?'

'Yes, Lynn.'

'Could you stop saying my name all the time?'

'I don't.'

'Yeah, you do. You say "Lynn" at the end of every sentence.'

'But, Lynn …'

'See?'

'Fine, I'll stop.'

'You look pale, Mum. Go for a bit of a walk, give someone a call. Go out, it would honestly do you good.'

'Yes, maybe I will, maybe I should …'

Lynn gets up and flashes a smile. She stoops slightly; she's tall, almost the tallest in her class, and awkward in her newly awakened body. She always wears these ugly, baggy clothes that hide her figure, but paints her face like a street-walker, as if her face wasn't attached to the body she hides away.

It's Lynn's birthday in two weeks. She has put her hair up with a biro. Good girl, Lynn.

Lynn rests a hand lightly on her shoulder, companionable and correct as Lynn always is, and then runs upstairs. On the table, an empty glass with a trace of brownish liquid left in it. Then she smells and hears the hot dogs, burning and turning to charcoal. She dashes to the oven and switches it off, but it's too late.

The hot dogs charred. The glass empty and the television off.

Lynn upstairs, her down here, and outside dusk creeping closer.

6. OLGA (1986)

She'd forgotten why they called her Olga. Until the day on which Olga's life was to change catastrophically, nothing too terrible had happened to her.

Olga had been to her lectures and then walked her dog, a golden cocker spaniel called Lydia. Olga was twenty-three years old and she was a nice girl. She had Russian ancestors, but couldn't speak a word of Russian herself, and her name wasn't Olga, she had a more average name, a Western European one, but that doesn't matter now.

She had got up early, having slept badly, and cycled to uni as usual. She hadn't managed to run into anyone — all the people she knew were studying other subjects, and she had no real friends, apart from one girl — so she'd taken Lydia for a walk instead, feeling a little bored. Then she'd had lunch at her favourite café, treating herself because otherwise nothing good would have happened that day, and strolled around the streets for a while. That was how she ended up finding the book.

It was a nice afternoon, and there was nothing better to do. The second-hand bookshop had just opened, and she went in out of sheer boredom.

Two older ladies were standing in a corner, chatting. There was a young man by the shelves, engrossed in a book. He was very good-looking, and Olga approached him instinctively, but just as she positioned herself beside him, pretending to look for something, he put the book down and ran out of the shop like a man possessed.

The till was unmanned, and no one but Olga seemed to have noticed his abrupt exit. For some reason his leaving like that put her in a great quandary; she wanted to run after him, but lacked the courage. And so she picked up the book he'd abandoned in such alarm, and began to leaf through it.

Of course, he might just have rushed out because he had to go and meet someone, but Olga wanted to believe this was part of some kind of adventure. And she was even more eager to piece together a tragic love story. Perhaps he'd fallen unhappily in love, and when he'd opened that book just then, he'd found his lover's initials there. And so he had run to her, to confess everything: how he'd suffered, how he loved her.

The old ladies seemed oblivious to the whole thing. Olga examined the first pages of the slim, dog-eared volume, but found no initials there. Nothing at all. No dried rose petals, no handwritten notes. She was about to put it down again, when she glanced at the title page and read: 'Saré: Ice Age, Book 1'.

She had never heard of a Saré. The book was old; it had a strange smell. She thought again of the boy who had made such a hasty exit and forced herself to believe in the love affair. It must have something to do with this book. She liked that idea.

The book only cost a few francs — all right then, she would have it, even if she didn't really know why. She turned the pages: a few numbered chapters, small print, the words sometimes only covering half the page. What was this? Some postmodern thing? It wasn't her kind of book, but she would be better able to embellish her tragic love story if she owned it.

She paid — a bored-looking girl had finally appeared behind the till, chewing gum, her hair dyed a reddish colour — and left the shop. She had been given a small paper bag, which rustled pleasingly in her hand. The day had now acquired a completely new aftertaste.

Olga went home, fed Lydia, and lay down on her old sofa (inherited from her Russian grandmother, who had also been called Olga). She drank tea and stared blankly at the ceiling for a while; no one phoned, no one knocked on her door. Then she quickly reached for the paper bag — the sound reassured her — and took out the book …

It was just after midnight when Olga finished reading. Lydia was sleeping curled up at her feet. Olga was sweating — her back ached from the awkward reading position, her feet were numb — she had been lying motionless, reading, for almost four hours, something she never usually did.

She got up tentatively. She was afraid, but unsure what she was afraid of. She went to the window. The street was tranquil, almost deserted; the shops were shut. For Paris, it was incredibly quiet. She sat on the window-sill, opened the window, and gasped for air; she felt like she was suffocating. Olga was afraid, inexplicably afraid. She had grown frightened of life.

The last four hours had put years on her, though she didn't understand that yet. She began to sob. She ran to the telephone. She had to talk to someone, and the only person Olga would describe as a friend, though she would never admit it, was Nadine: a plump, freckled classmate who was studying philosophy and went on women's rights marches. Deep down, Olga admired Nadine, because she was free and seemed to have so little regard for what other people thought of her. But everyone else she knew, the people Olga would have liked to call friends, thought Nadine was an arrogant crackpot.

'Nadine ... I need to talk to you ...'

'What's wrong? I mean, do you know what time it is? I was asleep ...'

'I'm coming over, on my bike ... I can ...'

'All right, all right, you do that. I'm at home, I'll wait for you. Go carefully.'

The previous semester, Olga had come off her bike on her way to Nadine's, and had broken her leg. Breaking a leg while riding a bike in Paris was pretty much the most embarrassing thing that could happen to a person!

Olga kissed Lydia, grabbed her green spring coat, and ran down the stairs. She had the sense that she was rushing out exactly as the boy in the shop had done.

She cycled fast, sweating, ignoring the traffic lights and the pain in her legs and her back. She rode for her life, as if trying to outwit the night and the darkness. By the time she reached the avenue de Breteuil, she was damp and completely out of breath.

She took the old lift up and jabbed the doorbell with her finger over and over. The shadows in the hallway had gone wild and were crawling up the walls like spiders.

'Okay, what's all this about? What's got into you?'

Nadine was wearing a red dressing gown.

'Forgive me ...'

All at once Olga could see that she'd been a bad friend. For months she hadn't dared to stand up for Nadine when other people badmouthed her, had ignored Nadine at all the campus parties, been rude about her demos behind her back. And for what? For some stupid guys who were just using her, and those bitches who had nothing to talk about but men and fashion.

Olga began sobbing again.

Nadine put her arms around her and walked her into the flat. They sat down in her tiny room, on the bed, and Nadine fetched some biscuits and a blanket.

Olga had to tell her story. She told it. She told Nadine about her boring day, about the shop, the boy, the book, how she'd read it and how frightening the book was, the images in her mind as she was reading it, and what it was like to feel that fear. Then she said that she'd suddenly realised she didn't have the courage to do *anything*; she didn't know why she was even at university, she was bored by it all, she had nobody, she thought everyone was awful, her parents were paying all that money to support their only daughter, and she didn't even know what for. Olga talked and talked. Nadine sat there, breathing deeply, nibbling on her biscuits, and glancing up at the window from time to time. It was a quiet night. Nadine liked everything Olga said; Nadine liked Olga. She actually felt proud of her friend, who seemed to have found herself at long last, although it had happened with such peculiar suddenness.

Nadine came from a modest background, financed her own life, and had been in Paris for seven years already. She was inwardly proud of being independent and able to look down on all these 'nothing people'. Nadine was a fighter and she loved the fight, though sometimes she was lonely and thought herself ugly and fat. Sometimes all her political work struck her as meaningless. Then she wanted security, and she would think of Olga, of her gorgeous figure and her light-heartedness, her long, dark hair, and she wanted to be like her ...

'Who is this Saré guy?'

'It's a woman. All it says is that she lived in the fifties but her writing only turned up in the early seventies, and that she killed herself when she was seventeen. That's it. I need to know everything. It's all so absurd, Nadine, so mad, the stuff she writes. She's great and terrible, she's full of hatred and longing ... I've never read anything like it.'

'Give me the book ... I'll read it.'

'Yes, yes, Nadine, you must ... for my sake.'

'It's all going to be all right. I'm here. I'm glad you came. I'll help you.'

'Nadine, I'm frightened.'

'Of what?'

'I don't know.'

Soon they fell asleep on the bed, their arms wrapped around each other. It was lovely. When she woke, Nadine studied her sleeping friend. Something had changed and she liked the change. Nadine suddenly felt that someone really needed her.

7. ME (2005)

I write. I am young, female, and I come from an 'exotic' country. No, I'm not famous or universally desired, though all the characteristics I've just listed suggest I should be. In fact, I am about to be abandoned, I live in a country that is not my own, and I'm having a kind of identity crisis. I'm serving all the clichés almost willingly.

A few days ago I read a story, and for some reason it gained such a hold on me that ever since, I've had the feeling of walking around pregnant with it. I have no idea why this story has impregnated me. I think, since I have nothing better to do, that I should try to focus on it. And for me, that means: I should write it down. Not an analysis, not a meticulous retelling, more like a way to understand things a little better.

So, this story is about a girl who seems to have been very unhappy and who caused other unhappy people to become unhappier still. Since I am currently doing a very good job of being an unhappy young girl myself, I think I have my own place in this story. I borrowed the story of this unhappy young girl and devoured it. I spent a long time thinking about why the girl was so unhappy and why she seemed to infect so many other people with her unhappiness. I didn't think about the great horrors of the world we live in, but about all the small, personal ways in which an individual suffers. Like this girl. And because I couldn't get them clear in my mind, I decided to sit down and write.

It's a grey spring evening. I find the absolute, clinical beauty of this city depressing; it looks like it wasn't built by humans, like it has always existed — with the harbour and the rain and these reddish buildings. But I like the nights in this city very much — they're long and quiet.

I think I have started down a path that might make it easier to live. That every tap on the keyboard will only make things better. Loneliness is creeping into my veins, as it always does at around eight o'clock in the evening. Then I decide to do 1,000 things, but of those 1,000 things 999 remain undone, and I sit there with nothing in my head. I have stopped taking pleasure in alcohol and art. It would be a very good thing to find a new identity; somehow, I have lost the old one. Maybe I should adopt a different biography, a different point of view, different legs and differently shaped fingernails, different thoughts, different tastes, and a bit of levity.

Yes, and love, of course. Must one write about love, if one is young, female, and most importantly from an exotic country?

I would like to have something to say, something about world peace and love and the colours of light and the colours of feelings, but I don't. I just want to write a story. Just a story in which I feature. What I'm doing there, I don't know. Not yet.

8. BROTHER (1968)

He enters his room in the halls of residence. Bathroom and kitchen are shared. His roommate is a boy from the English course, who is stupid, and an outsider. The boy seems so lost it makes people warm to him. He has a grant from somewhere or other, and sometimes he listens to the Doors because they're hip. He doesn't understand anything. The boy — they call him Garçon — is wearing a pair of old tracksuit bottoms and sitting perched on the bed, staring at a magazine. He thinks that Garçon is in desperate need of a girlfriend, for physical reasons if nothing else.

It's late afternoon and he's drunk three bottles of beer. He's been living in this room for six months now. Maman sends money every month, and Mone even came to visit him once. She wore another inappropriate dress and he was ashamed of her, and then cross with himself for being ashamed.

Garçon: Hey, Patrice, there's a party this evening, are you coming?

Brother: No, thank you. Things to do.

Garçon: Is it more of that incessant typing? What is it you're writing, anyway? (This is the first time the boy has asked about it, the first time in six months, though Patrice types for at least three hours every day.)

Brother: None of your business, it's private.

Garçon: Is it a novel, or something like that?

Brother: Hey, enough, all right? I've told you once.

Garçon: You never go out, it isn't right. (Garçon himself seldom goes out, and when he does, he loiters in a pub for loiterers.)

Brother: Are you finished now?

Garçon: All right, don't come, then. I'll go on my own. Marie will be there, by the way.

Somehow word has spread that he is sweet on Marie Bessonville. But he isn't at all. Everyone is always talking about it. He just wants some peace. But he never gets it. Paris is just as much torture as Marennes was, only more patient and cynical in the way it torments him. There is no peace. He doesn't want Marie Bessonville, he wants *her*. These thoughts are wonderful. The thoughts of her. Everything else is boring and routine, thinks Brother, though no one calls him that anymore except his sister Anne, who has stopped writing to him.

*

Two hours later. He is alone in the room. Garçon has actually gone to the campus party. He is happy. He sits down in front of his typewriter (a birthday present from Maman, a real investment) and starts to type. First slowly, then faster and faster. A can of beer (half empty) and an ashtray sit beside him on the little desk. He smokes more now than he did at home. A March evening in Paris is boring. But not for him; the hard-won peace and quiet is a precious thing. It's silent in the halls of residence, quieter than usual. A screeching in his head. He'll see her soon, if he concentrates.

He writes the year 1968, even if he's set it up so that they have missed one another in time; has left no possibility of being abandoned by her in the present day. She is always. Has to be. He types.

A knock at the door. Soft and hesitant, then a little more forceful. He can't believe it. Gets up slowly, stops, wavers, has a swig from the can, takes three paces across the room, then stops again.

But the knocking persists, and eventually he opens the door. He accidentally brushes against Garçon's radio in passing, and it falls off the edge of the bed. What's a radio doing on the bed? He is annoyed — no, angry.

It's Marie Bessonville. This is too much for him. She smiles. She's wearing a red blouse with a bow at the neck and a full, knee-length black skirt.

Brother: Hello, Marie.

Marie: I … I thought I'd just drop by because you weren't at the party. Can I come in?

Brother: Um … yes, come in. I was busy.

Marie: I didn't mean to disturb you.

Brother: Don't worry about it.

Marie comes in. They go into the tiny galley kitchen, where there's hardly space for two people to sit, but they manage it. Marie is quite pretty. Her presence puts him on the back foot and he doesn't know what to offer her.

Brother: Would you like some tea? Or I've got some beer left.

Marie: Yes, beer is fine.

He knows Marie from his literature course. She's popular and has a scandalous reputation. Her eyes are honey brown, set too far apart, with long lashes; she is tall, slender, and pale. She puts her hair up with a porcelain comb. Other girls who are jealous of her call her Porcelain Marie. And when they've had a drink, they just say: 'She does it with everyone.' Marie has something about her, so everyone thinks. He doesn't. He stays out of university life.

His attention is all on *her*. Since he moved to Paris, there is only her. He can't leave her alone, can't think about anything else. He has all but stopped working on the stories of medieval knights that everyone likes so much.

They sit there with their beer cans; he has got himself another, although his half-empty can is still waiting for him on the desk. He's disoriented. The room smells of cheap cigarettes. Suddenly, he feels ashamed of his mean existence. He gets up; the kitchenette is too cramped.

Patrice Duchamp is twenty-two and not especially fond of women. He's scared of them, his little sister Anne claims.

Marie: It's cosy here. I share a flat with my friend Claire — you know her, don't you? The blonde with the checked coat. The English girl.

Brother: Oh, right. I didn't know that. She's nice.

Marie: Yes. We get on well.

They go into the bedroom. He offers her his only chair and sits down on his bed, on the woollen blanket. He finds all of this somehow awkward. He thinks of his sister Anne. Suddenly he thinks that maybe she isn't all that bad, and that things wouldn't have turned out like this if he hadn't had that image in his head, Anne on her knees. Perhaps the problem wasn't Anne at all, but Marennes.

Marie: Are you sure you don't want to come out? I mean, it's a nice place, and they have cheap beer.

Brother: Oh, I don't know, I'm not really a …

Marie: Or a little walk, maybe?

Suddenly it occurs to him that she is sitting in his halls, in his room. This is Nanterre, and girls aren't allowed in boys' rooms. She must have bribed the caretaker; he doesn't want to know the details. He doesn't actually want to know much about her at all …

Awkward, stuffy, and ominous — that's how this feels. What might *she* be doing now? Bathing? Or screaming into the night, standing out on the street, naked?

Marie: Well, then … then I should go …

Brother: No, no … wait. We can go for a walk, or — just a minute, I'll put the radio on and …

He picks Garçon's radio up off the floor, switches it on and a chanson immediately streams out. He hates chansons, but he stays where he is and looks at Marie's shoes. Lace-up boots, the same brown as her hair. Marie looks at him and he takes a few paces over to the chair. He's forgotten to remove the paper from the typewriter, and now Marie is staring at it. (No, no, leave it, leave it!)

Brother: Marie!

Marie: What's that?

Brother: Oh, it's nothing, it's just … something I need to type up.

Marie: What …

Standing beside her now, he catches her scent. He grasps Marie's arm, bends to kiss her shoulder. He puts his hands on her waist and hides his face in her collarbone. That Rimbaud poem comes into his head and he feels an urge to scream.

> My sad heart drools at the poop,
> My heart drenched in tobacco spit:
> They squirt it with their jets of soup,
> My sad heart drools at the poop:
> Beneath the jeers of that rough troop

Who laugh until their sides are split,
My sad heart drools at the poop,
My heart drenched in tobacco spit!

He licks her face like a crazed dog, and she embraces him. Then he doesn't know what to do next, and imagines *her* doing all of this.

Marie Bessonville takes his hands, lays them on her breasts, undresses him, and he is soon naked, very naked, he has never been more naked. She kisses his lips. He hasn't made love to a woman before and such thoughts — always that image of Anne in his mind's eye — disgust him.

He is on top of Marie Bessonville and then he is inside her. Marie Bessonville has a beautiful body, and he fights his way further into her, wonders if his bedroom door is closed ... Marie Bessonville laughs and keeps throwing her head back in a provocative way. Marie Bessonville has led him here, step by step. He thinks of *her*, and now he wants to ... strangle her ... but his strength leaves him, a violent thrust, a great shudder, and he falls into the depths of Marie Bessonville ...

9. ICE AGE / BOOK 1 (1953)

A handsome Italian from the rue Capron and her. He was simply walking along and she asked him if he wanted to sleep with her. At first he just gave her an anxious look, then she took his hand.

And so he twisted and turned in her, like a corkscrew uncorking a bottle.

★

I will scream, my scream will be louder than life could withstand! When everyone is asleep ... I'll swim away across the Styx. I will push Zeus from his throne, I will roast him and give his flesh to my hyenas, tell them to eat their fill.

I will reign in the Ice Age.

I will tear out my heart and throw it to the vultures; I will govern cruelly and bring silence to the world.

I will jump up high, to the moon, so he can embrace me. My moon. I am his other side. We were lovers, once.

Somewhere on the bridge I will drink vodka with my hero, and then drown us in the Seine, out of sheer, suppurating love.

I would strangle you, if you were worth it. If you only knew that right now, while you believe you are loving my flesh, you are really discovering how trivial and stupid you are.

Headache, damnation!

Raindrops fall on the lungs. I leave.

Achilles, my dead love, is waiting nearby.

I marry the silence and I find happiness in unhappiness.

★

'What did you say your name was?' He speaks good French, but with an accent. Pitiful man … 'Saré? What kind of name is that? It's been a wonderful evening. Can I see you again?'

'I'll see you again.'

'What?'

'Nothing.'

'Good. I want to see you again.'

'Now get out of here, you pig!'

'Hey, have you gone completely crazy?'

'Go!'

'Hey, stop it, are you mad? What do you want?'

'Give me the taxi fare home. I don't want to walk. That's all.'

'I'll give you whatever you want. It was good. Very …'

'Will you just get out?'

'I work in the rue …'

'I know where you work, now get out.'

'All right. I didn't mean to upset you.'

She runs down the stairs. 'I'll meet you, my lizard, my darling one, lick my knee and heal me,' she thinks, and later she will write it down. She will shake all the trees out of their decades of sleep. Giants will come forth and they will stride across the globe and everything will melt together into a pulp …

At three in the morning, she walks down the rue de Choiseul and thinks about what it would be like to be kissed by the moon on a March night in Paris.

It's like a heartbeat, her old stilettos, her footsteps, small and lonely. She is seventeen and doesn't know why everything has turned out the way it is now. The Now has always been there. She leaves footprints in the black sand as she walks. And she can't get away. She is stuck fast to her existence.

Sometimes, people stare at her. She is wearing an old men's coat, stolen. Three sizes too large.

She didn't take a taxi after all, and pocketed the money instead.

A small boy runs ahead of his father, babbling away enthusiastically to himself. The March wind is playing badminton with him, but he doesn't know that. She calls out to him across the street to tell him; he recognises her, is pleased to see her, tries to go to her, but his father pulls him away.

A dog trudges beside an older lady in a little hat. How pathetic is the attempt to fight off death with a single weapon: beauty.

The dog recognises her, too; in a past life they might have been siblings, or maybe she was a fish in his silver aquarium. Now she can take her revenge, and she sticks her tongue out at him.

She has lost the thread, and no longer wants to play chess with little Eros. The streets and the gloom make her fearful.

She stands still and thinks for a moment about the future, which is just the past turned inside out. In the land of the slaughtered lambs, the sun rises … in her land, the moon rises.

She sits down on the pavement. A car honks its horn. And now, now she raises her glass eyes from the ground and looks at the world. And the street comes alive and she lets out a little laugh: this is how it should always be, if only her eyes could give life.

She would so like to eat a ragout now. Maybe the landlord at Le Coq will give her a glass of red wine …

10. APIDAPI (2004)

This period of stasis couldn't last; eventually, she bought prunes at the Asian market and didn't enjoy them, and she thought for a minute about her ex-husband's son, and then about the ex-husband himself. And imagined him having silent orgasms with other women. The idea still seemed very strange to her.

Then the telephone rang.

'Hi, it's Jan here. There's something I want to discuss with you. Are you familiar with Saré?'

'What kind of a … Sorry, who is this?'

'Jan, from your course. Art history. Cubism. That essay?'

'Oh, Jan, yes, sorry, I'm a bit … Where did you get my number?'

'Hey, listen, it would be really great if you could spare me an hour or two …'

'What's the issue? Because right now I'm quite — '

'Can I see you? This evening? Roelof Hartplein, at the Wildschut? It's not that far, if you take your Apidapi.'

APIDAPI!

'Um. All right. What's this about?'

'I'll tell you when we meet. The Wildschut, then. In an hour's time?'

'Okay. But — ' He has hung up.

APIDAPI was what swung it for the boy. The fact that he'd mentioned the name. She had a vague recollection of his face, a red-haired lad, that much she knew. At least he was offering her a way to kill some time. It was the weekend, and that meant the torture of trying to fill useless hours had begun.

She spent a long while standing in front of the wardrobe. Finally she pulled out a pair of tight jeans, old ones, from the time of the English Lover, and a white shirt. She had twenty-seven white shirts; she had recently counted them. She liked white shirts — they could say nothing and everything. Always consider the other side of the story — this basic principle was what had won her all the stipends and funding she'd got so far. She put on mascara and a muted shade of lipstick. She tied her hair back. Then she went down to her car. APIDAPI was waiting faithfully for her in the garage.

She knew the Wildschut; a friend of hers had introduced her to it, in the days when she still had friends and went out. It was a nostalgic place where she didn't feel all that comfortable.

Bob Dylan was playing on the car radio, and it was raining. She arrived early, looked for somewhere convenient to park, swore, considered turning back, but then squeezed her car in between the other cars, mopeds, and bikes. She still got wet and swore again as she ran into the café. It was half full: a few tourists, background jazz. She found a table for two in a corner. Ordered a glass of red wine. It was the kind of evening that made you want to get on a train and head off into the unknown.

Jan really did have red hair; he was rangy, tall, and awkward. She only had a vague memory of him, though he claimed to have written an essay for her. A fathomless abyss.

He shook her hand tentatively, smiling.

'Sorry I'm a bit late … the bus was cancelled. Do you like it here? I do — couldn't say why, though …' He was wearing a dark blue denim jacket and black trousers, much too long for him. Horn-rimmed glasses. She should at least have remembered those.

He ordered a mineral water, a vegetable soup, and a gin 'for afterwards'. She said nothing. What on earth had that essay been about?

'I don't want to bore you so I'll get straight to the point and tell you why I came to you with this … So, you're not familiar with Saré?'

'No.'

'She was an author. Well, a kind of author. She lived in the mid to late fifties. No one knows exactly. We don't know very much about her.'

'Uh huh.'

'She was seventeen when she died.' He paused for a moment and waited for his words to sink in. He had beautiful, deep-set eyes of an indeterminate colour. Somewhere between grey and green.

'An author at seventeen?'

'Yes, and what a writer she was! She left behind this little book, a school exercise book, you know? Squared paper … she left it in her room, in Paris. The concierge found it after her death. She threw herself in front of a train, you know?'

Every time he said 'you know?' he gave her a searching look, as if expecting a particular reaction. It made Laura feel uneasy.

'Almost nothing is known about her,' he went on, his voice soft and low. 'There isn't even a photo of her. Years later, this exercise book ended up in the hands of a publisher. It was one of these underground publishing houses, founded by student protesters from 1968; they mostly published left-wing literature. There was a small print run. It sold out almost immediately. In certain circles, the book became an instant cult hit, and people wanted more and more by and about this Saré. But Saré — Jeanne Saré — there was just no trace of her. And because no one knew anything about her, she became this myth … a martyr, who died for her ideals. In the next six years, there were four reprints, and several translations. But in those six years, there were also fourteen suicides in Paris alone, all copycat versions of Saré's death …'

He paused again, as his soup arrived and he began to eat. She had barely said a word, but that didn't seem to bother him. Now and then he looked up, as if trying to read something in her face. She didn't know what to make of him. She smoked, even though he was eating, and sipped her Merlot.

'A myth, then, from the not-so-distant past. Eventually the press started linking the suicides to the book. And for a while, it seemed to have been lost; almost all the existing editions were out of stock. You *are* interested in women, right?'

'Sorry?'

'Well, I mean, you've done a lot of research in that area. Your paper on Camille Claudel was sensational, I thought it was great.'

'Yes, sure, I've done research "in the area of women", if you want to put it that way, but that's not what I'd call it ...'

'No, no, there *is* a connection here: all of the fourteen suicides were women ...'

'But what was in this ... exercise book?'

'Well now, that's the really interesting thing. Thoughts. There's no plot; everything in it is open to interpretation, it's all madness or truth, depending on how you want to see it. It's one long stream of consciousness. Brief entries, moods, sometimes quite apocalyptic. But ultimately, it isn't about what's in there, it's about the person, the myth that apparently encouraged fourteen women to take their own lives. What I came here to ask you is whether you want to help me find out more about her ...'

'Help ...'

'Yes, I've done loads already. I've even made contact with some of the families of the women who died; I've been in touch with the literary institute in Paris; I've talked to a Bible scholar; read Greek and Roman myths, because she draws a lot of parallels. I want to know who she was. The stuff she said or left behind is nebulous. The women who died because of her: I want to know who they were, too. I need real lives, not theories. And you're good at that.'

'Well, that isn't entirely correct: I don't do much with literature, my focus is on the visual arts. Why don't you ask Dr Deen from the literature ...'

'I'm studying literature, too. I know the lecturers. This is about you.'

'Me?'

'Yes, you.'

'Why?'

'Because I know that you can burn, really burn for things. I've been to your lectures, I've written an essay for you, and I've been preparing to make this suggestion to you for the last year. I've been studying you.'

'Studying?'

'Yes, I need someone who can help me and ...'

'Now just wait a minute! There are thousands of stories like this. At certain points in time, all people need is a vision, a signpost. You saw it during the war, and in the post-war years — times when people have to start again from scratch, when they lose faith, when old ideals are being toppled, and …'

'No, no, I know all that. But this is different. You need to read this book. There's no solution there. It's absolute nihilism, but also filled with longing. She has lived through everything that's in there, nothing is invented …'

He seemed to be enjoying his dramatic performance. He stared at her; there was a twitch behind his glasses, and something in his eyes changed.

Laura thought about the time she had travelled to Cairo with her first grant, when she was looking at ancient Egypt, when she was happy, and had something to love … The waiter brought the boy's gin and he sniffed it before taking a slow sip.

'Please, you have to help me.'

'How am I supposed to help you?'

'I'm going to Paris for two months. I'll take time off from university. I'll write an article, a research paper. I want to find the person behind those words …' He was speaking much more quickly now and going a little red in the face.

Laura stared awkwardly at her empty wine glass, saying nothing. She ordered another.

Time stretched out. The rain eased off a little. Summer: there was so much of it left. And that made her think of the house in Belgium, the children, all those nice people and her sister, talking about her and giving her advice. The thought disgusted her. She took a large, hasty gulp of her wine.

'And you will love the material, you …'

'Love? Oh, you *are* funny. Look, I'm busy, and in any case I don't have any real interest in this whole business. I'm too old for apocalyptic writing and conspiracy theories.'

'These aren't theories, they're fourteen human lives.' He was disappointed in her and how she'd responded.

How old must he be? Why had she come to meet him in the first place? Her evening was gone, her emptiness and thoughtlessness gone, and now all that was left were pangs of conscience, a whole night of reproaching herself for the current state of her life. For the fact that everything was slowly slipping away from her. Laura was afraid of those nights.

'Let me give you this folder, and you can take a look and if you still aren't convinced by the material, then I'll ask someone else ... okay?'

'Fine. I'll take a look at it.' She was irritated; the boy was too insistent and she wanted to get rid of him as swiftly as possible.

He placed a thick, black folder on the table, bursting at the seams. She stared at it. He made another attempt at small talk, which very quickly foundered on Laura's monosyllabic replies, and then took his leave. Jan, the student, and Laura, the ice queen. What a lovely couple they made, she thought with a disparaging smile, as she got back into her APIDAPI.

By eight the following morning, she had read through the folder and looked at the images. There were pictures of Paris, articles from various yellowing newspapers; there were interviews, notes, and related material; there were philosophical essays and texts on ancient myths; and then there were the pages by this Saré. Photocopied. Did he have his own, bound copy?

Laura read and read. She smoked and smoked. It got light; the rain had stopped. Laura sat at her kitchen table and whispered something to herself. Then, suddenly, she burst into tears.

11. WOMAN (2004)

Milly's is packed. The Sunday evening crowd. June is nearly here. A lovely month, a month with no funerals.

'Lynn's birthday party, it was total chaos. There were so many people there, suddenly all these boys I'd never seen before. They're at that age, I thought. But it's still odd. I think so, don't you? What are you thinking about? Do you guys have plans for the winter break? What are you going to do? I still don't know. Lynn is desperate to go to camp, and then I'll have to do something on my own. Europe? Are you kidding me? Oh, I can't. Nah, it's too far … My mother? I'd rather die than go to Adelaide. No way in hell. I can't take her going on about all the things I should have done better. No, I'm fine. I'll go away, maybe Thailand or somewhere, I mean, I went before, it's an easy option … No, I dunno, just have a holiday. I think it would be good. I can't be bothered with it anymore, and I just can't stay in Sydney without Lynn. It's suffocating. I get migraines and I can't sleep at night … though that's kind of par for the course anyway. Yes, Lynn … oh, you know what, I think I'll let her go, why not. It's somewhere out towards Murray River, she's already all hyped up about the journey. She's fifteen and it's okay. I never had that kind of freedom when I was a kid — none, absolutely none — and I hated it. Even after all these years, going to Adelaide still gives me nightmares. I was never allowed to stay out past ten, it was only when I moved out, cos … But you know that. Yes, coming to Sydney and … the American road trip? What made you think of that now? Those four months we spent driving along the Atlantic coast … it was great. Everything was so big, I loved it. I came back a different person. And then I didn't want to speak to my parents for two months, stopped replying to their letters, and when my dad came to visit me in Sydney, I hid, I had someone tell him I'd gone away. I dunno why, I think I was just angry that they'd kept me so closeted away from life — from real life — all those years. And then eventually it was okay again. I had a boyfriend — the drummer — and I was happy. I like to think back on my student days, don't you? I just think I should have left Sydney afterwards. Why didn't I go to New York then? They gave me that offer. I would have liked to go, I like New York. I should have done it, but I stayed because of Frank ... Didn't you ever want to get out of Sydney? Why not? I always wanted to. But I stayed; too bad for me, right? Yes, Lynn, but I could have had Lynn in New York; I'd have had Max there as well and ... kept him. No, I'm not going to talk about it, it's okay, don't worry, I'm not going to go off on one. But then, why *can't* I talk about it, huh, Jen? Why not? I mean, why does no bastard ever talk about death? Wherever I go I get funny looks, I hear whispers, everyone thinks I'm about to blow my top and start a bloodbath ...'

BLOODBATH, FRANCESCA!

'Right? Right, Jen? I mean, everyone does say, there's that woman, the one with the dead kid and the mad husband, but you know, I go on living, and I can have a normal conversation. Can't I, Jen? Yes, all right, I'll stop. Would you order me another Scotch? I'm not drunk, I just want another Scotch.'

Jen reels away to the toilets; she's the one who's drunk, not Francesca. She just likes a drink and that's okay, why would it not be okay? She sits there contemplatively and thinks about the desert inside her: the immense, abandoned, dead road made of sand, always going downhill, never ending.

THE SWARMS OF BIRDS IN MY HEAD. CIRCLING BEHIND MY PILLOW. THE NIGHTS ARE GROWING LONGER AND I AM GETTING MY BREATH BACK. I THINK OF YOU, MAX! I THINK OF YOU OFTEN AND IN MY DREAMS WE ARE WALKING ACROSS A BIG DESERT, JUST YOU AND ME. WE HAVE ALWAYS BEEN TOGETHER. YOU WERE ALWAYS THERE, IN MY THOUGHTS, BEFORE MY EYES AND BEHIND MY DREAMS. WHEN YOU CAME INTO THIS FUCKED-UP WORLD, MAX, I THOUGHT WE WOULD BE GREAT FRIENDS. I WAS MISSING

SOMETHING, I HAD YOUR SISTER BUT THERE WAS STILL SOMETHING MISSING — BUT YOU, MAX, YOU WERE THERE. IN MY HEAD, BEFORE YOU EVEN CAME INTO THE WORLD. AND I ALWAYS WONDERED WHY YOU WERE SO QUIET, AND WHY YOU DIDN'T GO OFF TO PLAY LIKE OTHER CHILDREN AND GET UP TO MISCHIEF LIKE YOUR SISTER, AND THEN ONE TIME I WATCHED YOU, IN YOUR ROOM, AND I SAW YOU, MAX. SAW YOU TALKING. WITH SOMEONE WE COULDN'T SEE, WITH ANOTHER MAX, MAYBE. THAT WAS IN NOVEMBER, AND IN JANUARY YOU WERE GONE. I WANTED TO BE THE PERSON YOU WERE TALKING TO THERE, MAX. I WISHED I WAS THAT OTHER MAX YOU SPOKE TO … I AM COMING FOR YOU, I WILL FIND YOU AND PICK YOU UP AND TAKE YOU TO YOUR LAND OF CANDYFLOSS. I'LL DO THAT, MAX, AND I WILL GO ON EVERY CAROUSEL IN THE WORLD, RIDE EVERY PINK AND BLUE HORSE.

'I miss you so much, Max …' she whispers, watching her friend as she makes her way back to the table with two fresh, full glasses. Good girl, Jen.

At the funeral, Jen had worn jeans and everyone thought it 'unimaginable' that she wasn't wearing black, and then she'd looked at her friend and seen this indescribable fear in her eyes; she was afraid for her and for her life and her future. In Jen's eyes, Francesca saw her world shatter and thought that she was the only one who had any inkling, any sense of it all.

'You actually should go to Europe, you know? I mean, you're always raving about Greece, maybe if you go it'll help you get back in the swing of things. Or Rome — you've talked about Rome a lot, and maybe from there you could take a trip to Paris …'

'Oh, Jen, what would I do with myself over there for two whole weeks? I mean — starting some kind of grand tour now, all on my own. What would I do with myself?'

'I've got a cousin in Paris. She can show you the city. If I give her a call, you won't have to hang out on your own. Book a hotel. One of these five-star places with all the bells and whistles, and have a good time! Frankie, you can't carry on like this!' Jen is tipsy and sentimental, but it suits her. It is just before midnight, Milly's is packed to the rafters, and the whole place is smoking and spinning. Go to Europe, go far away, to Rome, to Athens … or into the desert, it all comes down to the same thing …

There they sit, two women in middle age, telling each other their stories; stories with no beginning and no end. There they sit. The one works, has two sons, a normal life, and looks younger than she is; her name is Jen, she has brown hair, and comes from an orthodox Jewish family from whom she has emancipated herself. The other is just an F for female, a woman. She is exhausted, a bad mother who has lost everything she once had. And this other woman wants to tell a story with an ending. She wants to know how it ends.

She wants to tell the story of how it felt to come home one day, on a hot January afternoon, with two kilos of tomatoes and fish from the fish market, wrapped in paper, like they do in Sydney's fish markets … To get out of the car and open the front door. To go into the house, her house. And call her son's name, and her husband's — he had the day off — and get no answer. Her daughter was staying with her grandmother. To go upstairs and then to find her husband, the man with whom she had shared a bed for eight years and shared her life for days and months and eternities before that, lying in the hallway, outside the children's bedroom, in a puddle of blood and brains. And then to run on, hurdling the body, desperate to see her son, see him hiding under his bed with wet trousers, red-eyed and trembling. To think he would have seen this and would never speak another word. That's what she was thinking as she went to him. She saw the whole world buried beneath her as she stepped into the kids' bedroom. She didn't need to look for him anymore. Because there he was, her five-year-old, lying on the bed, eyes open and staring straight ahead. His face had a blueish tinge. And it took another five hundred years for her to understand that he was dead, too. She spoke to him, she kissed him, and kept trying to convince herself that he was still alive, because he still looked so alive. But then she had to put her ear to his chest, had to feel for his pulse and lift him up before she understood that he wasn't looking at the ceiling, but had ceased to be. He had been suffocated, they told her, with a pillow; his pillow with the bears on it, eating honey with spoons … The big man couldn't bring himself to shoot the little man, so he suffocated him with a bear pillow. Francesca would have liked to tell that story about the end, if she could only have found the words for it.

12. OLGA (1986)

Olga mostly stayed at home now. She didn't go out. She declined invitations, was often absent from seminars, seldom went to her lectures. Sometimes she talked to Lydia. She forgot to go food shopping. But every evening she sat at her desk, copying something by hand.

Line for line and word for word, she was writing out the yellowing book she had bought a few weeks before. She was hoping that little by little, the copying would help her get to the heart of this book. But ultimately that didn't matter; the main thing was that she was doing it, and it seemed to give her a purpose.

She had lent the book to her best friend, and four days later, when Nadine still hadn't given it back, Olga had got angry and cycled over and snatched it out of her hand. She'd berated Nadine, who didn't understand why Olga was so angry and was initially quite offended. But when two weeks had gone by and Olga still hadn't been in touch, her friend began to worry about her.

Olga, on the other hand, had barely given a second thought to this argument. She was content and thinking only of herself. Olga's life was purposeful. The book existed. Everything else was trivial and ridiculous. She was filled with strength and faith. And that was because of the book, just as everything was because of the book. She studied it, she knew every line of it now, she read and read and wrote and wrote … There was a magic in this book that she had never experienced before. The book also lent a kind of enchantment to everything that happened around Olga. She was slowly becoming happy. And slowly starting to realise what it meant to be happy.

One evening, there was a knock on the door. Olga lived on a small street in Bercy, where people seldom just dropped round.

Olga had been looking forward to her evening of writing. Suspecting that Nadine was on the other side of the door, and guessing that Nadine wanted to have some kind of discussion with her, Olga was incensed. She considered not opening the door. But Olga was still a nice girl, and a smart one, too: she knew not answering would make Nadine suspicious. She mustn't let that happen. So she opened the door and said at once: 'I'm glad you're here, I'm sorry I've been so impossible lately.'

Nadine's face brightened and they hugged. Everything was fine again. They went into the small kitchen, where Lydia was asleep on the floor, sat down in the corner, drank coffee, and ate the Belgian chocolates that Nadine had brought with her. Lydia snored; she wasn't as young as she used to be …

Olga was wearing an old-fashioned dress that Nadine had never seen her in before, black with white polka dots. She had cut her hair a little shorter; Nadine noticed that, too. Olga's eyes shone. She seemed euphoric. Nadine was slightly unsettled, but she didn't ask any questions.

'I haven't seen you at uni. People are starting to ask about you — even Michel was asking after you. You like him, right? I think he fancies you. He's a good-looking guy, and I find him less awful than some other men you've liked.' Nadine was trying to sound light and cheerful.

'Oh — what? I don't like him at all, I have no interest in him. Anyway, all those uni people are idiots and phonies. Except you.'

'Well now, there's another new thing.'

'How so?'

'Well, I mean, you've got a new haircut, you're wearing an odd dress, and no one's seen you for two weeks … so there's something going on. Are you in love?' Nadine had thought about the book often; she hadn't got round to reading it, had done no more than leaf through it. The book was dog-eared and Nadine hadn't liked the fragmented look of the text. All the same, she couldn't really say what had stopped her from reading it.

'Don't be silly, didn't I just say … There's nothing going on. I just wanted to do some thinking and be on my own for a while. Last semester was really stressful and I needed to sort myself out a bit.'

'There's so much going on at uni: people actually want to demonstrate now, and I'm organising a protest, too. Want to join me?'

'Against what?'

'Well, you know, I think we need some real change; the humanities are being dismantled, all those cutbacks. And a lot of students have started to think the same. I mean, just look at everything that's happening here and …' Nadine lectured a little while longer about a new world order, women's rights, the need to repeat the protests of the previous decades, and so on.

But Olga wasn't really listening; she was just thinking about the moment when she could return to her work.

'Do you not like my dress?' she asked Nadine suddenly, with a smile.

'What? Um, I actually think it suits you, it's just a bit old-fashioned …'

'Yes, I bought it in a costume shop, in Montmartre. I thought it was beautiful.'

'Have you been listening to a word I've said?'

'Of course … But you know me, that's really not my thing.'

'What *is* your thing, then?' Nadine was offended. Olga didn't give a damn about the wider world. Nadine used to think she was still too young and perhaps also a little foolish (though in a naive, almost cute way), but now she just found Olga's attitude egotistical and ignorant.

'I'm going to find out soon …' Olga shot back. In the past, she'd always managed to avoid answering that kind of question. .

Nadine stiffened, looked at her friend, then got up and walked out of the kitchen.

'Well, when you've found out, you can let me know.'

Olga didn't prevent her from leaving, much as Nadine had hoped she would. She stayed where she was, staring at the half-open door after Nadine had disappeared from the flat. Then she returned to her desk.

It was late evening, quiet and peaceful, and Olga's room was transformed into a fortress of silk, softly enveloping her heart. She saw the whole world from above, and it was a wonderful, hideous sight. That peaceful night, when she decided to bid her previous life adieu, was when Olga dreamed about Saré for the first time.

13. ICE AGE / BOOK 1 (1953)

I will write the book! I will cut my heart out of my body and lay open my brain so that everyone can see in. I will rub off the ashes, rub every speck of dust from my skin, until I get to the core.

I walked and walked; after I had reached the earth, reached dry land, after the North Wind had carried me there in its tender arms, I stood and waited for … God. He did not come, he did not answer, he had slammed the door. Soon I called on all the snakes of the underworld to rise up. I became great and I became UNIVERSE. I learned to slowly disintegrate … I saw the corpses, who had given up praying to the purgatorial flames.

Everything was trivial: the world had turned into a shadow, half-dead people floated around. But I just wanted to go back.

They all begged me to take them with me. But I promised to shoot them in the back, if I had enough powder.

I wanted to leave. I wanted to leave … I reached Babylon and tore down all the walls, destroyed the gardens. I wanted to skewer all love, since all lovers had become mute. And love mutated into suffering.

Ophelia pursued me, screaming: 'Nothing, nothing is coming.'

I became Saré. I perfected myself and the wind went on applauding me.

I would be victorious, would cut off Ophelia's head, since she never ceased lamenting … From Media to Syria and from Byzantium to Atlantis — everyone, everyone would have to sleep. The ultimate sleep!

I walked on … In my final poison glass I would dissolve God and the devil together and drink them down, in a single draught. Then we would all be even.

★

She stopped writing. She was a seventeen-year-old girl, with empty eyes and desperate skin, cold and raw. The girl had gone away and sought out loneliness as her ally.

The girl had no one; if her family found her, they would get her locked up in an asylum. The girl was a little shapeless, not beautiful. But she had wonderful eyes and a voice that seemed to come from a past era. The girl lived in an attic room in the Latin Quarter, sometimes went out stealing, and when it was dark she spoke with the night. She knew no one and no one knew her. The girl despaired; her loneliness and her fear grew so great that she became the mistress of sorrow. Three times she had tried to find a love. Once, when she still lived with her family, in another world, in a nightmare rather different from this one, and then twice more in Paris. But love had left only emptiness behind.

So she told her story to the world, though the world wasn't interested. The girl's pain grew so deep and so silent and so hard that she could rule over all the world's sorrow. And since that was the way things were, she thought, she could carry everything with her, suck up everything bad and frightening and chilling into herself, and thereby conquer her fear, at last.

The girl withdrew further with every passing day. Things lost their colour … Each time it rained, she climbed onto the roof of the building. She looked down at the city. The sight made her afraid. The girl knew that the fall, if a fall befell her, would be a very long one. And week after week and month after month it grew colder in her house, in her palace.

Sometimes she would steal red wine from the little wine stall in Montmartre and drink one glass after another, sitting alone on the window-sill. She hoped that the emptiness would recede, but it only grew.

Sometimes she would lie in a lukewarm bath and dream, or write her thoughts in an exercise book that she had kept from her school days. And every line was more melancholy than the last, every sip of red wine mixed with a sip of loneliness, and the girl drank it down in dutiful silence. Again and again.

Sometimes she would smoke cigarettes, tearing off the filter. Sometimes the night sang songs for her and they were long, sad songs of love and peace, but the girl found neither the one nor the other.

Time passed and the girl became pregnant with her fear. The fear grew inside her like an ulcer and ate her up. Her cries lost their meaning. The girl became mute; every night she cut out a piece of her tongue. It didn't hurt any longer. She did the same with her heart, until at last in place of her heart there was just a cavity behind her ribs. She crouched inside this cavity.

Eventually she decided to squeeze her own existence out of herself, like juice from an orange. She made a pact with the silence and complained no more. She would just walk and understand everything, by not understanding anything …

The wind caressed her ankles and she learned to fly, above all the city's rooftops … 'I will die in the bed of my dreams, then,' she thought to herself. 'Wherever I walk, the snow obliterates my footprints. I will lie down to sleep when all the snow has fallen from the sky …'

She sat up. It was late in Paris, and she was sitting on her bed. She had been dreaming.

Saré, the girl with the empty eyes, switched on a small lamp and whispered over and over again: 'It will be fine, everything will be fine … Everything will be fine, everything will be fine …'

14. BROTHER (1968)

He is standing on the Pont d'Arcole, looking down. There's a lot going on outside. People want to change the world. April 1968. Students are protesting; unions too. Mother is worried and writes. Sometimes he calls her from a phone box. He doesn't care about the turmoil.

> My sad heart drools at the poop,
> My heart drenched in tobacco spit:
> They squirt it with their jets of soup,
> My sad heart drools at the poop:
> Beneath the jeers of that rough troop
> Who laugh until their sides are split,
> My sad heart drools at the poop,
> My heart drenched in tobacco spit!

He thinks of these lines of Rimbaud's often.

Sometimes he also thinks of Marie Bessonville.

The world seems restless. Nanterre is restless; it's almost impossible to sit at his typewriter, there's too much noise, including Garçon yammering away. He walks up and down, and the bridges of this city are getting to know him. He likes the bridges. He doesn't like the people. The dream of freedom seems on the point of bursting, and there is growing disappointment among the city's inhabitants.

He thinks of Marie sometimes. She's probably out at some demo now, pseudo-socialist that she is. His head hurts, and he is constantly receiving telegrams from Maman. But the worst thing is how difficult it is to write in these times ...

He has given his lecturer a couple of his stories, which have been printed in the student paper. He is beginning to hate his moral cowardice ... Everything is hateful except *her*. But it has become so hard to keep pace with her!

He stands there, smoking. People walk past him. He is of medium height, medium build, a stranger.

Back in his room he finds a card that Garçon has brought upstairs for him. A card from Anne, his younger sister. She writes: 'I'm in Paris, I've left Marennes and I'm not going back. Mother knows. And I don't care, so please spare me any kind of attempt to make me "see sense". I'm staying with a friend, 16 Rue Manin, by Parc des Buttes Chaumont, drop round if you like. I hope you're not angry with me. Anne.'

He thinks for a while. He goes over to the desk; Garçon is in the shower, humming loudly to himself.

It's five o'clock in the afternoon and the halls of residence are deserted. Unreal. He wonders if he should go now, to see Anne. Then he sits down abruptly, pulls the cover off the typewriter, and stares at it with vacant eyes. He types an A and then an S. Nothing happens. *She* has gone, she's stopped speaking to him. It's time for him to find her.

He doesn't know what is in store for him.

He gets up, grabs his jacket, and runs out of the room. Downstairs, by the exit, he sees Marie Bessonville with Fred, the stupid Englishman. He tries to walk quickly past them, but Marie comes running up and throws her arms around him.

Marie: Patrice ...

Brother: Hello!

Marie: I've been looking for you.

Brother: Yes, I, I ... My sister has moved to Paris.

Marie: How lovely. I'd like to see you again.

Brother: You're seeing me now.

Marie: What's wrong? Why are you hiding from me?

Brother: I ... I just haven't been very well for the past few days. Everything's all right.

Marie: Come with me, come now, just for a little while!

Brother: But ...

Marie takes him by the hand and pulls him away, waving at the Englishman, who stares stupidly at them both. This all makes him very uncomfortable. Marie takes him to the metro and they ride into the city; all the way there, Marie looks at his hands, and he says nothing. They end up in a park he's never been to before. She walks by his side the whole time. Then they sit down under a tree, not a soul in sight. The sky is threatening a light rain.

Marie: I need to talk to you.

Brother: Did we have to come here for that?

Marie: I like this park, and it's quieter here at this time of day.

Marie's hair is up and she is wearing black trousers and a loose, white men's shirt — a little unusual, he thinks. He stares at her arms and her legs and he feels embarrassed again. He thinks about that evening in his room and instantly blushes.

Marie: I like you, Patrice, and I don't know why you're afraid of me. I mean, I'm not that bad.

Brother: I'm not afraid, I'm just a bit ... well ...

Marie: No, Patrice, you *are* afraid, and you've been avoiding me ever since that evening. But it was good, wasn't it? I thought you liked me, too.

Brother: I don't understand what you want from me.

Marie (surprised): What I want? I thought we wanted the same thing ... and you ... I don't understand you, Patrice! Do you ... ?

(Marie takes a small bag out of her pocket: grass. Marie is modern. Recently a lot of places have started to smell of this stuff, the university toilets and the courtyard. She starts to roll a joint.)

Brother: Marie ...

Marie: Why don't you come to the protests? It's important! Why do you never come with us when we go out? Why don't you like people?

Brother: What makes you think that? I'm just busy.

Marie (loudly): Busy? Busy? Doing what? Writing your stories — well, fine! But stories have people in them too, and you honestly don't have a clue ...

Brother: How would you know that?

Marie: I've read them.

He feels ashamed.

Brother: That's not all I'm doing. And anyway, it's just a hobby.

Marie: It isn't a hobby. Literature is all you're interested in; you don't go to any other lectures, you don't care about anything else … Everyone thinks it's weird.

Brother: I don't care what they think.

Marie: And what about me? Don't you care about me, either?

Brother: You were afraid of me the other night, weren't you?

Marie (lowering her eyes): Well, you know, you were so strange, those things you did, and then you wanted me to do the same to you … You were different, that's true, but no, I wasn't afraid. I liked it, Patrice. (Marie blushes a little. Perhaps she isn't so modern after all.)

Brother (looking away): I'm sorry. I don't know what's wrong with me, either.

Marie leans over and kisses him. At once, he is calm and contented. And there is no one but him and Marie Bessonville — pretty Marie. Maybe it's luck — that she is here with him, that she was in his room, that it happened, because Marie is popular. Marie is desirable. But he hasn't really *seen* her before now. He doesn't know her. He puts his arms around her and gives her hair a gentle pull. This evening, he feels like a different person.

Suddenly, impetuously, he pulls up her shirt and kisses her breasts. Marie tenses, breathes faster; everything clenches within her.

He senses a force of some kind — and then, finally, he sees *her*. She is standing behind the tree, staring at the two of them. He shakes his head and looks at Marie in shock.

Marie: What's wrong?

Brother: Nothing, nothing …

Marie: Kiss me.

They kiss. He slides his right hand between her legs, looks around; the tree is covering them and their fathomless depths. His strength grows, because he can sense *she*'s there. Marie has helped him to reach this point. And is helping him now, guiding his hand. He satisfies Marie, she moans and hisses and murmurs indistinctly. He smiles. He has to explore Marie's body again at once, it's so beautiful …

A few minutes later, they lean back against the tree, and Marie looks up at the sky.

Marie: It's going to rain.

Brother: Yes.

Marie: Do you have to go?

Brother: I'll come and see you afterwards.

Marie lives in a flat, which she currently has to herself. Her flatmate is away; she told him this three days ago, when they bumped into each other in the corridor.

Marie: I'll be waiting.

★

An old building, with no concierge. He walks up the stairs, knocks. Loud music is booming out from the third floor. He knocks again, more assertively. An unshaven guy in a dressing gown throws open the door.

Brother: I'm looking for Anne.

Guy: Anne? Oh, right, come in.

The flat is old; smoke hangs in the air, and the wallpaper is tattered and covered in posters of bands. There's a guitar in the corner, empty beer cans and unwashed dishes scattered everywhere. It smells musty.

Anne appears from another room; she is barefoot and has a cigarette in her mouth. She has changed. She's stopped wearing red lipstick and got a strange haircut — she looks unkempt. She lets out a laugh and throws her arms around his neck, which she has never done before. He's confused.

Anne: I'm so glad. I didn't think you'd come. And then I would have come to see you … Eventually, I mean, when I'd stopped being angry.

Brother: What are you doing here? Whose flat is this?

Anne: Oh, they're friends of mine. Jean used to go out with Catherine, do you remember Catherine? She had this cool car, what was it again?

Brother: And what do you intend to do here?

Anne: Don't know yet. We're protesting. It's great. There are eight of us here, and it's really exciting. And then I might get a job as well. Jean's been here for a while now, and he knows some people.

Brother: Anne, this is absurd. I mean, you might think it's all fun and games to start with, but ...

Anne: Come on, Brother, it's fine. I know what I'm letting myself in for.

Brother: What about Mother, she'll ...

Anne: I think she'll make her peace with it eventually. I've spoken to Mone, she'll explain it to her. I just couldn't stay there any longer.

Brother: Anne ...

Anne: You could take me out to dinner, I'm ravenous.

He agrees to the plan. They go downstairs. Anne has got changed and is now wearing a long skirt and a t-shirt that says 'Destruction' in English. He thinks it odd. He looks away.

They walk and walk; he doesn't know what to say. He thinks about Marie being back in his life. He thinks how much he is looking forward to typing again tonight, when everyone is finally asleep. When it's quiet.

15. APIDAPI (2004)

It had been raining for days, long enough to drive anyone mad. Laura called in sick, although she wasn't sick. She sat on the window seat, drinking grappa and eating prunes. More rain. It suited her mood.

Her flat, her carefully designed domicile: Laura stared at it with dead eyes. Her books didn't speak to her. The phone seldom rang. Her sister called once, asking what her plans were for the summer and why she couldn't just say yes to Belgium. Laura told her she didn't know yet.

Laura sat on the window seat and thought about her husband, her ex-husband. It was funny, knowing someone for seven years and then suddenly not knowing that person anymore, as if he'd never existed. She had lost her taste for the prunes. On the sofa, beside the stairs leading up to the bedroom, lay the folder. The images she had seen as she was reading flashed through her mind, but she wanted nothing to do with all that.

Wasn't the future just the past turned inside out?

The doorbell rang. It had been so long since anyone had rung her doorbell that it made her jump. She heaved herself up off the window seat and opened the heavy door cautiously, very cautiously. The red-haired boy with the glasses was standing in front of her. He was wet through.

'Hi … Can I come in?'

'What are you doing here?'

'You haven't been in touch, so I just thought I might …'

'Oh. Right. Um, okay, come in.'

She gave him a towel and sent him into the bathroom. Then she became conscious that she had no make-up on, was wearing an old pair of dungarees, and that her feet were bare. She was uncomfortable with him seeing her feet … She hastily pulled on a pair of old socks and tied back her dishevelled hair.

He came out of the bathroom with his hair tousled, in a white vest and socks. His sodden trousers clung to his legs.

'I'm sorry about this … It's a wonderful place you've got here.'

'Would you like some tea?'

'Oh, yes please.'

She went into the kitchen — tiled in black, with glass-fronted cupboards. The boy followed, taking everything in.

Laura put some water on to boil and made camomile tea — the only sort she could find. She fetched her bottle of grappa and leaned against the fridge. 'Terrible weather, it just refuses to stop …' she muttered awkwardly.

The boy drank the tea and kept looking about him. 'It's really lovely here … I mean that.'

'Well, there comes a time when you're too old for flat-shares.' What a stupid thing to say, what made her think of that?

'True. I just came because I wanted to ask …'

'I've read through the folder and the book. It's interesting, but I don't know what any of this has to do with me.'

'Didn't you think it was an interesting story? Didn't it move you?'

'Many things move me, including the poor children in Africa, and yet here I am.'

'I beg you …'

'Listen, kiddo—' that was entirely the wrong tone to take, again! Never mind, carry on — 'You want some advice from me? Go and find someone in the literature department, explain everything to them, apply for a grant, travel to Paris, and write a thrilling dissertation about it. The topic is certainly an original one.'

He looked awkwardly into his steaming cup. For a second, she felt sorry for him. She couldn't think of anything better to say. She was being honest. Trying, at least.

'But I don't want someone from the literature department, I don't want to write a dissertation. I want you to help me. Could I possibly have a little shot of that grappa?'

'Oh, of course, I'm sorry.' She poured him some from the bottle. He drained the glass quickly and looked about him again. 'You're not happy at the moment, are you? That's why you haven't been at the Academy all week, am I right?'

'What? No, I've had a cold.'

'I want you to help me, to come with me … to Paris. Please. I can't do it without you.'

'Excuse me, but we don't know one another — and I find this a little intrusive, you dropping round like this — where did you even get my address? I told you my area wasn't literary studies, it was the visual arts …' It *is* the visual arts, present tense, darling! 'This really isn't my field, I mean, and I don't know what it is you want from me.' All of a sudden, she realised she had begun to use the polite form of address, which she never did with students. It made her smile to herself. She just couldn't put her finger on exactly why. She needed to pull herself together.

He said nothing, apparently untroubled by what she'd just said. He had clearly been expecting this resistance; but soon he would have to go, to give up, leave her domain. Then she would go back to the window seat, to the prunes she had stopped enjoying.

The woman from the black folder had tried to summon an apocalypse … but the apocalypse never came. That had been the way since … since forever. You couldn't start anything; everything had already been started. It was the end that was missing.

'I need you. It's really important …' He was tenacious.

'But there's nothing I can do!'

'Yes, there is! You can save me!'

'Oh, come on. Really? I'm not interested in the story, my French is terrible, and I don't want to — are those reasons not enough for you? And now you're harassing me.'

'I'm not harassing you! You're just going through a bad patch and feeling defiant or something …'

'That's enough! I don't want to do this. Find another supervisor.'

'I don't need a supervisor, I need a partner.'

'Partner? Partner?'

'Yes, a partner!'

She finished her grappa and poured herself another. She was bewildered and annoyed. This was all too much. Her mind suddenly turned the clock back … the dead baby … Oh, perfect, that was all she needed; the black thoughts had returned. She sat down at the table.

'Honestly, I can't …' she said, trying to take a rather milder tone.

There was shock in the boy's eyes as he stared at her. He must have finally accepted her refusal.

The boy had freckles on his nose. Laura liked that. He looked so lost, all of a sudden.

Then he leapt to his feet. 'In that case, I'd better go. I'm sorry. I'm at the Academy every day. You might still change your mind … There are a few weeks left before the summer holidays. I really hope you reconsider, and please forgive me …' he didn't wait for a response; almost flinging open the door, he rushed out into the street.

Laura watched him go. What had just happened?

It had stopped raining. She went to the window seat, but didn't touch the prunes. She held her breath. The world was silent and calm, and she should be, too.

Then she caught sight of the folder that was still lying on the sofa. She sat down and opened it.

16. ICE AGE / BOOK 1 (1953)

She is lying in the bathtub, which is full of sea monsters. She is alone. She is naked and doesn't know if she should climb or fall. Everything turns the colour of dead leaves. Nothing moves, and as the armies of ants scale her brain, she feels ticklish all over. She lets her head drop back into the bathtub, then looks up, her eyes full of water. She picks a towel up off the floor and dries herself. Then she takes a dress and pulls it over her naked body; she likes it that way. Then into her coat. She goes out, and the door stays open and howls after her. She runs down the stairs; she's hungry, and needs cigarettes.

She runs through the streets. Then she is standing … somewhere near the rue Fortuny, looking about her. She doesn't know how she got here. It's a lovely evening, with summer on its way and the city packed with gawkers trying to trample time to death.

*

Why did I forget everything I once knew?

I cannot stand you, you penitents, you poor creatures, coming to life in your ecstatic songs about forgiveness … I don't want forgiveness, I came to take everything, I know it. I could vomit when I think about it all, all the senseless songs of the universe, which itself is nothing but a few specks of dust. I came only to leave and tear everything away with me. I don't want your love. Time stops crawling on my skin.

*

She stands still and the sight of her arouses pity. She has grown thinner, dark shadows have appeared under her eyes, and a passer-by throws some coins at her feet, which makes her laugh. She doesn't want to move; she wants to crush time's skull. She wants to kill her hunger. And so she stands there, on the square, on the tarmac, for eight hours, until all the people have gone, until the sun has been defeated by the moon, until the moon becomes a shadow once more, trying to challenge herself to a duel. She stands and stands and talks to the bedrock beneath her feet. Some people look at her; some don't notice.

The earth grows soft. The birds begin to lament, and she is still standing there. That is the decision she has made.

Sometimes, yes, sometimes she thinks about all the people she has known. What it was like to have another life. It was troubled and terrible, but she had food and warm bedclothes and a canary to talk to. She left it all behind. She set off to end the world.

How awful it is to have drunk loneliness with your mother's milk.

She started walking at dawn; her legs had become rocks, they creaked and crackled. She walked, learning to walk again one step at a time. She walked, and the streets were deserted.

The empty city rolled from side to side. She found a half-smoked cigarette on the ground and picked it up. Walking had become her sole purpose. Fear devoured the morning, and the smell of hot croissants wafted through the streets of Paris. Trams clattered by in the distance. She found some matches in her pocket and smoked — a new beginning.

She thought of the girl called Fanny, who had paid for stories with her blood, though she didn't know it. In some other life, Fanny would understand.

She knew a baker's apprentice in the rue de Charonne who would sometimes slip her the leftovers from the previous day. She took the half-empty tram there.

Another, more handsome apprentice was opening up the bakery today. He gave a start when he saw her.

'Can I have a croissant?'

'Sorry?'

'Can I … I knew Pierre here; you must be new. I'll tell you a story, and you can give me a croissant in return. I'm hungry. Do you understand?'

'I'm not allowed. What kind of story?'

'Doesn't matter, choose one.'

'Um, I'm not sure … Don't you have any money?'

'I want a croissant!'

'All right, all right.' His dialect gave him away as a southerner. She found it calming.

'Will you give me one?'

'All right, wait.'

He gave her a warm croissant and jotted something down in a dog-eared notebook.

She bit into it. It was a miracle. She had promised him a story. 'There's a courtyard round the back there, come on, let's go, and I'll tell you a story … It's still early, no one's going to come.'

'But I have to work …'

'Don't worry about that. You can close up for ten minutes.'

He obeyed, eyeing her the whole time. He must have been about her age. He locked up the bakery and followed her. They went into the yard behind the building and sat down on the flagstones. The city was starting to wake up.

'What do you want to hear about?'

'I don't know. You don't have to tell me a story, it's fine, I'll pay for the croissant.'

'No, no, no!'

Her voice was so loud it made him jump. She told him about Antigone, she told him about freedom.

She saw that he was moved. How pitiful. She said nothing and he kissed her and held her tight and all at once it was warm and the whole world smelled of fresh rolls and she sank down into a place where she didn't exist. He didn't know her … he knew nothing, nothing … and for a moment she thought it would be wonderful to know nothing and to smell of bread rolls.

'What's your name?'

'What?'

'Your name?'

'Saré, Saré …'

He said nothing more, and so she walked away. He watched her go.

The sun blinded the city. The sun crept into her and began to thaw something there. But the ice between her ribs was a place the sun could not reach.

17. APIDAPI (2004)

It had been a beautiful June: lots of tourists, lots of sunshine, good weather. Positivity. She had started giving lectures again.

The boy was laying siege to the front entrance of her apartment block again, like he had on so many other days. She'd given up counting how many. He would come over straight after his lectures and stand outside, not speaking. She had tried to talk to him once, but he refused to say anything. He didn't want his folder back, either. He just stood there, waiting. But every evening at eleven o'clock sharp, he left; just picked up his bike and rode away. He disappeared.

Laura couldn't help but smile every time she caught sight of him outside her block. There was something comical about him. The way he got on his bike, always a little perplexed and clumsy, and rode off without having achieved anything.

In the early days, when this had first started, Laura had considered letting someone from the Academy know — student welfare, or the police — but she didn't. What would she have said? He wasn't bothering her, after all; just standing there, waiting. She could already hear her cynical colleagues saying to her: 'Every one of us is waiting for something. He must be in love with you, sweetie.' By which they would have meant: 'Go to bed with him, then he'll see how cold and hollow you are, and you'll be rid of him once and for all.'

Laura stood at the window, looked down at him one last time, and then went into the bathroom. In front of the mirror, she began to take off her clothes, staring at herself all the while. She saw her pale skin, her breasts, her strangely protruding ribs, her nose — which had turned pink from drinking grappa every evening, the hard line of her mouth; she saw her age and the listlessness that had taken possession of her body.

Laura van den Ende, how could it have come to this? How did you get so tired and so old?

She turned the taps on, checked the temperature, and was mesmerised, for a moment, by the sound. The sound of the water was the sound of her childhood. The smell of the rose-scented soap. Splashing in the tub — a childhood sensation.

Then suddenly there were the buses, the buses to Sindangbarang, along one coastline of a country with 13,600 islands ... the country that has the most sunsets, as she had always said, at age twelve, at thirteen, even at twenty. There had been water everywhere; they'd always taken boats and little ships from one place to another, or sometimes the small, stifling buses, there and back. People had hung out of the doors and windows, all shouting and breathing heavily. And then in monsoon season, the three of them — Laura, her little sister, their mother — would sit on the veranda, waiting for her father and eating mangoes. In monsoon season everyone was quiet, even the children grew silent and thoughtful and ate plump, ripe mangoes. They sat on the veranda, played chess, sometimes, or Mother would read aloud. And when it stopped raining, there were parties and everyone danced. Laura and her little sister weren't allowed to go; even after twelve years of the ocean, twelve years abroad, twelve years of a foreign language, twelve years on another continent, Mother hadn't found a way to be part of life there. The house smelled of coffee. Papa always brought coffee back from his business trips, from ships laden with the stuff. All the time they lived there, when he was working, when he was happy ... until Mother left him for Europe, until she had worn his mind down so much that in the end, he could no longer say or think or want anything. Laura and her sister and Papa. They went to see the Borobudur temple. The most magnificent building in Java, watched over by five hundred Buddha statues ... Years later, Laura had written about that building and its history.

She had dreamed about it night after night once they were back in Europe, once they had started their new life in the land of bicycles, which was suddenly supposed to be their home.

Papa always used to tell stories about the ocean and how you could talk to it. He would tell them about the fishermen of Goa and how golden the sands were there.

Laura and her father on the beach in Krui, at night, a stop on their journey ... Him, smelling of coffee, hugging her and saying: 'Look, look, Laura: this is all there is, you can't expect anything more from life, you shouldn't expect anything more. Here, Laura, this is paradise, you just have to smell it.' And she had smelled it that night, and seen it, too. Laura, who was nine then, and Papa, the big white man with the loose shirts and calloused fingertips. With the coffee smell on his neck and a pair of sunglasses that kept sliding down his nose. He'd never exchanged his outdated sunglasses for a new pair.

And then the five years of boarding school in Jakarta, surrounded by other white girls who all had funny names. Their names were so foreign and their scents were so foreign and what they said was stupid. Laura missed the beaches of Sindangbarang, and the coffee smell of home, and her little sister. She missed the salt in the cracks of her elbows, missed her turtles and her rain; remembered travelling to visit the Ranakpur sculptures with Papa, all magnificent and filled with wonder, these stone elephants standing there so mysterious, waiting for millennia for something that was known only to them.

And her mother ... she had spent years sitting there reading English newspapers. She had tied her girls' hair up with brightly coloured ribbons, never let them run around barefoot; met her friends for tea at the Hyatt, got to know all the embassy wives who came and went over the years, and never spoke a word of Indonesian, never stopped mentally converting the rupiahs to guilders — never, ever stopped doing that — right up until they left.

It was awful having to play golf with all the Phyllises and Lucies, and sometimes in the evenings Laura would sneak off and write long letters to Papa — wherever he happened to be just then — asking him to please come and get her soon. He didn't come. No one came to get her. She snuck out at night, lost her way in the narrow streets of Jakarta, and then went back to her boarding house, not knowing where else to go.

Laura and her sister Alice, the two white girls. Names their mother had chosen for them, names passed down from their aristocratic ancestors in far-off Europe. Names they were supposed to wear with dignity. The names, at least, should retain their pedigree.

Every summer, there was talk of spending the holidays in Haarlem; yes, this year, for sure. And yet they never got away, there was always the coffee to think of, and no one ever went away without Papa. Not once in all those twelve years, and that was fine.

Little Alice with the straw-blonde hair, which all the children of Sindangbarang wanted to touch ... Alice, who was the better swimmer. Alice, who now had two children and a farm in Belgium. Alice who, when they first arrived in the Netherlands, refused to speak a word of Dutch for three months. When did she start being nice? When did she start turning into her mother? Dressing like her, speaking like her, eating like her, and talking about the same rubbish? When Mother broke off contact with Papa, maybe? Or when the row over the money started? Or maybe when they called him secretly one January night, dialling the code for Jakarta from a telephone box, in the cold; Alice and Laura standing together on the corner of a street in Haarlem, having crept out of the house, not wanting to break their mother's heart, to make her disappointed in her daughters for missing the Papa they no longer knew, who spoke fluent Indonesian and knew nothing but the country of 13,600 islands? When they called and a young woman's voice, making an effort to sound European, breathed an 'Allo?' into the receiver?

Yes, maybe then ... Or maybe they had stopped smelling paradise much earlier. The forgetting had darkened every corner of their brains.

But whenever she heard gushing water, Laura also heard the voices of Indonesia, the voices of a distant land where she had once known what paradise smelled like.

Her mother still read English newspapers and invited her friends to tea, to the big house in Haarlem on the North Sea coast, a sea which was cold and uninviting, unlike the ocean of Laura's childhood. And her daughters didn't exchange a single word about that other place for years: neither of them ever mentioned Indonesia, neither drank coffee (tea in every possible variety!), neither said that they longed for something different, that they were lost and alone in this cold and scentless country. Eventually, Laura moved out. Alice called her just once while Laura was studying in Amsterdam, sounding tearful: 'Laura, Laura, I can't stand it anymore. Let's go back, let's go and live with Papa. You can study in Jakarta, can't you, you can …' Then she just sobbed — and her older sister had had nothing to say. By then they had spent eight years in the Netherlands. Laura stayed silent, and soon Alice started talking about new friends and her holiday to Sicily.

The land of sunsets was like poison to their mother. She'd finally lost her husband to that country, to a foreign country she did not love. To the country, to the ocean, to the coffee, and to an Indonesian woman seventeen years her junior. And that was that. Laura had never had the courage to go back, not even once she'd stopped calling her mother at weekends. And over time, both Papa and Indonesia had been forgotten, too.

Just once, one night after a lot of sex and a lot of kissing with her husband, the only man whom Laura had learned to love since her father, had she begun to remember — and until dawn her husband lay with his head on her belly as she talked and talked. And afterwards, he said: 'I want to go there with you, I want you to show me all those places.' She didn't reply. But inwardly, she thought for the first time that maybe she could go back, with him at her side.

The bath. Laura snapped out of her reverie. Then she let the water rinse away all her thoughts. But suddenly she felt the language of her childhood returning; she was letting it thaw on her tongue. And she remembered that a boy was standing outside who would wait there until eleven, and for some reason this thought amused her so much that she laughed out loud.

18. OLGA (1986)

She was still wearing the old, polka-dot dress. Had there ever been a life before the book? She had copied it all out. She had learned what it was to weave a cocoon from her own loneliness ... Olga felt physically old. Each day she waited for nightfall as it crept slowly towards her. She waited for her dreams. She waited for *her* to appear in them. Step by step, Olga was walking towards madness.

She was horribly afraid. Afraid of waking up, of these hot drops called time dripping onto her temples like hot wax. How many more hours and days still lay ahead of her? And how was she to kill them?

And Olga was afraid of people, from whom she now felt entirely removed. Olga feared the morning that was looming in the sky.

She got up, crawled out of bed and went to the window, threw it open, stared out at the light-drenched city, and began to sweat. She felt sick, and pressed herself against the cold wall to calm herself a little. Full of fear, Olga pulled on her clothes. She forced herself to take Lydia for a walk, to have a cup of coffee, and cycle off into the day. She couldn't stay at home during the day now — there, the spectres would come and devour her brain.

She could no longer stand to look in the mirror, to be aware of her own smell. Her room, her footsteps, her everyday existence were all a great prison. And sometimes she would find herself suddenly furious, with a boundless urge to destroy things.

The streets had emptied out. Olga cycled through the Marais in the cool evening breeze. She was riding around aimlessly; she had asked a neighbour if she could feed Lydia today, unable to bear the thought of having to go home.

She had received a letter from her mother that had made her cry. The things she wrote! Some drivel about savings, and then: 'look after yourself, Paris is a big city, be careful and work hard and don't worry about us, we're happy when our daughter is happy'.

Olga thought of her mother and remembered the wallpaper of their flat in Parthenay, a faceless little town. The kitchen with its spice jars; the striped towels in the bathroom, all hung up according to size. How had she stood it there? How had she survived the Sunday walks and the neighbourhood weddings, the days and nights? Luckily, she had forgotten.

Reading the letter, Olga had been angry. Her parents had slaved away all their lives so they could own little spice jars and towels and put some money aside — money their daughter was now squandering pointlessly in the city.

Why had she gone to university? Her mother hoped her daughter would become a teacher one day. Why had she come *here*? Why hadn't she boarded a plane at the first opportunity and got as far away as possible?

She rode west, more slowly now. A café on the corner was still open, and she could hear people chatting. Olga slowed down even further. Then someone called her name. She braked and scanned the customers for a face she recognised. Then she saw Michel, the blond boy from the literature course she had found so charming just the previous year.

'Olga, how are you? Where have you been?'

'Hello, Michel.'

'I've been hoping to catch you for days. I wanted to ask if you'd like to go for a drink with me.' He was in his mid-twenties and had carefree blue eyes and a broad, obliging smile.

'I'm not sure. I'm really busy at the moment.'

'Oh, come on. I'm free now, and I was about to head home, but now that I see you … You look wonderful, that's a great dress!'

'Thanks.' Olga still lacked the courage and the determination to act on the things she had thought about, she was still too afraid. So she sat down at a corner table and had coffee with Michel. She felt lost. She didn't know what she was doing, but even worse, she didn't know what else she should have been doing.

Michel told her about university, about a concert he'd been to the previous week; he smiled as he talked, and once he even placed his hand over hers. She felt wholly indifferent towards him and wondered why he was showing so much interest in her all of a sudden. Months ago, when she had worshipped him, he'd more or less ignored her.

Eventually he paid the bill and they got up. He convinced her to leave her bike and let him give her a lift. In the car, he pushed a cassette into the tape deck. An unfamiliar melody. Pop. Olga didn't know a lot about music — Olga didn't really know a lot about life in general. That was something she had realised over the last few weeks.

They went to a club and drank beer. Olga was a lightweight, but she went on drinking all the same. He talked and talked, and she started to lose the thread.

At some point they danced, and he held her tight, pressed against him, and Olga felt safe in a way that seemed suspicious to her. They kissed. Then Olga had to go to the toilets and throw up. A Black girl with immensely long plaits held her hair back, but laughed at her as well. She staggered back to the dancefloor and moved in time to the music. Someone pressed against her hips and put his arms around her waist. It wasn't Michel. Eventually Michel appeared and pulled her away from the unknown man.

He kissed her again and asked if everything was all right. Then she asked him to take her away.

She fell asleep in the car, with no idea where they were going. He helped her up the stairs and whispered something she didn't catch.

The flat was large and full of cassettes and wine crates and photos of people she didn't know. He liked to take photographs, he said, and offered her another beer. Olga drank and thought about Nadine. How good it would be to be at her place now.

Olga sat on the sofa and accepted one of his cigarettes. She had an urge to smoke, an urge to get back the life she had once loved without ever harbouring a doubt.

He turned the music right up and she felt her head was going to burst, but she didn't say anything.

The boy sat beside her and stroked her hands and told her she was beautiful.

Olga let it all happen. She wanted to come back to life, wanted to feel things again; to stop thinking, dreaming. She took a swig of her beer and coughed.

The boy unbuttoned her dress. She was just thinking she would have to call Nadine and tell her everything, when something fetched her back to the present moment.

He was on top of her. The sofa was too narrow and the music too loud. He murmured something, but she couldn't make sense of his words. He was breathing loudly and he grabbed her breast, but she stayed motionless; something in her had died.

She felt the unfamiliar weight of a naked male body bearing down on her and her head stopped working ... She reached for his hand and put it between her legs, which usually turned her on. She gave a little cry; he carried on, asked if everything was all right; she saw his penis and took it in her hand, in the hope of feeling some emotion.

She slipped out of her knickers, pushed the beer bottle away, got on top of him, and the boy groaned. She was no longer thinking about him. She let him take her body. The pain it caused her reminded her that she was alive.

He swam through her body, without ever touching her.

And then she hit him, and hit him again, and again.

He was taken aback, and fended her off; then he got angry and slapped her in the face and told her to stop it.

She laughed; it was good to exist again. She scratched her thighs until they bled. She laughed again. He told her she was sick, and got up. Olga lay there — naked, blood-smeared — then she drew her knees up to her chest, curled into a ball, and sobbed.

19. WOMAN (2004)

THIS FUCKING CITY DISGUSTS ME.

The beach is empty, free of tourists. Evening is approaching and the water is calm. The odd ship off in the distance. Eyes heavy and full of sand. Silence in every pore and a can't-go-on in every breath. But the evening is so patient. No stories to listen to for miles around. Sadly, she's heard them all already.

Many years ago, there was a carousel on this spot. A little fairground. One night, a gigantic wave came and destroyed everything. It was a sad sight: all the little horses and the candy-floss stalls, rusting away on the beach. That was many, many years ago. Now time has wiped it all away.

A few shredded thoughts remain, thoughts of a daughter who is tall and pretty and who will soon be going away to make the most of her school holidays.

The cigarette smoke rises into the sky. The bottle is buried in the sand, so the Scotch won't spill. Her thoughts swing back and forth.

In the distance, someone is singing, probably up in the harbour bar, which even at this time of year is stuffed full of tourists eager for adventure, trying to escape their everyday melancholy.

She kicks off her sandals and takes a few steps towards the water.

'I'll get over it,' she thinks to herself. She used to enjoy the taste of wine, and listening to music in the bath. Hale and hearty. She read books and smoked and wore her father's old gumboots in the rain. And now …

It wasn't too far from this city, on the seafront in Port Macquarie, that she had met Frank. It had been like a dream, a daydream. Frank was the man who had fathered her two children. Who had later shot and killed himself, after suffocating their son. She had loved Frank on the beach at Port Macquarie. And even six, seven, eight years later, she'd still been able to call up that feeling.

The drive for love, this all-destroying drive — it's everywhere, it could send you mad. What is it for, when it only ends in loss? The masochism of it, vomit-inducing! The water plays about her ankles.

Someone told her she should take a holiday. A holiday from life, maybe? She needs to go away and let go, she decides. And she doesn't know why she is feeling that need now, in particular; perhaps it's the palm trees, perhaps the memory of the rusted carousel horses. No matter where the trip takes her, there has to be a trip.

Her knees are wet, her jeans are wet, her shirt is wet, the water swallows down everything she owns. She swims out.

MAX, I'LL FIND YOU …

The lights dawdle on the surface of the water and the noises from the harbour grow more distant with every stroke.

20. ME (2005)

People should be banned from making promises! How many do you need to hear before you realise you've been conned? If I wasn't about to be abandoned, I wouldn't be sitting here and writing now. But that makes no sense.

I'm fully aware that sounds childish. Or maybe not?

Ever since the day death entered my life, I have been trying to discover whether I'm living. I don't want to blame my parents and a traumatic childhood for the way I am, fuck that. 'Very early in my life it was too late.' I even know which book I got that line from, it's by Marguerite Duras ...

My phone is silent and I don't want to sleep yet.

I came across a photo somewhere today, when I was looking for something to do. Worn out from all the attempts to reach people who are scattered all over the world and who could be my friends and lovers ...

Then I gave up and stared at the black-and-white photo. Two girls in a park, in that city of churches. The smaller one is me. I have sad eyes; little feet in worn-out shoes. The photo looks like it's from another century, when people had different beliefs and different lives. Is that — was that — really me, and is the present an extension of that self? Was I frightened back then that I would be abandoned, and is that why I look so sad?

I feel sympathy for me, for that child.

I wonder when things got like this. For me.

I have no orientation; never did. I blunder around in other people's stories, trying to find my own. I can never find the right street, I get lost ... How can I find my story in this one?

21. BROTHER (1968)

Time has become indigestible; there are protests everywhere, but he keeps to his vow of silence. They praise his good honest talent. Marie loves him, Marie Bessonville tries to love him. He is afraid. His sister goes on demonstrations and hennas her hair. He writes at night, when everyone is asleep. Garçon has learned to ignore the noise. Sometimes he wants to hurt Marie Bessonville. He has dreams, and every morning wakes up nauseous from them. He sleeps badly and there are deep shadows under his eyes.

Mother sometimes telephones, and then he has to go downstairs to the recreation room. He finds it embarrassing to talk to her when other people might be listening. He feels desolate and wants to control Marie, but she's like water. The harder he grasps, the faster she runs through his fingers. Everyone likes her and they don't know why she wants him. At night, he dreams of *her*.

People are listening to rock music and going to festivals; they don't want to learn and live like they used to. That's the age he's living in. More and more lectures and seminars are being cancelled because of the stupid protests. Anne is living with some idiot, and he sometimes imagines her doing the same things she did that time in her room.

Spring is beautiful and ripe for love, but all he feels is anger and disgust. He writes short stories that are praised and printed in minor magazines, at the recommendation of his lecturers. And he lives in the constant fear that *she* might be discovered. She doesn't even know he exists; they have missed one another — he's sure of that.

Once, he tells Marie Bessonville that he would like to go somewhere with her where they won't be disturbed. They go to a restaurant in the

Latin Quarter and eat fish and salad. Marie is wearing men's trousers and a blouse with a plunging neckline. He is disgusted by the thought that other men can see her breasts, but he doesn't say anything. Marie smokes. She has been waiting so long for this moment.

Marie goes to the demonstrations every day. Marie has beautiful hair, tied back in a loose knot.

After they have eaten, they wander aimlessly around the streets. Marie asks if he wants some grass. He says yes and she drags him into a basement; he doesn't know where they are. Marie is a real Parisian and she knows the city like the back of her hand. At her side, he feels lost.

It's a club, dark; Janis Joplin is playing. He doesn't like the music, and it smells of marijuana. Couples are lying around everywhere. He's surprised that Marie knows such places — the woman is a mystery. He thinks that Anne must hang around in these clubs, too. Marie goes to the bar, gets two glasses of wine, and hands him a cigarette she has rolled. He smokes, not knowing what to say.

Soon, they are kissing. He feels her knee pressing against his leg; he's excited. Someone is smoking an opium pipe, and people are dancing sweatily in the cramped space. They are sitting on a musty sofa. Here, now. With her and her knee. Everything he could ever have dreamed of: her knee.

All at once, he thrusts a hand between her legs. Marie seems to enjoy it, she doesn't stop him. She moans softly, but no one looks around.

He feels his body getting heavy. He likes the way she smells; she is wearing a little perfume on her throat and he likes the scent, floral and light. He moves his hand between her legs and kisses her neck. He takes her hand and puts it on his crotch; his trousers are too tight now, everything is too tight …

Marie: I love you.

Brother: We need to go …

Marie: No, we don't. I want to be with you.

Brother: Why do you love me?

Marie: That doesn't matter.

Brother: I don't know what's wrong with me.

Marie: I can open you up. I can look inside you.

Brother: I don't know if that's a good thing.

Marie: I don't care. I'll tell you anything you want to know. I'm no saint.

Brother: I've hurt you.

Marie: I wanted you to.

Brother: I'm sorry.

Marie: Stop it, stop apologising! I'm here, aren't I? This is what I want!

Brother: You're strong.

Marie: Maybe. I want to walk this path with you.

Brother: You're crazy.

Marie (laughing): I don't like your stories.

Brother: I know, neither do I.

Marie: Why do you write them, then?

Brother: Just because. So that …

Marie: You have so much paper in your room. Garçon says you type every night. That's something else, isn't it?

Brother: I don't want to talk about it.

They don't talk anymore. They kiss. Then they go back to her place.

22. ICE AGE / BOOK 1 (1953)

Having everything is like having nothing. When you reach a certain point, you have to stop and wait to turn to stone; you have to summon the willpower to want nothing, and provoke life with your wanting.

I walked the streets of the kingdom of the dead, looking for my shadow; it had betrayed me. In my loneliness, which became my blessing, I searched for traces of my own self, but everything had been obliterated. I spoke to God. He said he was tired, he said he was disappointed. I told him he should leave it all to me, but he just shrugged.

I wandered the streets of Atlantis; everyone had perished, everyone had drowned, and been buried in the eternal cold of the water. I walked the streets, looking at the empty houses and the empty alleyways. A continent filled with dreams lay beneath my feet …

I went to my oasis, three hundred years later, and saw that it, too, had dried up. Everyone had ceased to WANT. I lit a fire of annihilation.

A life without words, a life that freezes to death and stops breathing. I want snow to start falling, flakes large as madness.

I take my dagger and cut out my heart. I lay it on the table and hack it to pieces. I carry on long after it has stopped beating. I watch, calmly.

I swim north, towards the North Pole, to where life must cease. Once I dined beside Tantalus, who slaughtered his own son to serve at a banquet for the gods; I tasted it … As I was going to Hades, I lost my way. I found myself in No Man's Land. The thing that makes us lose our way — is life.

I reach ʒero. I will be able to walk. Why did I ever leave the desert? Ophelia, I curse you. I will have all the nunneries burned down. I will turn your inferno into your happiness. Ophelia, I curse you.

★

Dawn was breaking and the book took on a life of its own in her hands. The morning light laid itself on her knee. The water in the bathtub, in Ophelia's pond, sloshed back and forth at the slightest twitch of her muscles.

Her hair, encircling her, took all desires from her. Hunger was the only sensation that had not been numbed. She tried to distract herself from it. It didn't work.

All the gods had grown tired and fat. Naked, she got out of the water, which had lost its transparency in the night. She rose and walked across the floor, dripping. She had consumed nothing now for forty-five hours. There were no more boundaries. The world map dissolved on her belly, flowed into her navel. For twenty hours she had sat in the bathtub, looking for the way BACK.

She had barred all ghosts from entering her attic room. The army of disillusionment knocked at the door.

Light pierced the window, the light she had once tried to catch between her thighs. The light of the sun.

She stood at the little window in her room and looked down at the city. She thought about the baker's apprentice and his kisses. And the warm bread he gave her in payment for those kisses. She got dressed and ran down the stairs.

23. APIDAPI (2004)

When that warm June neared its end and July greeted the city with rain and the red-haired boy was still standing outside her building until eleven on the dot — so far, he'd missed just one evening — Laura decided to go downstairs. She had begun to feel sorry for him. Her conscience was starting to prick her; the boy might be neglecting his studies.

She threw open the door and walked over to him. He was standing by the building's vehicle entrance and staring into space, his hands thrust into the pockets of his jeans. She'd almost got used to seeing him here like this.

He hadn't come on 28 June. She'd felt strange about it, but decided that he'd given up. She was relieved and concerned at the same time. Then, on the 29th, he had turned up again, and it had made her smile. If he arrived outside her building and took up his position before she got home, they would ignore each other. Not even a glance. Never. She would walk briskly past him and go in through the front door. Sometimes Laura watched him from the bedroom window, hidden behind the blinds, smoking, drinking grappa. When her sister called and embarked on one of her sermons, the sight of him was a nice distraction.

Now she was walking over to him. He was carrying an umbrella but hadn't opened it, even though it was raining.

'All right, that's enough!' she said, standing so close she could smell him. He smelled like a child. How old must he be? Twenty-three, twenty-four?

'I'm glad you came,' he said with a smile.

'That really is enough now.'

'So you're ready, then?'

'Ready? I've told you: I'm not going anywhere. Why won't you stop?'

'Just agree!'

'Go away, or I'll report you to the police. I swear, I'll report you!'

'Come to Paris with me. I don't care if you call the police or not — I'm going to stand here as long as you keep resisting. You have to come with me.'

'I don't have to do anything. I'm warning you, now. Stop it.'

'Come with me.'

'Okay, fine, I'm calling the police!' Laura yelled. And then flinched at her own voice. For the first time since he'd begun this siege, she considered the neighbours. What must they be thinking …

'You do what you think is right.'

Laura ran back inside and slammed the door behind her. She climbed the stairs, her breathing heavy and rapid, and pressed herself against the wall. She picked up the telephone. She hadn't planned to actually call the police when she'd said it, but now she was angry; his stubbornness had made her lose her cool. She didn't know who to call. She didn't even know the number for the local police off the top of her head. Maybe she should phone the rector and explain the whole thing to him. But what would he say? Everyone would assume the boy had a crush on her; of course they would. And in any case, she didn't particularly like the rector. And the police? People have a right to stand wherever they like, and he wasn't directly harassing her …

Laura's whole body was so tense that she felt she was on the verge of getting cramp. She stood in her book-lined living room and closed her eyes.

She saw her husband, saw his face so precisely, so clearly in her mind's eye it was like he was standing in front of her. Laura felt the hysteria rising through her. She looked out of the window — the red-haired boy was still there. Well, it was only just after nine.

She went into the kitchen, took a cigarette and a swig from yesterday's half-full glass of grappa. It tasted miserable. She coughed. Then she sat down at the old oak table — a gift from her friends for her thirtieth birthday, not long before she accepted the chair at the Academy.

There was a log jam in her head, and for a few minutes all she could think about was the man she had married. The man with whom she had spent seven years, with whom she had a dead child. She thought about his boxing gloves and his silent orgasms, his way of looking sideways and raising his eyebrows when he disapproved of something. She hadn't phoned him once since the divorce. And that was more than eighteen months ago, now.

She had no interest in the stupid book. Or Paris. Or the red-haired boy.

She saw the face of her eco-warrior brother-in-law, thought of the Lover she could go and meet, of her friends who were doing yoga or going to Portugal and stretching out in the sun, keeping an eye out for young, tanned men and discussing religion. She felt afraid. What could she wring from all the time that lay ahead of her? Yet more evenings alone with her grappa?

Laura stubbed out her cigarette in the glass, went back into the living room, and picked up the phone again. It was raining heavily now, but the boy was still down there, seemingly indifferent to the dreadful weather. Laura leaned against the wall and took a deep breath …

She remembered her first time. In Amsterdam, in student halls, in a bed that was too small even for one person. There was no lock on the door; someone was making a racket in the room next to hers, the place smelled of alcohol, and then there was a tiny spot of blood on the bedsheets. She thought of the boy whose face time had wiped from her memory. Who had smelled of beer. Thought of how it had felt to sleep with someone who meant nothing to you, how it felt to get drunk because it hurt, and how it felt to be lonely without being able to admit it.

She thought about the view from the plane over Indonesia, when she left the country for good. How it felt to live … to study, to mature, to become an adult and cold and jaded and dead inside.

She thought about all the trips and the single rooms in large hotels; thought about having to build a reputation for herself, the money that gave you independence. Cairo, New York. How had life felt then? She was afraid. She had forgotten so much. She had entered the year of forgetting.

Laura ran down the stairs, flung open the door, ran out into the rain, and shouted at him: 'All right, I'll come with you, I'll come, for fuck's sake. I'll come with you.'

The lad, entirely calm, not showing any hint of delight, nodded and pointed towards the front door. He was soaked through. Strange that both times he had entered her flat, he had been dripping wet from the rain. He took off his trainers; she threw him a towel, and he dried his hair. She went into the kitchen and put the kettle on. It was already dark outside. She set two cups of camomile tea down on the table. Took the grappa bottle down from the shelf. Looked at him. Then fetched two glasses and poured.

'I'll put a plan together. I'll bow out at whatever point I choose. You will accept the plans I make, and you'll do as I say. You'll accept money from me if it's necessary. You won't talk about the project at the Academy. You won't start any wild love affairs, you'll make yourself available, and you won't get sick. Don't smoke weed, get drunk, or tell me your whole life story, and don't try to talk me into anything. When I decide there's nothing more to be gained from this business, you'll accept that, too. If you can't live with any of these rules, you can leave now.'

'I'll agree to that.' He sipped his grappa. 'I won't get drunk, or high, or fall in love. I'm not lazy and I'll accept any help that's offered. I speak barely any French, but if I need to, then I'm a quick learner.'

'I suggest you tell me everything you know about this story; what you don't know, and what you want to know. I'll take care of the organisation. We'll fly out later this month, once the holidays are well underway. I don't really like flying, but it will save us a long, tiring car journey and hours of having to make conversation. I'll do some research before we go. Don't you have coursework to do over the holidays?'

He shook his head. 'No, all finished.'

'That's good. By the end of next week you'll have a research plan from me, and you'll study it thoroughly — understood?'

'Sure thing.' Now his face began to radiate something like joy.

Laura wondered what the hell she was doing.

He smiled, his expression beginning to thaw. He looked out of the window, at the canal and the torrential summer rain, at all Amsterdam's dismayed tourists. It was nice that he expected nothing more from her, that he was being obedient. To some extent, she found it reassuring.

'However, I do think there are some things I need to know about you.' She lit another cigarette.

'You can ask me anything.'

'How old are you?'

'Twenty-five.'

'Do you come from Amsterdam?'

'Well, partly. On my mother's side. My father is Danish. I lived in Odense until I was thirteen.'

'And you're studying …'

'Literature and cultural studies.'

'Odense …'

'Yup, not much going on up there.' He had such a strange smile.

'What did you do before university?'

'I did an internship at the archaeological institute in Copenhagen, went on a dig in Turkey. Then I went travelling, mostly in South America. I signed up for a history course in London, but left after two months. I wanted to write a book about the perception of art in South America; who knows how I came up with that idea. I even wrote 140 pages of it, then I lost my motivation. Eventually my father reached the end of his tether — no more money. So I stopped, and — well …'

'I understand.'

'You understand?'

'I mean …'

'Okay.'

'Odense …'

'Yeah, Odense. I really wanted to be a jazz musician. Jazz is my secret passion.'

'Jazz in Odense … sounds exciting.' They both laughed.

'Thank you. This means everything.' He said that before he left. At eleven on the dot.

24. WOMAN (2004)

The air outside is chilly, but the Scotch burns in her throat. She is sitting there on the couch, her slim legs tucked under her buttocks.

The television drones dully away. The end of term is coming up, and Lynn's off somewhere, celebrating. Her daughter is not supposed to see her drunk, but that was just impossible to manage today. *Indiana Jones* is on. Harrison Ford is currently looking very disconcerted, but soon Sean Connery will turn up and everything will be all right again. The way it should be.

Her mother called earlier. She'd known who it was before her mother had even said anything, just by the sound of her breathing. She asked after Lynn. Francesca replied the way she always did. Her mother is seventy-one now and looks fifty. Her mother was married to her father for forty-six years. He was a naval officer. Of those forty-six years, he spent almost twenty-five at sea. It doesn't seem likely that her mother was happy about that. But she always reigned supreme, a domestic goddess. A pretty woman, born in Adelaide, patriotic. There wasn't much to talk about, they both knew that.

Harrison is sweating as he leaps onto the tank ... Francesca empties the bottle. Lynn won't touch alcohol, Lynn hates alcohol, she's scared of it. Lynn wears vulgar make-up but dresses in clothes that make the rest of her look like a boy. Lynn can't see that those two things don't go together. Lynn was little; she was at her grandmother's when her father and brother died. No one talks about it in Lynn's presence. Lynn is proud and pretty; she has long legs, full lips. Good girl Lynn.

Lynn is afraid of losing her mother, but sometimes Lynn hates her mother, and her mother knows it. Lynn hates her because of the Scotch bottles, because of the silence that has spread through the house in Surry Hills, because of the suffering that has been inflicted on her just for being her daughter, just because she is part of this family and no other.

Lynn creeps quietly into the house, hoping Francesca will be in bed. 'Mum? Why are you still up?'

'Couldn't sleep, sorry, darling.'

'But, Mum …'

'Did you have a good time?'

Lynn has baggy jeans on and her glasses are a little smudged, her lips bright red. She is wearing a checked shirt, three sizes too big. She asked for it for her birthday. It looks terrible. It's such a shame for that wonderful body to be draped in a sack.

'Yeah, it was okay. But I'm tired now. Sunday is when the fun really starts. Everyone's really stoked. Mum? You've been drinking, haven't you?'

'Sweetheart, I just wanted to chill out a bit, you know.' She finds speaking difficult, but her head is still clear. 'Granny called …' Just don't stop talking, or Lynn will start thinking. It's no good, when Lynn thinks. 'She wants to know if she can come and see you, after camp. I told her you'd give her a call yourself, all right?'

'Mum, I don't think it's okay that you've been drinking. Again. You promised.'

VERY OFTEN, VERY OFTEN, SWEETHEART. I KNOW. I'M SHIT. I THINK YOU CAN GO NOW. YOU DON'T HAVE TO DO THIS TO YOURSELF, HERE WITH ME AND THE LOVELY HARRISON, LYNN, MY GOOD GIRL …

'I'm sorry, love, I wanted … a bit of couch time and TV and …'

Lynn sits down beside her and looks so lost in her awful adolescence, in her inability to express herself, in her urge to run away. Francesca would so love to give her the security she needs.

'But Mum, I can't go away at all if you're going to start again, I can't …'

'Lynn, listen to me.' Her tongue feels like it's died. She tries to master herself: talk, talk to Lynn. Her good girl mustn't be scared. If Lynn gets scared, like she was back then, all will be lost. 'Lynn, I'm doing fine. There's one thing I want you to know. I love you. I'm going to go away, too. When you're off at camp, I'm going to fly to Europe. To somewhere over there, and try to find myself again. And I want you to know that I'm doing it for us, Lynn. For no one but us. All right? And Granny can come back here with you when school starts again, because I'll still be …'

Lynn turns off the TV angrily. She stares straight ahead, her lower lip drooping a little. She would cry if she only could.

'I'm going to try to make everything better, okay? I know you think it's all shit, I know that, but I can't pretend to you, Lynn. The two of us have to get through this.'

'Mum, I honestly think …'

'No, listen to me when I'm talking, and stop acting like you don't understand any of it, Lynn.' She is raising her voice now.

Lynn recoils slightly and stares at her trainers. Her mother has never been violent, not even when she's drunk; her mother hates nothing more than violence. Lynn knows that, and she isn't afraid. Not of that.

'We only have each other, Lynn, that's just the way it is. I'm sorry it upsets you, but I'm your mother, and we have to make the best of it. There's a past we both share, Lynn.'

'Stop saying "Lynn" all the time. Stop saying "Lynn" all the time!'

'I'm sorry, I just really want to explain. I want you to understand.'

'So, where are you going to go?'

'Greece, maybe. I want to take some time to think things over, you know?'

'Uh … I reckon you could do that here.'

'No I can't, Lynn. Here, I'm constantly forced to remember.'

'Does Granny know about this?' Bringing Granny into it, Lynn's favourite tactic. Granny, her patron saint, who caters to her every whim, to compensate for the misery of living with her mother.

'Forget Granny, forget everyone, it's just you and me, try and accept that for fifteen minutes, okay? For my sake, Lynn. Accept it! You're here, and so am I, and that's all; there's no one else. What I'm trying to say is that neither of us is very happy at the moment …'

'We haven't been happy for years, Mum.' And it has been years, too, since Lynn said anything so honest. The sentence stabs, like a thin wire, deep into her heart.

'Yes, I know.' A brief silence. 'I'm done with it. I want to fight for the two of us, Lynn.'

'Oh, Mum … we've been here before.' She gets up, pours herself a glass of milk from the fridge, turns her back to her mother.

'I want to try, Lynn. I'm only human, too.'

'We'll never get there, though! You'll never get there. I know it …' All at once she is much older, Lynn is suddenly as old as her mother. Lynn is suddenly a broken woman. Lynn has always avoided these discussions, always fled to her room, to her bed covered in heart-shaped cushions and a teddy that belonged to her brother — her only memento of him.

'Lynn, why would you say that?'

'Mum, why don't you give up? Why aren't you tired of it all? Why don't you just say we'll never get there?' She sounds so helpless. Lynn is fifteen again. Lynn has no language, Lynn is mute and closed up like a safe, scared of herself and of her mother. But Lynn is trying to speak.

Her mother stays quiet and waits.

'I mean … everyone knows it; everyone says it, except us. Frank …' She hasn't spoken that name once in all these years. She expelled the word "Dad" from her vocabulary. The term doesn't exist for her anymore. Lynn decided that at the age of seven. 'Frank went nuts, Mum. Frank was insane, everyone knows that, I mean … You knew he was sick, you were hoping he'd get better or something, I don't know. He went nuts and then, Max … Mum, we *know* all this.' Lynn is still standing with her back to her.

Her mother is crying, and can't move. She can't see Lynn's face; Lynn won't allow it, as long as she's talking.

'Frank went nuts, Mum, he killed Max, he killed himself, and he … he killed us, Mum. That's what happened.' Lynn won't say anymore.

She knows; the clarity is terrible. She won't move from where she is sitting. Any attempt to touch her daughter would be impossible.

Then Lynn turns and looks at her. She hasn't shed a single tear; her face is stony.

Francesca tries to stop crying.

Lynn isn't scared anymore. Lynn is so unbelievably strong. Death has made her strong, while her mother has lapsed into impotence. 'Go abroad, Mum, do it, but don't say everything will be fine and all that, and don't say I'm the one you're doing it for, I don't want to hear it … It isn't true … I mean, it's not like it's a terrible thing to say, but don't say it, okay?'

'But Lynn, I do love you!'

Now they are looking one another in the eye, mother and daughter. All at once Francesca realises that her own language is just as pitiful, just as meagre and impoverished as a fifteen-year-old's.

Lynn looks at her mother. She believes her. Then she lowers her head and walks out of the kitchen.

The woman without a face sinks onto the floor, lies down on the cool tiles, lays her head on them and tries to scream, but she can only gurgle.

25. OLGA (1986)

Olga was sitting naked on the bed, Lydia asleep on the bedside rug. An old dog now: tired, calm, and contented. Olga had the shivers and hadn't left the house for five days. Her neighbour had taken care of Lydia all that time, at least there was that. The room smelled unpleasant. Olga, who now felt only a slight fever, stared at her legs and knees. She used to know how to like her body.

Sometimes Olga knew that *she* was there, somewhere close by. She just had to learn how to see her. Olga thought she felt hungry, the other kind of hunger, too. This thought was encouraging. She had stopped going to uni. They must have assumed she was ill. Olga almost smiled at the thought.

Olga no longer knew who she was; she'd forgotten her past. Somewhere, in a hallway, years or maybe days ago, perhaps in another life, she had seen a word scratched into the wall: 'destruction'. She hadn't paid it any attention, but it had lodged in her memory. In the white-painted hallway: 'destruction'. She had retained it, for whatever reason. And in her mind, she had changed two letters: 'distraction'. That's how she'd remembered it. She hadn't been able to stop thinking about the word in the last few days, perhaps because she herself could have written it. Perhaps a part of her had always known that she would go into that shop one day… On the last page of the book, that's where the word had been.

There was a knock at the door. Olga didn't move; Lydia gave a start, began to bark and ran to the door, then looked hopefully back at her mistress. Olga got up and moved across the room like a ghost, asked who it was.

'Olga, it's me, Nadine … Please open the door!'

Olga hesitated, then slowly turned the key in the lock.

Nadine's expression was fixed; her face white as a sheet, older and a little narrower. She looked different from usual, in a knitted jumper and wide-legged linen trousers. They stood like that, facing one another wordlessly for a long time. Then it occurred to Olga that she was naked and that this was the first time Nadine had seen her like that. And it occurred to her that her body had changed; it must have lost some of its former beauty.

'Olga ...' Nadine stepped inside, trying not to catch Olga's eye. She greeted Lydia with an anxious pat on the head and went into the kitchen. Olga slammed the door shut and stumbled after her. For a moment, she felt warm.

'What's going on?' Nadine burst out when Olga appeared in the kitchen. She ran into the bedroom, pulled the cover off the bed, and threw it at Olga.

Olga wrapped herself in it.

Nadine took apples and a box of tea from her bag, as well as spaghetti, tomatoes, and cheese. She still wouldn't look Olga in the eye.

All at once, Olga became aware of Nadine's beauty: her softness, her calm, her poise, her pale smooth skin. She looked at her friend and couldn't help but smile.

'Olga, talk to me ...' Now Nadine was whispering. She got pans and plates out of the cupboard. Olga leaned heavily against the wall, then sat down on a chair and watched. The dog wandered in, looking bored.

Olga thought she needed to say something: 'Nothing's going on. I'm tired. I've got no motivation. I'm not going to go to lectures anymore. I want to be alone.'

'Olga, you can't just ... What are you intending to do?'

'To think. Suddenly, I understand. I was so stupid before.'

'That really isn't what I was getting at. Olga ... I'm worried about you.'

'I'm just thinking things over.'

'Did something happen with Michel? Everyone acts so weird when I mention your name. What did you do?'

'I slept with him, and I hit him.'

'Did he ...' Now they're looking at each other. Nadine has a kitchen knife in her hand; Olga's face is reflected in the blade. Nadine's hand is trembling.

'No, I just wanted to. I wanted to hit him.'

'Why would you do something like that?'

'Something like what? I had sex. Full stop.'

'Olga, you've changed …'

'Do you love me?'

Nadine froze. She was about to chop the tomatoes, but now she lowered her hand, leaned on the table.

Olga repeated the question.

This day would be etched into Nadine Leavit's memory, always there, just waiting to be summoned.

'You know …'

'Do you love me?'

'Yes.' Nadine stared down at the tabletop and opened the packet of spaghetti.

'What are you doing? What's all this for? What are you doing?'

'I'm cooking. For us.'

'You're cooking …'

'Yes.' She was standing with her back to Olga, trembling slightly as she slid the spaghetti into the pan. She scalded herself in the process and flinched. Nadine was a practised cook and that sort of thing never happened to her. It was unbearable. She turned back to her friend: 'Why are you naked, Olga? What are you doing?'

Poor Nadine didn't understand anything. And the moment at which Olga could have explained it all to her was long gone. Maybe that moment had never even existed.

They said nothing more. Nadine cooked. Olga didn't get dressed. She watched. They ate. Nadine was incredibly pale. She did her best to start a conversation, but it misfired every time. She fed the dog.

Then they sat there. Nadine stared at the table, stared at Olga's hands. They were lying on the table; sick, sweaty, and soft. Nadine grasped Olga's right hand and started to cry, something Olga had never seen her do. But she wasn't moved by Nadine's tears. Olga was hoping *she* would come to her — tonight — come and tell her what she should do.

Nadine laid her head on Olga's hand; she sobbed and her body grew increasingly tense. Olga offered no response.

After a while, Nadine went into the bathroom. She came back with her face washed and some colour in her cheeks. The flat lay in twilight.

Nadine fell on her knees before Olga. Nadine embraced Olga so hard she thought she was going to suffocate. Nadine started to kiss her, her hands, her face, her shoulders, trying to impart some life to her.

Olga would have liked to taste a little of that life, but she knew it was no good. All of a sudden she knew it was just as well Nadine hadn't read the book.

'Please don't do this, I'm so frightened for you … please …' Nadine kept saying words, but language had lost its meaning and they both knew it.

Olga led Nadine to the bed. Lay down beside her.

Nadine was confused; Olga wasn't.

Soon, Nadine fell asleep snuggled against Olga, who lay there motionless. She found her slight fever strangely soothing. Nadine slept restlessly and twitched often.

Later, Olga sat up, careful not to wake her. She knew that Nadine would have liked to spend a night or maybe several nights with her, but that wasn't going to be possible, not at all. Maybe once it might have been, and Olga would have learned to love her in the way that Nadine wanted her to.

But there could be no thought of that now.

26. ME (2005)

I have decided that if I am going to understand history better, I must travel to a homeland I don't have. I need to seek out the people who are on the point of leaving me. So I am on a plane. I haven't spoken a single word all day, I suddenly realise. I can't decide if I should find it liberating or oppressive, the fact that this silent life comes so easily to me.

I used to talk a lot but, ultimately, I was always mute, since I couldn't really communicate, couldn't commune with others. Perhaps it's down to that sense — the feeling I have now, on the plane — that I'm always missing out on something, something happening in another place and with other people.

As a child I used to frighten myself by playing a game called What If I Was Someone Else. I would walk along the street, imagining I was every other person I saw, imagining myself transplanted into these foreign bodies, trapped in them. It gave me a thrill of horror. I made all kinds of plans: if it actually happened, how would I prove to other people that it was really me and not someone else?

I never felt that I *was* someone else. I don't know why the prison of your own identity is so solid, so constricting, that as a child I didn't even entertain the possibility that I might one day escape from it.

The people around me are strangers and the conversations behind my back, in front of me, to either side, repulse me.

The land between orient and occident is waiting for me, not exactly with open arms. Naturally I am lying to myself when I claim that I'm going there to remember the life I imagined for myself before that life began. Naturally I am lying to myself when I claim not to know what I am doing in this story.

27. ICE AGE / BOOK 1 (1953)

She had ignited love, in the form of a stolen candle that she had placed on her belly. Love was now dripping onto her belly and onto her lap; she had burned love down to nothing and it had gone out.

She closed her eyes and saw her palace; she was lying in a glass coffin, hovering above a thin layer of ice.

She was sitting in a pavement café. She'd persuaded a young postman to treat her to a meal there, but then he had got scared and run away. He'd left his café au lait; she finished the plate of salad and drank his coffee.

It would soon be autumn and she would have to consider how she was going to pay the rent on her shabby room and buy some proper boots. She had to consider how to evade the authorities, and when it would be time to go BACK. Once her hunger was at least partly sated, she felt better, and the ice palace melted away inside her skull leaving a blue puddle.

Sometimes even she herself had believed she was sick. But now her despair destroyed everything inessential around her.

She had given up her name, her face, her voice. She had stuffed herself, filled herself with hot wax. She would have to go soon; humanity wasn't worth so much as a handful of earth …

Her greenish coat, a men's coat, was too thin for the time of year, but she was learning not to feel the cold. She asked the old man at the next table for a cigarillo and he gave her one, grinning stupidly and staring at her fingers with their bitten nails. She lost herself in the smoke. Her stomach grew calm and settled, demanded more, but she took her notebook out of her coat pocket — creased and stained — and laid it on the table. She looked at the stains, smelled the death in the ink; she traced the letters of her crooked handwriting. The old gentleman with the cigarillo glanced in her direction once more before turning away.

The days were getting shorter. She would have to marry the longest night in the world, and when they made love, months of darkness and Arctic quiet would be conceived.

She wrote the words down in her notebook; she had to save paper, had no desire to steal, had to remain as inconspicuous as she could. She wrote the English word *destruction*. She had read it somewhere. She'd regarded it as hers. It belonged to her. It was part of her secret alliance with the notebook.

It was a nondescript Thursday in Paris.

★

How wonderful, we will not know each other, we will no longer know each other, since there will be nothing more to know. You and I, I and you, won't know each other any longer. We will walk every seabed, crawl through all the air holes; we will build a palace of mist, we will be victorious; I will give you everything, even my death. I will hibernate with you, kissing, in the great nest of the giraffes, in the land that belongs to no one. I will scratch all the beauty off my wings. I will invent love with you, the way I want it. I will watch over you as you sleep, and steal your dreams.

There are little puddles on the streets, we will cross them in our silken ships. Let me stay, we don't know each other any longer, let me stay, let me hold you, let me watch over your footsteps, let me love — stupid, aimless love — but let me do it anyway, let me, just let me, I will eat up your pain in poems that I will engrave on your body. I will tend every wound, just let me, don't say anything.

Let me trickle darkness into your wine; let me tell you all the world's secrets, on a little hill, on a cold January afternoon that will stretch out endlessly; let us not recognise one another any longer, just let me …

★

The girl in the old coat got up, cradling the creased notebook in her hands like a sick cat, and wandered off into the evening.

She felt the city lights flickering on her face; she heard the footsteps of the passers-by; she saw bicycles and cars go past; she felt the hidden knots that hold all this together. But she could not loosen them. She walked and walked, pressing the notebook against herself like a breastplate.

28. BROTHER (1968)

The constant noise of police sirens outside, and the student halls in uproar. Marie is out demonstrating. Anne was arrested, and he had to go and pick her up. Mother is dying of worry. Mone wants to bring Anne home, writes imploring letters. They won't do any good. He can see the steps his sister is climbing and he despises her: her bare breasts under those long men's shirts, her features grown harsh now.

And the longing is suffocating. The longing for Marie. His inability to climb out of his own shell makes everything so difficult. What is the point of protesting? Why keep trying to change things? All he can do is pour scorn on it, since no revolution is capable of changing human nature. And if anything does change, then it's only for a short while before the past comes crashing back all the more forcefully.

One of his stories has won a competition. It was about the role of Christian sacrifice in the cultural history of the West. He will receive a little money and be published in a literary magazine.

He needs to reorient himself; old people admire him, and young people don't know what to make of him. Marie sometimes leaves little notes on his door. 'I miss your skin. I'm waiting.' It drives him crazy.

He hides away. They only put up with him here because they know Marie likes him; he's under her protection. Otherwise, he's a nobody.

He feels sorry for Mone, who now has to stand in for Maman's other two children as well. He goes to see Anne and takes her out for dinner. Mother dutifully sends him money, while Anne doesn't get a single franc. He tells Anne about his literary success.

Brother: Mone's coming to Paris soon. In two weeks.

Anne is wearing a headscarf. She looks very sweet, but her fingernails are dirty. There is always something vulgar about her, he thinks.

Anne: I know. She's written me a million letters. You gave her my address, didn't you?

Brother: They're your family, whether you like it or not. There are certain things you have to do.

Anne: I only do what I have to.

Brother: The whole thing is moronic! These silly protests!

Anne: Well, that's your opinion. Are we supposed to just sit here and watch while everything rots, while people get exploited by the capitalist system, while …

Brother: Anne, that's not what this is about. It never has been.

Just then, their food arrives and the global revolution is forgotten. She is always happy to accept money when he offers it. She's looking thin. She scoops up great spoonfuls, filling her cheeks with food.

Once again, he is torn between disgust and fascination, between pity and disdain. He thinks of Marie Bessonville's breasts, plump and firm. He has always denied himself beauty, but with Marie it's impossible.

Anne: Oh, Brother … you're so distant from us. You always were.

Brother: I think it's silly that you always call me Brother …

She chews, her mouth overfull.

Anne: So distant … Where *are* you, anyway? Where do you live? Are you afraid of life? Is that why you write stories? So many thoughts and so little life.

They are sitting in a cheap café, strangers to one another. Paris is in uproar; Paris is hungry. Anne is hungry; her brother is sated. The same blood flows through them — how alarming …

He walks her home, to the dilapidated building where she and her comrades live. He is embarrassed to be strolling through the streets with Anne.

Anne: I'd so love to have a bicycle — could you get me one? That would be wonderful. I don't want to have to steal one.

Brother: I'll see what I can do. You don't need to steal anything.

She smiles, kisses him lightly on the cheek, and runs up the stairs to the front door. He feels miserable. He takes the metro into the city. Goes to a phone box and calls Marie. Marie picks up. He is relieved. He would dearly love to tell her everything, everything.

Brother: Marie ...

Marie: I knew it was you ...

She promises to be at Sainte-Chapelle in an hour. He kills time until then. He thinks about *her*. Then Marie arrives. She strides across the street, proud and dignified; she draws everything to her: eyes, time. Everything clings to her, the present moment clings to her. She is wearing a blue dress with a low neckline. He relishes the sight. She embraces him, hasn't seen him for three days, and he can smell her perfume. Hand in hand they stroll through the streets. He feels alive again. Abstraction of connection, perfection in a bend of the knee. He is young at her side, and life tastes of life when she's there.

29. APIDAPI (2004)

The tourists broke into the city that summer from west and south, north and east, like a mob, plundering and greedy. Not even the wet evenings put them off.

The final lectures were sluggish; students already dreaming of far-off places, the sea, and adventure.

Laura van den Ende had spent the whole day in the national archives, doing research. She'd had four cups of coffee and five cigarette breaks. She had grown accustomed to the blue of the screens and was now scanning through images in her mind. All on a single topic: Saré.

Two weeks before, she had begun to look into Saré's book, which also contained a few drawings; she had got hold of various editions in various languages from San Francisco, Paris, and Berlin; had enlarged the drawings and covered the wall of her study with them. At times she felt like a teenage girl who was just discovering heavy metal.

At least the boy — the Freak, as she now thought of him — had left her in peace.

She drove towards Helstraat, where the Madame Jeanette bar was waiting for her. She parked illegally, would get a ticket. It didn't matter. The terrace was empty. The bar did good cocktails, martinis that she had sunk in ridiculous quantities on the evenings she spent there with him and ...

Laura had got divorced eighteen months ago. She'd flown to Canada and considered the matter closed. She had finished her second doctoral thesis and then ... nothing; then a hole that was larger than all the ones before.

She had got divorced because ... something had happened. They had stopped going to the Madame Jeanette, stopped drinking; and he had started fucking other women. He no longer shaved, he was rude to her, they yelled at one another, objects flew across rooms.

Sometimes he would sleep on the couch, and sometimes he didn't come home at all. Once, in a drunken state, he'd brought a little blonde girl home with him.

She drank her martini and leaned back in her chair. She took her phone out and dialled a number, unfamiliar digits, let it ring a few times, then there was a peculiar 'Ye-es?'

'Laura here.'

'Oh. I've been waiting for you to call.'

'I'm in the Madame Jeanette, do you know it?'

'Is that the place on Helstraat?'

'That's right. Can you come? I'll wait.'

'Now?'

'Yes.'

'I'll be there in twenty minutes.'

She hung up and thought about how absurd this project was. The Freak and Laura the high-flying art historian.

That book of Papa's, back in Sindangbarang: the only thing she could remember was that it had been written by a woman. It contained a poem she'd learned by heart, at the age of ten, for no particular reason. The lines had fascinated her, though she didn't understand them:

> To have your heart I cannot slake my lust:
>> I crave your kisses' lambent blaze outpoured:
>> I crave as Christian yearns for Saviour Christ
>> To feast upon the body of my Lord.
>> You are my hallowed Godhead: this I crave:
>> Your blood and body in my flesh to hide.
>> Yours, the sweet flesh I hunger to receive,
>> Till you in me, and I in you, have died.

When she recited it to her mother, her mother was horrified and told her it was obscene and heretical. But she'd never forgotten the poem.

When he arrived, she was already at the bottom of her third martini. He was wearing an old pair of jeans and army boots. He looked ill at ease in the unfamiliar surroundings.

He definitely hadn't done military service — it would definitely have been civilian, definitely in Odense — divorced parents, growing up between two homes, that kind of thing.

The Freak studied her closely. He had an air of sadness about him, lighting a cigarette, saying nothing, then leafing through the drinks menu.

> You are my hallowed Godhead: this I crave:
> Your blood and body in my flesh to hide …

Laura looked at him. 'We can leave in ten days. I'll buy the tickets and book a hotel. I've put some bits and pieces together — here's the folder. I say we concentrate on the women who died by suicide; you can look up addresses for the relatives. How's your English?'

'Passable.'

'Good. I've made a list of what you'll need to put in place before we go. Why are you staring at me like that?'

'It's wonderful. I was afraid you might have changed your mind.'

'I keep my promises, don't worry. I think three weeks to start with …'

'Three weeks isn't enough.'

'That's for me to decide. After that we'll see, once we're in Paris.'

'Okay, okay.' Lounge music. He ordered a whisky.

'Tell me a bit about Jakarta,' he asked her, out of the blue. How did he know?

'Why would you ask me that?'

'There are 12,087 hits on your name online.' He wasn't handsome; he had an everyman kind of face.

'12,087, really? My father worked there. There isn't much to tell.'

'You're a very private person, aren't you?'

'What are these questions in aid of?'

'And why did you make me come here?'

Now Laura was angry. '"You are my hallowed Godhead: this I crave:

/ Your blood and body in my flesh to hide …"' she recited. 'Do you know it?' Laura drew on her cigarette, which felt heavy now. She was watching him closely. She felt superior.

But he surprised her: 'Ricarda Huch: "To have your heart I cannot slake my lust". What made you think of that?'

Laura was spooked. She stubbed out her cigarette. 'You know it?'

'Yes, Ricarda Huch: a poet with a real social conscience, but little recognised. Why?'

'No one knows that poem! No one!'

'Well, you do — and so do I. So …' The Freak With The Everyman Face knew her childhood poem.

She hastily ordered another martini.

30. WOMAN (2004)

'Francesca, stop it now, wake up.' Jen is on the phone, informing her that she has looked at a few really great hotels, and there's a lot of really great stuff in Athens. There are plenty of flight options. Good connections. She could go next Wednesday.

'I don't mind, just book it,' Francesca says, waking up.

Lynn is going away; she will be grown up and different when the two of them see one another again..

Jen will take care of everything. She's glad. Lynn is at school. It's a sunny Friday morning. Jen hangs up. She falls back onto the bed. How to start the day? What to do?

MAX, LAST NIGHT YOU WERE THERE, IN MY DREAM. FRANK — YOU WITH YOUR SAUCER EYES; LYNN HAS THEM TOO, GOOD GIRL, YOUR FAVOURITE — I DREAMED ABOUT YOU, TOO, BUT I DON'T REMEMBER IT NOW … SOMETIMES I WONDER IF YOU WOULD HAVE DONE THE SAME TO HER, IF MAX HADN'T BEEN THERE, IF SHE'D BEEN THERE IN HIS PLACE. WOULD YOU HAVE EXECUTED HER THE SAME WAY? WOULD YOU HAVE BEEN ABLE TO DO IT, LOOKING INTO HER EYES? SOMETIMES I WONDER WHEN IT STARTED WITH YOU. WHEN EXACTLY — WHAT WAS THE PRECISE MOMENT IN OUR LIVES WHEN YOU STARTED PUMPING YOURSELF FULL OF ANGER? YOUR BROTHER WAS AT YOUR FUNERAL. HE TOOK MY HAND IN HIS AND MURMURED SOME WORDS, BUT HE COULDN'T COMFORT US. I WAS SORRY FOR HIM, BECAUSE HE WAS YOUR BROTHER, FRANK, AND HE WAS ASHAMED OF

YOU. HE DIDN'T UNDERSTAND IT, FRANK, AND YOU KNOW WHAT THE WORST THING IS? IT'S THAT RIGHT THEN, I SUDDENLY KNEW THE ANSWER. I KNEW WHY YOU'D DONE IT. I JUST COULDN'T TELL HIM. I COULDN'T TELL ANYONE, BUT WE BOTH KNOW IT, FRANK, WE BOTH DO …

31. OLGA (1986)

The day wasn't a special one. Olga had decided to lock the door and yell a No into the face of the world. She had plastered the walls with the pages she'd copied out, stopped collecting the post, closed the curtains. But then she'd pulled a dress over her naked body and gone out. It was the day that Olga met death for the first time. The weather was warm and summery. Olga met death in a backstreet in the Marais. On a bridge, he came and beckoned to her; he looked nice and so Olga thought to herself: 'Aha, death and the maiden — ' and burst into a loud laugh. Death didn't speak, but he transmitted his thoughts to her, and they made Olga giggle. 'You old slut! You left me here on my own,' Olga thought to herself, leaning against the side of the bridge. Somewhere, people were celebrating life; somewhere, there were people who didn't have a clue. Death and the maiden now walked side by side. He wasn't so terrible; he was actually nicer than life, by whose side Olga had always walked before. 'You depressive shit, leave me in the lurch, would you? I could have done everything you wanted … You set longing on me, like a dog, to suffocate me, but I'm still alive, do you see? I'm coming, don't worry. You'll get what you want, you nasty piece of filth! I'm walking, see, I'm striding, and with every step I'm giving up on a little more of this city. To hell with it! And with everything else, too — people, places, feelings — I make thoughts light up like stars. I hate you. I hate you so much that I'm prepared to kill you, and I'll do anything just to make you STOP … You lied, it's all lies.' As Olga thought this, she began to cry. Finally, she could admit to herself that she didn't want to go on living. She thought about the men who might once have been able to get through to her. Always the image of *distraction* before her eyes, thinking of destruction while making love ... No, not like that. Maybe she'd never had the organ you needed for life. Once, once she had loved a rabbit that her father brought home as a stand-in for the puppy she really wanted. Then Olga had begun to love. The little girl loved so desperately that she stopped sleeping and eating, so worried was she that something might happen to the animal. She didn't want to go to school, or church, or on Sunday outings with her family; all she wanted was to be with the rabbit, who didn't even appear to register her love. Her parents were concerned. They tried to talk the little girl round, to warn her off loving so intensely. And Olga said: 'But I can't help it.' And perhaps that had always been true. It's just that between then and now, she had forgotten. One day the little girl came home and the animal was gone, along with its cage and its carrots. Gone. Olga wanted to run away and find her rabbit. She could make up for all of that now, couldn't she? Now that everything false had been banished from her life and she had returned to herself, she would find it.

32. ME (2005)

Now I am here, where I was before. Travelling didn't help. I'll go out in a minute and buy some drinks that will make the evening sing more sweetly. What a crazy thought: I am entirely composed of banalities. There are people who might only meet you once in their life, maybe just one chance and then ... then they see your hair, your jeans, your eyes focused on a rustling newspaper. That's how chances are missed. That's how lives are ruined.

Maybe in another life, I met the unhappy girl on the street, misjudged her, didn't recognise her, had no desire to share her pain, and now she's pursuing me?

Do you remember me? We were once very close; you were there and so was I, and then we ran over the bridges and sometimes sat in the parks. Do you remember me? Do I remember you? Would I spot you in a crowd, somewhere among thousands of others? Would you still be so unique?

33. ICE AGE / BOOK 1 (1953)

I will dissolve myself; no one is capable of replacing me. Hence the book. And it isn't my mission to save souls. I'm frightened. I step over myself and keep walking. I practise it. Peace brings: fat bellies, disgust, the rape of your soul. I have left bite wounds everywhere, but no one has found their way to me. Not even you! You, a nobody!

I cut out my tongue … destruction. In order to live, I need to extend myself, I need a malleable soul, a body with no limitations. I am not made for these compromises; I want a sentence with no full stop.

My Golgotha is the SELF. My agapē is a failed attempt. The source of semeia is nothing but a dream … still no stigmata …

There is a roaring sound that sometimes takes on colours.

Do you see me, standing there, wordless, since there is no more logos *for me?*
ON THE RIGHT SIDE STAND THE MEN
ON THE LEFT — THE WOMEN
I REMAIN BETWEEN.

I injure the twilight, scratch at the sky above my head, stretch out my arms. But I still don't touch the sun. Somewhere between my heart and my despair a child was conceived, but it must know nothing of life; it must stay there, in its non-existent place, if it is to live, and I will never bear this child. And so the child, my embryo, can die inside me, protected from the future.

Tonight I will cut off my hair …

The moon marries the sun out of sheer loneliness; I marry loneliness itself.

34. BROTHER (1968)

'La belle chienlit' begins. 'When France gets bored' is how *Le Monde* captions the start of a new era. He is baffled by it all; wants nothing to do with it, regards it as a waste of time.

He has to get Anne out of police custody once again. He calls Mother. He betrays Anne. He's angry, really angry; he can't help it and he needs money.

Marie takes him everywhere with her. She criticises his fantasies, teases him, calls him 'my little reactionary', but his writing is winning prizes and a small amount of money. He is bitter. Marie Bessonville and her horde of stupid ideologues, as they call themselves. 'French students are preoccupied with the question of whether the girls of Nanterre and Antony will have free access to the boys' rooms. All in all, it is a vastly diminished idea of human rights.' So the papers say. He smiles at the lines. Because that is what their revolution amounts to, in reality.

Now the unions are demonstrating. Many who join them are kicked out of university. The world seems to have forgotten all the rules of play, and how to compromise. The banlieue around the campus has become almost a no-go zone for the authorities. The student halls are occupied, people smoke pot in the hallways, and all they listen to now is rock and roll, which is 'hip'.

Marie talks about communism, existentialism; she quotes Sartre.

He can only think of Marie's body now. Everything else seems meaningless.

They talk about the National Liberation Front; they want to liberate Vietnam. Marie is very hot on 'freedom'. Once, in a club, he says to Marie:

'I believe in freedom, but a different kind. It's not about demanding things from life. If we're going to have anarchy, then make it total, then unleash everything, including total violence. Against everything and for nothing!'

Marie is horrified and stoned; she slaps him in the face. Then she drags him off to the toilets and 'apologises'.

He writes at night and suffers from insomnia. Mother sends money. She worries. Mone comes to Paris, weeps, stays in a hotel; she wants to become a dressmaker and help Maman, she says.

Marie moves to the inner courtyard of the Sorbonne, which is drawing in all the idiots from Nanterre. The fight is set to continue. Marie asks him to go with her. He insists that it's nothing to do with him.

Marie meets Henri Weber and is charmed by him; Patrice hates him, but then he gives in and does go to the Sorbonne after all. The lecture theatres are closed and people have begun to arm themselves. Anne is proud of him and tries to forgive him for snitching on her to Maman.

Anne: It's good that you've finally started engaging with reality a little bit.

He says nothing. She has cut her hair short. In the evening, he takes the metro back out to the banlieue. He's tired and complains of headaches. Marie tells him she loves him. That night they are taken away; the police have stormed the courtyard, arrested everyone, and he runs straight to the police station. Marie is soon released: her father pays, he's proud of his daughter, so Marie says.

The Latin Quarter is completely sealed off with barricades, according to the newspapers. Marie rejoices. He doesn't understand why she is still with him.

But by this point, he has been accepted. His existence is unobtrusive and somehow neutral. That saves unnecessary discussions. Garçon disappears, scared shitless. In times like these, betrayal is not forgiven.

People avoid the Latin Quarter, and the students stay, making camp-fires; everyone is crazy. On 13 May the unions call a strike in solidarity. For the victims of repression. Europe is in turmoil.

Marie gives notice on her flat — the area is too bourgeois, the ambience too rarified. She'll stay in one of the occupied buildings, she says, but then she sleeps in his room, in Nanterre.

In the morning, as soon as she leaves his domain, he starts dreaming of the night, when she'll return to him.

At least the paper he types on is quiet and won't take to the barricades.

Tens of thousands come out to march on 13 May. He wants to hide himself away somewhere.

He takes painkillers and tranquilisers, and can't sleep when Marie doesn't 'come home'.

This is his castle now, his palace of dreams — the bed, and Marie in it. Sud Aviation goes on strike, and so does Renault, but he has no interest in that. When Marie stays away for a long time, he types diligently. The clacking of the typewriter keys is louder than all the shouting put together, he thinks.

Around eight million workers are on strike.

'Up until three years ago, women couldn't even open a bank account without their husband's approval. How sick,' says Marie. 'Everything needs to change now.'

Marie also talks about the people at the *Revue Arguments*; she wants to get something published in it, political and erotic essays, she says, as eroticism is a part of politics too, these days. He thinks it's silly; after all, she isn't a member of those dissident circles in which the people who work there move.

There are calls for a people's government. What is that supposed to mean?

His insomnia grows more severe.

He goes to visit Anne, in a left-wing housing project in one of the *villes nouvelles*. She tells him about the youth welfare office, which is after her, but that her friends won't let them take her. He keeps his mouth shut, feeling a closeness to his sister that repels him. Anne is proud to have been there when the 'pigs' were halted by the boulevard Saint-Michel barricades. She can take some credit for that, she says.

Their mother writes begging letters: he mustn't 'drop Anne'. Maman can't see any way of getting her home, and legally, she will be an adult soon in any case. He doesn't understand Maman. He'd have thought she would swoop into Paris like a fury and fetch her daughter home by force, but she's too tired for that these days.

Marie drags him around with her, hangs out with people in a house on the passage Saint-Émilion. An 'underground meeting point' as they call it now. A lot of people Marie knows are there. They drink whisky and cheap wine and one guy says he has some opium. Then they smoke opium. He doesn't say no; he thinks about *her*. And about Marie's breasts. Then Marie dances and is happy. They celebrate a 35 per cent wage increase for the workers.

He feels a little nauseous, but then ... all at once, she's there: Saré, his woman. She comes towards him, her head shaved. He touches the bald spots lightly. The others dance; someone yells across the crowd. She sits on his lap and strokes his hair.

Brother: Stay here, with me.

Her: I have to go soon.

Brother: You belong to me.

Her: Stop lying to yourself.

Brother: I love you ...

Her: You poor boy.

Brother: Stay.

*

Later, in the room in his student halls ... He is lying down, and Marie is sitting on the floor, smoking, naked. They have the room to themselves; no one else is around. All the caretakers have fled. Summer will soon be here.

Brother: I was ...

Marie: Are you feeling better? I was worried. You slept so long. We brought you back here in Marc's car.

Brother: Oh.

Marie comes to sit on the bed. The silence eats into every pore.

Brother: Why do you love me?

Marie: Just enjoy it while it lasts.

She crawls over to him, the cigarette still in her hand. He has slept properly for the first time in weeks. An incredibly calm feeling. Marie kisses him. Gets back out of bed. She goes to the typewriter; her nakedness is shocking, dazzling. He watches her, not knowing what she has in mind. She removes the cloth that covers the pile of papers. Picks up a few pages and starts to read.

Brother: Put those down!

Marie: I want to know what it is.

He leaps up and dashes over to her, but she refuses to give him the pages. She wriggles free, runs to the open window, and holds the paper out of it.

Marie: I want you to tell me everything, or I'll throw them out — I'll do it, you know I will ...

Brother: Yes ... yes ... all right.

He has to keep his promise. Now they're sitting side by side on the bed. He reads aloud to her, his voice wavering.

35. OLGA (1986)

Summer lay over the city. Her parents worried, and the university sent people, but Olga didn't open the door. Olga's dog knew everything.

Olga came to like her existence. Days passed. Olga turned away. Olga no longer had any desires. Sometimes she thought she was happy. Olga didn't recognise herself in the mirror now, and every night she tried to decapitate her fear; she didn't quite manage it, but she wouldn't give up. The post-mortem of her ego continued.

Olga wanted to renounce everything, to stop viewing anything as a sign, to stop seeing signals in the sky. She just wanted to lie in lukewarm water. To regard emptiness as belief. To eat bread rolls, to stare at the dog as she slept. What must Lydia have been feeling? Olga was young and her departure was dignified, full of splendour and full of rage.

Singing the song of death and the maiden, Olga began to make her exit.

In the mornings, someone would knock on her door. Sometimes letters were slid under it. Once, Michel was sitting on the stairs when Olga arrived home. He was holding a little bunch of flowers, half lowered into his lap. He got up and stared at her, blocking her path.

'Hello. I wanted to apologise.'

Communication had been failing utterly for hundreds of thousands of years. And it was more depressing still to think that the very attempt had been so absurd from the beginning. The greatest love of her life had been a rabbit. Wasn't that pitiful?

'What for?'

'Here, these are for you ...'

Olga took the flowers and carried them in the same way she used to carry Lydia when she was still a puppy and too lazy to walk. She went back out into the street. He followed her.

'Olga … come on, stop! What's wrong? Everyone's looking for you. What's happened? People are worried.'

'What people?'

'You don't look too good, Olga.'

A slight shrug from her. She unlocked her bike and pushed it along beside her.

'Shall we go for a coffee? My treat … it's chilly out here.'

'No, thank you.'

'Olga!' he almost shouted, indignantly, coming to an abrupt stop on the pavement.

She still had a little sympathy for him. 'I want to be left in peace. I'm leaving university.'

'Olga, I want to talk to you, please …'

She was surprised at his insistence. He followed her wordlessly into the nearest café, where he ordered coffee and lit a cigarette. He was agitated.

'I've fallen in love with you …' he blurted out, and then looked away. 'I tried to shake off this feeling, but … you know, everyone says you've gone mad. Your behaviour is really very, very strange, Olga, but I just can't stop thinking about you. I want to say sorry for the night when I hurt you. I want to help you; I'm guessing you aren't well. Tell me everything and I promise you …'

'Oh, that's funny,' Olga groaned.

He seemed offended, but he swallowed his annoyance.

'I'm serious, Olga. I want …' he had turned red. She was a stranger to him.

Olga saw it. How much more she could see, now. 'I think you should just leave it be, Michel. I used to be in love with you — isn't that funny? But I was in love quite often and I never got anything back, or at least, no one felt the same way I did. It isn't revenge, it's just how it is, there's nothing I can do about it. Come on, let's go for a walk — it's a lovely evening, isn't it?'

'I spoke to Nadine. She told me you're depressed.'

'So? Maybe, maybe not … I want to go for a walk.'

He paid and they left, Olga still pushing her bike. He talked about his siblings, about Paris, about his dream of getting his pilot's licence one day. He seemed still to have hope.

She looked at his hands, the corners of his mouth, and thought that actually, it was a shame to give up a life, to throw it away just like that, for nothing and more nothing, even if life had become meaningless to you.

He bought candyfloss and ate some; she didn't want any.

She thought about *her*. About repeatability; she, too, would have a successor. Always. On the carousel of life — chained to little wooden horses. Then Olga let out a laugh. 'It's me! It's me! I ...'

'Pardon?'

'Oh God, it's me ... I ... I'm her!'

'What? What are you talking about?' A shred of white candyfloss was stuck to his lips as he turned to her with a look of bewilderment, almost panic.

'I know now.' Olga was happy. She looked up at the sky, sat down on the ground, laughed. Now she understood all the signs *she* had left behind for Olga. Distraction. She understood that moment in the bookshop, the boy who'd run out. She understood her desire to cut off all her hair.

Olga hugged Michel, who had given her his day, who had made an effort to understand her. She turned to him and kissed him on the lips. The world had switched perspectives. 'You'll help me — won't you?'

He laughed; he didn't understand any of this, but that wasn't important.

IF YOU LOVE ME ... I WILL TEAR MY HEART TO PIECES AND FEED IT TO YOU EVERY MORNING. IF YOU LOVE ME, YOU DON'T NEED TO UNDERSTAND ANYTHING ELSE. YOU WON'T KNOW WHAT THE SUN WAS LIKE BEFORE YOU SAW IT IN MY EYES. IF YOU COULD ONLY LOVE ME ... THIS WILL BE A WONDERFUL EVENING, WITH SO MANY WONDERFUL EVENINGS STILL TO COME. IF ONLY I COULD ... MY SKIN IS MY ARMOUR. SUFFOCATING. WOULD YOU MAKE SPACE FOR ME IN YOUR IMAGINATION, WHERE I CAN BE COMPLETE? WOULD YOU DO THAT? FOR ME? IT IS WONDERFUL! YOU DON'T KNOW ANYTHING, YOU DON'T UNDERSTAND ANYTHING OR DO ANYTHING. THE TIP OF YOUR NOSE IS COLD, I WOULD LIKE TO WARM YOU, IF I ONLY COULD ...

36. ME (2005)

I'm transcribing a conversation from today. My friends have been asking me to talk to them — friends who are well informed, do yoga, eat a balanced diet, watch films at the art-house cinema, and yet still have empathy and worry about other people — and so I do. I haven't been myself for a long time, they say.

Am I having suicidal thoughts? — I don't know, no, not really.

Am I depressed? — Depressed how? No.

Do I suffer from insomnia? — Well, yes, but I'm actually trying not to sleep.

Do I have people who are looking after me? — I don't want anyone to do that.

Am I having an identity crisis? — What on earth is that supposed to mean?

Am I having enough sex? — Who's to say what's enough?

Did I have a difficult childhood? — Probably no more difficult than any other.

Was I an outsider at school? — How funny: you mean there are alternatives to that? I'd like to hear about them.

What are my parents like? — My mother is my mother; my father is dead.

Am I serious about wanting to start treatment? — Yes: I would like to be treated with absinth, filterless cigarettes, and Marlon Brandos.

Do I find that funny? — No, I'm being entirely serious.

37. APIDAPI (2004)

A hot July morning after long days of rain. Schiphol Airport crowded and noisy. People battling the heat, their clothes sticking to their skin.

The Freak was wearing thick sunglasses, which he didn't take off even when they were inside. The air-conditioning units hummed. Laura was sweating between her breasts. All her previous lovers had felt such triumph at having got their hands on those breasts. But the Freak hadn't looked at them even once. Perhaps he was gay. That would certainly stop things getting complicated.

They hardly spoke a word all day. He read the *National Geographic*; she turned the pages of a novel from the airport bookshop. It was cramped on the plane; her thighs felt numb. She hated flying. She couldn't eat, and gave her food to the Freak, who devoured it all. He was so pale, his face so transparent. Those stupid glasses and his ridiculous trainers.

She wondered what he was like with people his own age, what he looked like when he orgasmed. With a man or a woman? She couldn't help smiling again.

A few days before, Laura had compiled a research plan. She'd thought of her APIDAPI, which would be all alone in the garage for the next three weeks. A sad thought, having to drop her protective armour …

Laura swallowed her anti-anxiety pills, which she ordered on prescription any time she had to get on a plane, and tried to listen to some music through her headphones and 'out-think' her nausea.

She was sitting in an aisle seat and kept her face turned away from the window, staring instead at an overworked mother with two young children. One child was asleep in the crook of her arm; the other ran up and down the aisle as the mother called his name over and over. The flight attendant eventually brought the child back.

Laura thought about her nieces. The girl she had begun to like after she turned three, who had more or less been the reason for her own marriage, was a little blonde, smiley creature with a cute accent. Sometimes she used to write Laura postcards on which she had drawn a flower and scrawled the three words she could write (thanks to Laura): 'Laura loves Lina'. That was before she'd started school and forgotten her entirely carefree life. Lina reminded her of herself as a child. Lina, whom she had sometimes taken to nursery and picked up at the end of the day like a good aunt. She had forgotten, now, what it had felt like to want a child.

Landing: Laura was tense in anticipation of the torture. From above, the city was revealed in all its beauty and horror.

Charles de Gaulle Airport crowded and noisy. Laura — tetchy, tired, and melancholy — didn't know what she was doing in this city. It was perfect for nights of passion, for adventure and madness, but not as the destination for a research trip.

The Freak seemed relaxed and happy pushing a trolley with all their luggage on it. There had been some discussion about the hotel; he didn't want to stay there at her expense, but having him go off to a cheaper bed and breakfast seemed overly complicated to Laura. It wasn't kindness but pure egotism that had made her book two rooms at the Maine Montparnasse. She'd had money to spare for the last few months; she could afford it.

The July sun heated the tarmac, and the streets of Paris seemed to be sweating. She hailed a taxi and he got in, obediently. It was unbearably hot in the car. She had been here for the first time with her mother, not long after they'd left Indonesia. Their first holiday without her father. Mother had always raved about Paris. But on that trip, Laura herself hadn't liked it; she had longed for rain, for water, for her father.

The hotel was on a quiet side street, but quite centrally located. She told the Freak she didn't want to do anything else today, and hurriedly pulled the door of her room closed behind her. She found herself unbearable, too.

The Freak just nodded genially, without saying anything. His room was on the same floor, three doors down.

She had a shower, unpacked, ordered coffee and water on room service. Stared down into the hotel's rear courtyard, smoked, investigated the mini-bar, discovered gin, sampled it, smoked again. Lay down.

When she woke up, it was dark. No word from the Freak. She got changed; the heat wasn't so oppressive now. She put on some lipstick and left her room. There was a small restaurant in the hotel. She was hungry, and she ordered a fish soup, a salad, and a Cognac. An older gentleman in a suit was playing kitschy lift music on the violin. With some effort, she managed to order in French, and the protective armour began to fall away.

She sat there for a long time, flicking through a copy of *Le Figaro*. The darkness felt good.

'I thought I might find you here ...' It was just before eleven when he turned up, freshly showered and shaved. He sat down at her table.

'Will you have a drink? I wasn't feeling great earlier.'

'Yes, I realised that. I'll have a glass of wine. I've been looking through the folder again. And then tomorrow, I'll — '

'We'll split the work between us. I'll go to the national archives. I've applied for a temporary reader's pass. And you can get on the phone.'

'On the phone?'

'Yes, call all the numbers on the list, all the victims' relatives.'

'Right, I'll do that. Can't I come to the archives with you?'

'What for?' She smiled. 'Don't you trust me?'

'No. I mean, yes ...'

'It's to save time. The first thing I'm going to do is find Saré's death certificate, and see if everything corresponds.'

That was the end of the conversation. He drank his white wine. She sipped her Cognac, which tasted wonderful.

'The first time I came to Paris, it was because of a girl. I was in love. I was eighteen and I idolised her. And then I came here to look for her, because I didn't have her address. She'd moved here to study — I knew her from Odense, you see. Eventually I got hold of her address. And I went there. We hadn't seen each other for two years. I'd saved up, worked, want-ing to come and be with her here, and then ... then I went to see her and it was ... it was a brothel. A kind of brothel. Like an upmarket one. I wanted to kill myself. But then I realised I should never have come. I understood then that you can't wait in this life, not for a single second.'

He looked at her; she didn't respond. He put a few Euros on the table and left the restaurant.

38. WOMAN (2004)

The sky was clear and full of stars. She couldn't quite believe it: in the middle of July, like a tourist who'd strayed from her tour group, she had done a spur-of-the-moment bunk and was now in a taxi to downtown Paris. Unbelievable. How was she going to explain this to good girl Lynn, and what was she going to tell Jen? 'So, I'm not actually in Athens, I changed my flight …'

Then it occurred to her that no one was expecting an explanation; they had left her to her own devices, and they might even be glad that she and her misery had absented themselves from Sydney for a while.

Paris was a city she should have come to visit in times of love. She asked about hotels, but the driver took her to a run-down *pension*. He was judging her based on her appearance. She didn't want to disappoint him, and found it funny rather than upsetting. Not today. So she got out at the *pension* and booked herself into a run-down room.

Then she set off towards Saint-Germain. She walked aimlessly up and down the streets, among the pedestrians, with a sudden sense of liberation.

Finally, she went into a bar called Le Rostand. The language was sweet and foreign, and it felt good not to understand it. She treated herself to a glass of wine, though she didn't really want to drink; she wanted to be careful. The world was already nearly perfect. She had slept on the plane and now she was wide awake. Was this a surprise trip? Had she flown to Paris so that she wouldn't have to return to the gods she'd once prayed to, the gods who had then betrayed her? Why Paris? Fate had decided, in the form of a last-minute deal.

Perhaps now she could be released from her prison after all these years, just for a short while. She hoped so. Piano music was coming from some-where, and she started to relax.

WE MET IN SUMMER. HE'S A GENIUS, I THOUGHT. WE SAT THERE, NOT SAYING MUCH. I THOUGHT THE TWO OF US COULD BE A GREAT HOT-AIR BALLOON, FLYING HIGH. I WAS THE FIRST WOMAN HE'D BEEN WITH AND I FOUND THAT SO ROMANTIC. HE WAS MY FOURTH. I SAID HE WAS THE SECOND AND HE BELIEVED ME.

THEN HE GAVE UP HIS ACADEMIC AMBITIONS. WASN'T A GENIUS ANYMORE, JUST BECAME A MONEY-MAKING MACHINE. WHEN HE DIED, NO ONE KNEW WE HAD SO MUCH MONEY. NOT EVEN ME. HE NEVER TALKED ABOUT IT.

SOMETIMES, AT NIGHT, WHEN HE COULDN'T SLEEP, I WOULD WAKE UP TOO AND COME DOWN TO THE KITCHEN. AND HE'D BE SITTING THERE, WRITING DOWN A LOAD OF NUMBERS, AND WHEN I ASKED WHAT IT WAS, HE SAID IT WAS NOTHING. AND THAT NOTHING SCARED ME.

HE LOVED OPERA. WHEN THE CHILDREN WEREN'T HOME, HE WOULD PUT THESE ARIAS ON, REALLY LOUD. I HATED OPERA. ALWAYS HAVE DONE.

ONCE, BEFORE WE GOT TOGETHER PROPERLY, WHEN WE WERE JUST GOING ON THE ODD CINEMA DATE, HE ASKED ME WHY I LOVED MYTHS AND I SAID IT WAS THE GREATNESS AND THE PATHOS. I SAID I WOULD ALWAYS LACK PATHOS AND TRAGEDY AND THAT I WAS SCARED OF LEADING A HUMDRUM LIFE.

HE UNDERSTOOD THAT SO WELL, SO BLOODY WELL.

HE GAVE ME THE PATHOS OF REVENGE. HE GAVE ME THE GREATNESS MY LIFE WOULD NEVER HAVE HAD OTHERWISE. AND WHAT BLOODY GREATNESS THAT WAS, A GREEK TRAGEDY CUBED, HE GAVE ME THAT.

The wine was good and there was more of it. No one stopped her drinking. She smoked. The time passed quickly, but not quickly enough.

Outside, couples were walking around: sad-eyed men, vagrants, shop assistants, salesmen, girls in short shorts, teenagers with lost faces wearing a mask of self-assurance for show — like Lynn. Outside, people.

And Francesca — who had now left the bar, drunk as she was — stopped walking abruptly and smiled. She ducked down one of the countless little side streets, strolled past a row of little junk shops, and thought about the money that death had given her. The money she didn't know what to do with. She stopped when she reached an old man with dreadlocks, who was selling second-hand books and back issues of *National Geographic*, yellowed and worn. She asked if he had anything in English.

'Here, Madame,' he said, pointing to one of the piles. She went through the old volumes. A little book caught her eye, an edition from the seventies.

Ice Age / Book 1, the cover said. Francesca didn't like the title. All the same, the book spoke to her for some reason. What was it, she asked. The man shrugged and grinned. He probably didn't understand what she was saying. Francesca bought the book, paying more than he'd asked. She was in the mood for wasting that fucking money.

Afterwards, instead of visiting Notre Dame, she went into another bar and had two whiskies. She flicked through the book; on the first page someone had written in fountain pen: 'Melissa, don't despair.'

39. ICE AGE / BOOK 1 (1953)

Shit. I can't feel my limbs anymore. Green dragons dwell somewhere between my ribs. My cigarette conceals a story; the imprint of my lips spells out something that no one can decipher.

Hades is full, no space for me. I have nothing inside me but hollow spaces.

The carnations on my blouse are drying out.

Washing lines spin a cocoon around my palace, fencing me in, like a prison. My palace of sand, water, and tears.

My friends are dead. And the loss clings to my eyelashes.

The nights suck on my nipples, but there is no milk. Poor nights.

The heart is an open wound, nothing more.

Once you have begun to treat the wound, you will never find the way back to yourself.

I despise myself for being so impotent.

I would like to pass through your ear, take everything your brain has stored. But your brain is empty, the effort would be all for nothing.

★

She has shaved her head.

An old woman gives her a few francs and murmurs a prayer as she leaves. God save her soul, she feels sick to her stomach. She sits down on a bench and waits for a storm to come. A young man is sitting opposite her reading a book; he glances up suddenly with a look of alarm and whispers something to himself, then walks over to her.

'Hey, are you all right? Is there anything I can do?'

She stands up and walks off, and he follows her; then she asks him for a cigarette. He doesn't have one, but he goes to a tobacconist's and buys her a packet. And she nods. They don't have a lot to say. He just walks beside her. She turns a corner, cuts down a narrow back street and stops on the rue José-Maria de Heredia.

Je déchiquetais sa plainte pour la jeter au feu.

The sentence scutters through her mind like a hunted animal.

They eat crêpes and he says that she looks ill, that he comes from Greece, and that he is in Paris to attend university. His father went missing in the war. His brother has an olive plantation.

They go into the Parc du Champ-de-Mars. He discovers that she is not wearing any clothes under her coat and starts to cry. Yes, he starts to cry.

The world seems like a severed limb in the cosmos, swimming lost and aimless through time. That's what she thinks.

Nothing happens. Nothing. She finally asks him to kiss her body; he kisses her neck. It makes her realise this is pointless, and she gets up and whispers: 'Adieu.'

Then she is gone, as if she'd never existed.

40. BROTHER (1968)

The holidays bring disappointment. His mother asks him to come home, at least for two weeks. He claims he can't. He uses a trip to the coast with Marie as a pretext.

But Marie has withdrawn from him. She lives in the seventeenth arrondissement now, on the outskirts of Paris. Empty factory buildings there are being occupied now, and she is living in one of these factory halls with five other people; it seems to be the modern way. He, meanwhile, refuses to leave Nanterre.

She left a note: 'I'm frightened, Patrice. Why are you writing all this? I feel like I don't know you. I don't know what to do. I think I need some time to reflect, to understand it all. I've taken the first thirty pages; I want to go through it all again. And why are you writing as if you were a woman? What is she to you? You need to explain everything to me, Patrice. I feel so lost right now, and I miss you, but I know I need to be alone for a while if I'm going to understand. And then I'll come to see you, in my own time. Please understand and be patient. Your Marie.'

They haven't seen one another for sixteen days; he's frightened and scarcely able to think, write, eat, exist. He wants Marie Bessonville, and he curses her. Maybe it's time to kill *her*. Maybe only then will he be available for Marie.

He meets up with some people from his courses. They call themselves men of letters. They go to the Café de Flore and read and drink. Sometimes he buys a little opium, from people he met through Marie.

Anne announces she wants to go to Algiers, to volunteer with the Red Cross. She talks about a 'pure way of life' and he realises she is grown-up and broken in a way he never wanted her to be. He goes to visit her and feels guilty. Mother and Anne have stopped speaking; Mone is now the only one who writes her the occasional letter, in secret.

He thinks about his family. He feels like weeping. One of the French lecturers is enthusiastic about his short stories, and recommends doing an internship at a publishing house. He gets an introduction to Satyricon Press and is granted an internship there, due to start in September. He can't muster any enthusiasm for it.

Marie Bessonville shows up at the end of July, when he's just decided to leave Paris for a week. She is wearing short trousers and a baggy men's shirt, and his eyes bore through her. She brings him chocolate, but they can't kiss yet.

They don't know where to start. Marie's hair plays with the breeze; his longing grows beyond the confines of his body. They go for a walk.

Marie: I've been thinking. This thing you're writing is monstrous.

Brother: I'll stop soon, it's too draining.

Marie: Why are you writing it? Do you really believe the world is that ugly?

Brother: Yes, I do.

Marie: But you don't live like —

Brother: I'm frightened of it.

Marie: Things can't be that bad, though, surely?

Brother: I think they are.

Marie: But you love me, don't you? Isn't that beautiful?

Brother: It hurts.

Marie: But …

Language falls short when emotions are dancing. She kisses him and he closes his eyes. He is prepared to commit murder when Marie Bessonville is with him. He is prepared to murder *her*. The thought shocks him.

They go to her place; none of her friends are there. The huge building is dingy inside, and it smells of rosewater and waste paper. There are sleeping bags lying in the corners, but Marie has a bed from colonial times, screened off with a white curtain as if it were a mosquito net, protection from the horrors of the world.

They undress and put their mouths on one another. He finally sees that she loves him. This love is frightening; he won't be able to overcome it. He is trapped in lust. They have sex on the floor, unable to make it to the curtained bed; they knock their heads against the wall and the bare floor. The world shrinks and transforms itself into a cave. The world is between Marie's legs. A girl with wonderful eyes and damp palms. Marie would have to copy herself in triplicate to sate his lust.

Now they are sitting naked in the kitchen with its makeshift furniture. He's starting to enjoy the empty space. Marie drinks tomato juice. He stares at her pubic hair. He relishes the sight.

Brother: Tell me something about your family.

Marie: Oh, there's not much to tell. My father's a good guy. We get on well. Maman is kind of different; she's very withdrawn, more like my brother. I lived with Papa after the divorce, that's what I wanted; and Jean stayed with Maman. But we saw each other a lot. And some weekends we swapped over. I liked the arrangement. It was very free.

Brother: And your brother?

Marie: Jean? He's studying medicine and wants to be a paediatrician. Very serious.

Marie giggles and comes to sit on his lap.

Marie: I love your body. It's a whole world. There's so much to discover there.

Then they fall silent. He wonders how she imagines his past. She's met Anne once. Perhaps to Marie, his past life tastes of Anne: relaxed and quintessentially French. Maybe with a dash of conservatism, a little more than in her own family, but charming and stylish all the same. Marie can't understand the hell of his past, and nor should she.

They make love, love, love, that's the only reason they exist. That's what he thinks.

Marie puts the sweat-soaked men's shirt back on, and he doesn't ask where she got it.

Marie: Have you always dreamed about it, always wanted to be like her?

Brother: Dreamed? No, not exactly. I've just always written about her.

Marie: Just? I've never read anything so terrible.

Brother: You think it's terrible?

Marie: This character, this language, it frightens me — it's disgusting.

Brother: No, that's the despair.

Marie: I don't find any of it poetic in the least, Patrice.

Brother: I'm going to do my internship at Satyricon Press, and then I'll find a job, and then I want my own flat, and I'd like you to move in with me.

Marie: Oh, I've won you over; you're mine! That makes me so happy!

Brother: Would you move in with me, then?

Marie: I'll think about it. Tell me you love me.

Brother: I've missed you so much.

And for a moment, the thought enters his mind: Marie could become *her*.

41. OLGA (1986)

The morning was sweet, the man asleep by her side. It had been a wakeful night and now it was cool, after the rain. Olga was sitting on the edge of the bed; the room was half empty. The furniture had distracted her. She'd put a lot of things out on the street.

The gentle man with his pilot dreams slept peacefully. They had made love. He hadn't understood anything, and he'd stroked her skin and apologised constantly, she didn't know what for.

She had thought about her past, while the man focused on her body, as if on a voyage of discovery, though with no map to his destination. Olga had lost something, something that had given life meaning, and searched blindly in no man's land.

Nadine had sent a postcard; she was in Provence. 'I'm afraid for you. I want you to laugh again. Please let me come and see you. I will try to understand. Nadine.'

How quickly the summer had passed. How quickly the cold could arrive. He was sleeping so peacefully.

Olga got up and fetched a cigarette. In the corner, Lydia growled in her sleep. She was getting old now. Time to go, Lydia, thought Olga. She recalled the smell of her childhood. She remembered Lydia as a little puppy.

The world was no longer so sad. Olga opened the window and looked out: the city was not yet fully awake. She smiled and took a deep breath of the fresh air. *If you love me, then help me to overcome death …*

'Morning … What time is it? Why are you awake already? It isn't even properly light yet.'

'I don't know, either.'

'Everything okay?'

'Do you like my body?'

'Of course!'

She saw him sit up in bed. He looked at her naked body and she knew that it had reawakened the lust for her inside him. All night, she had tried to inhale his scent, to suck it up. He smelled of mint and leather. The world had nothing more to say to Olga. She turned around.

'I want to ask you something, Michel.'

'Yes?'

'No, don't get up, don't come any closer.'

'Okay.'

'I want to know if you're afraid of death, and if you believe in God?'

'Hmm. I don't know about fear — I don't think about it very often. And I think that when I'm old, I will have stopped being afraid.'

'And now? What if it happened now?'

'What are you talking about? Oh, come back to bed …'

'And do you believe in God?'

'I don't know. My mother is very religious and we always had to go to church on Sundays. I think I do believe, but I don't like the Catholics. Maybe I should become a Buddhist or something, like François — do you know François? He became a Buddhist and next year he's planning to go to India. Please come here, Olga.'

'My name's not Olga.'

'Sorry?'

'I said, my name's not Olga.'

'What do you mean?'

'It's getting quite autumnal, had you noticed? I like autumn, it's an honest season. Loss becomes so visible.'

Lydia had woken up and jumped onto the bed. He shooed her off it, and the dog growled at him, put her tail between her legs, and went into the kitchen. Michel was watching Olga intently; there wasn't much tenderness in his eyes.

'I'm very lonely, Michel. I think it's an illness I was born with, and I don't think I can cure it. I can't believe in God and I'm not afraid anymore.

I even feel a need for loneliness. I don't know if you'll understand, but I wanted to tell you that. There's nothing more to say about it. I do love people, though — and before, I didn't even know I was lonely.'

He was standing beside her, naked. He had a slightly feeble physique, but she had learned to love his smell. And then she realised that she'd said all this for Nadine, that he was simply an intermediary — between her and her friend, who had no idea what was going on here.

'Olga ... you think far too much. You're a wonderful woman, but your head is too heavy. We need to change that ...' He caressed her gently.

They made love again. Olga wanted to cling to this moment. Lydia stood in the doorway staring at her mistress with a languid expression. The dog didn't know what to make of all this, but she was patient.

'I'll pick you up tomorrow around four, okay? This was lovely.' Michel blew her a kiss before closing the door. Olga waved and smiled.

Then she called after him: 'I'll keep you ...'

She wasn't sure if he'd heard her. She washed her hair, fed Lydia, and for a moment it felt like everything was just as it had been before she'd walked into the bookshop.

She would have liked to see that boy again, the one who'd caused her to pick up the book. She wanted to ask him what he'd been afraid of — though she already knew the answer.

She put on a pair of white jeans, a grey shirt, and an autumn jacket. She combed her hair. She put on an old woolly hat. She looked so calm and contented.

She wrote a few lines to Nadine, asked her for some small favours.

Then she packed the sheets of paper on which she had written out Saré's notes into a shoebox, put the key to the flat in with them, her grandmother's old ring, a half-empty pack of Gitanes, and a black-and-white photo of herself. She must have been about fifteen in it. It was the day she had got Lydia. The photo showed her with the little animal in her arms, in the garden of her parents' house. A cheerful girl, happy and full of possibility. Her large, blue eyes were looking straight into the lens, and the wind had tousled her long, dark hair.

She put what little money she had left on the table, and wrote her landlord's name on a banknote.

'Come on Lydia, it's time.' Lydia barked just once and ran after her mistress.

Olga took the bus towards boulevard de Denain. People sat in silence or were engrossed in their newspapers. The Gare du Nord was packed, as usual, flooded with a wild confusion of people and noise. Olga strolled through the crowds. Clocks were what created this mad rush. No one knew that they didn't exist, that you could forget about them, that time was an illusion.

She stood in front of the huge board that showed the departure times. There were trains to everywhere and trains to nowhere. Olga chose one that was going to Beauvais, because it left from Platform Eight, towards the end of the concourse. Lydia studied the mass of people with her naive curiosity, and sniffed the air.

Olga knelt down beside Lydia, stroked her, and kissed her on the snout.

'I love you so much. You're the best dog in the world,' she whispered in her ear. Lydia wagged her tail and licked Olga's palms. Then the two of them walked to Platform Eight.

The platform wasn't busy. People with bored expressions were looking vaguely into the distance. Olga walked up and down. Lydia played around her shoes in a way she hadn't done for a long time. It had once been her favourite pastime, and Olga had always had to hide her shoes when she wasn't wearing them. She let Lydia be. She had a few minutes left.

LET US SHAKE EVERYTHING OFF. ALL OF US. I KNOW YOU, BUT YOU DON'T KNOW ME. HOW LONG DOES IT TAKE UNTIL A PERSON CAN LIVE BETWEEN DAY AND NIGHT?

She had to lean against the wall of a kiosk to keep from losing her balance — the words had been so clear in her head. Spoken by a wonderfully sad voice. She could have wept with joy, but she didn't want to attract attention. Her breathing was deep and fast. *She* had spoken to her.

She quickly pulled a pen and a crumpled sheet of paper out of her coat pocket and jotted the words down so that she wouldn't forget them. Then she wrote down Nadine's name and address and added: 'Please send to this address.'

Then the bellow of a horn, a few loud voices calling out. A woman with a baby in her arms. The Lyon train had pulled in, stopped; people were getting on and off. Olga walked up to the furthest end of the platform, calmly, without attracting attention. She listened to the announcement telling everyone to step away from the platform edge. A whistle, and the train began to move. The heavy locomotive picked up speed.

Olga glanced at Lydia, and jumped.

PART 2

42. APIDAPI (2004)

'Every single archive, all the registry offices, all the newspaper cuttings from 1940 to 1960; really everything. I've searched all of it. Phoned the police station. And there really is no room for doubt. There's no birth or death certificate, no record of the suicide, and not one mention of her name appears in any of the newspapers. Until the book was published, that is. You'll just have to believe me on this.'

The Freak looked aghast. 'But that can't be true.'

'This person never existed. The publishing house that holds the copyright doesn't exist any longer, either. It was dissolved in 1989. It was a small press that mostly published adventure novels, science fiction, erotic anthologies, and a lot of left-wing rubbish. It belonged to Patrice Duchamp and his wife. Have you heard of Patrice Duchamp?'

'I can't understand it ...'

'Have you heard of Patrice Duchamp?'

'As a publisher, yes.'

'Have you read anything by him? He's an author, first and foremost.'

'Er, no, I haven't read any of his books. Should I have?'

'Well, he's won a few prizes over the course of his career. Written some good science fiction, if you're into that kind of thing. I know one of his books: *Jerome* — it's quite dark. He sets out a couple of interesting theories. As far as I know, he hasn't published anything in recent years and lives a very reclusive life. He taught literary history at the Sorbonne for a few years. I'd say we need to go and see him.' She paused.

'Do you really believe someone else wrote these things?'

'The fact is: it wasn't Jeanne Saré. Or maybe she wasn't seventeen, or mad; wasn't a missing person, and didn't kill herself at the Gare du Nord. Or she was called something entirely different. But that brings us back to the first theory: she never existed, not like this.'

'I don't get it.'

They were sitting in a café. The Freak had proved very professional, following all her rules to the letter. The two of them had adjusted to one another, and had even had a few glasses of wine together in the evenings. The Freak was a good reader.

Laura had rented a little Renault, out of sheer longing for her APIDAPI and because she hated the metro. She, too, had thrown herself into her work. And the more time passed, the more pleasure Laura was taking in this story.

She gradually began to feel something like contentment. She thought of Amsterdam less and less.

The Freak treated her with absolute discretion, always leaving her alone when she withdrew, not asking any personal questions. There were some days when she genuinely liked him. When he stayed cool in a traffic jam, for instance, and tried to calm her down when she started swearing. Or when she forgot to do something, and he was instantly ready to take care of it for her. Over the last week, they had seen each other at breakfast or dinner, and worked separately during the day.

The morning was beautiful and sunny, the café largely untroubled by tourists, and they had been able to find seats outside. He asked for a cigarette. (He only smoked when something unusual happened, as if using the cigarette to mark the moment.) Laura ordered another slice of chocolate cake.

'And what do you have to report?' she asked eventually.

'I've tracked down six people. Checked the addresses. Family members and loved ones of the women who killed themselves. No one wanted to talk to me once I told them why I was calling. The suicides that can be directly linked to the book happened between its publication — so, 1974 — and 1986. One family had emigrated to the USA since. One girl had no family at all. With one, I got quite a long way. A girl called Olga Colert. She … wait a minute, yes, here … she threw herself in front of a train at the Gare du Nord on 12 September 1986. She left some letters, and a dog. For many years a friend of hers, Nadine Leavit, was the editor and publisher of a feminist women's magazine called *Olga*. She publicly denounced *Ice Age* and gave it a bad name, and that's partly why it's been out of print since 1989.'

'Aha.'

'Yes, she's a very dedicated women's libber. Unmarried, one child. Lives in the third arrondissement. She sold the magazine four years ago and retired. Spent three or four years working for the Red Cross in Ethiopia. She must be forty-three or forty-four now. And she's my best hope, because apparently Olga wrote letters to this Nadine. There's an edition of *Olga* from October '89, in which Madame Leavit herself wrote about Saré and the suicides. Have a read. We need to get her to talk.'

He was excited. Sometimes Laura wondered what had made him read this book, what had so fascinated him about it.

'Well, I would suggest,' said Laura, 'that from now on we concentrate on Duchamp and Leavit. And you need to take over the writing. Document everything.'

The Freak nodded wordlessly. The past seemed to be at rest. Life seemed to step closer to the pair of them. She had found the right bait for it.

'I'm very happy ... that we're here,' he said suddenly, looking her in the eye.

She nodded and smiled politely. Sometimes she found him a little unsettling.

43. WOMAN (2004)

Francesca was confused. She had read a book. A book from 1974. She couldn't comprehend it. And this book, this angry little book was full of … Francesca. It told a story about her. And she felt betrayed and glad at the same time. Someone had written down her thoughts: how could that be? Someone had KNOWN everything.

She'd read the book in a single night, in the oppressive heat, and the next day she still couldn't sleep. She walked the streets like a hungry hyena, on the hunt for someone who could help her. In the late afternoon she realised that this was hopeless and that many years separated her from the existence of the woman in the book. The girl — yes, girl, because she didn't have time to become a woman — had thrown herself in front of a train in 1953, at the age of seventeen.

Francesca went back to her *pension*. Lay down for two hours. Then ordered a coffee and a bottle of cava on room service, and took a long shower.

She got a map of the city from reception and went round the corner to an internet café, which was full of teenagers playing shoot 'em ups. She spent the next hour and a half in the smoky room, which should have been impossible to endure for more than ten minutes because of all the shooting, writing down every result for the search term 'Saré', every name and every piece of information she could find.

Afterwards, Francesca went to a phone box (she didn't have a mobile) and threw in all the loose change she had for a long-distance call. A long-distance call to Boston.

A deep, raspy voice picked up after several rings.

'Hello?' His Australian accent had never disappeared completely, even after all those years in the States.

'It's me, Francesca. Leo, I'd like to ask a favour.'

'Fran?' He was the only one who'd ever called her that.

'Yes, it's me. I need to ask you something.'

'Oh my God, Fran! Where are you? Is everything all right?'

'I'm in Paris. I'm looking for something, and I need your help.'

'Good grief, will you tell me how you are first? It must be five years or more since …'

'I know. I'm calling from a phone box.'

'I'll call you back. Which street? No, wait, do you have your cell phone there?'

'Oh, Leo, it's not …'

'Give me two minutes.' And two minutes was exactly how long it took. Some people never change. Leo called, and once again she had to pull herself together so as not to immediately succumb to his so-familiar voice.

'I'm listening.'

'I need an address. In Paris, or maybe just France. For someone called Nadine Leavit.' She spelled out the name.

'Fine. Got it. I'll find that for you.'

'She's in her mid-forties, and she used to publish a women's magazine called *Olga*.'

'Okay, that makes it easier. Where shall I call you? Cell phone? Do you have a landline?' His tone sounded more business-like now.

'Pension Monceau, Room 47.'

'Right, right. I've made a note. What are you doing there, Fran?' Everyone used to call her Frankie, at university, when she was going out with Frank (who later became Frank L.) and the two of them went about as Frank and Frankie, but no one ever called her Fran.

'I'm on holiday. And right now, I'm looking for something …'

'Okay, I see.'

'So, what are you up to?' Her voice, her tone grew milder. She didn't have to explain anything. He hadn't changed when he went to the US. Not him.

'I'm at home, working. I don't know what to say, Fran. I'm so surprised. How's Lynn?'

'She's at camp. All grown up and very precocious.'

'Good girl Lynn, remember that?'

'Yes ... good girl Lynn. And how's Anna?'

'Anna ... Anna left me, eight months ago. She's pregnant by a gynae-cologist now. Expecting the baby in the next few weeks.'

'Oh, that's ... How did it end up like that, Leo?'

'Well, how do these things usually happen?'

'I think about you a lot, you know. You ... us.'

'Fran.' He fell silent; he'd lit a cigarette. Did he still smoke as much as ever? Durry-Leo she used to call him.

'Listen, I should go. I'll wait for your call. Okay?'

'Okay.' The okay sounded American. 'Fran?'

'Yes?'

'I've missed you.'

She didn't respond. She hung up. A storm was about to break. Should she make a quick dash back to the *pension*? She used to love summer rain so much.

She thought about the book, then Leo, then love, and then she leaned against the glass wall of the phone box, trembling.

Leo had studied maths; he was said to be very gifted, and he and Frank were an unbeatable duo. He had gone to the States seven years ago and was working for the government there on surveillance and satellite systems. He'd got married, but never had children. He had loved Frank, he'd loved Fran; they'd shared their youth like little chicks share food.

The storm broke, and Francesca stayed in the phone box, looking out at the downpour.

MY OCTOBER DAYS WITH YOU, REMEMBER? THE TRIP WE TOOK AND THE COASTS AND THE CITIES JUST WAITING TO BE CONQUERED, AND DO YOU REMEMBER HOW IT FELT? DO YOU REMEMBER, YOU BOY WONDER, YOU? I SHOULD NEVER HAVE WHISPERED TO YOU. AND DO YOU REMEMBER WHAT IT WAS LIKE WHEN YOU TOOK ME TO HOSPITAL,

WHEN LYNN WAS COMING, WHEN THE CONTRACTIONS
STARTED? THE DAY IN AUTUMN WHEN LYNN WAS BORN ...
YOUR LITTLE SUNSHINE, YOU CALLED HER, DID YOU WISH
EVEN THEN THAT FRANK'S CHILD WAS YOURS? FUCK THESE
SECRETS, LEO.

Francesca sat on the floor. It had grown stuffy in the small booth and
she'd stopped crying. It was over; something was over. She lit a cigarette
and tentatively opened the door. The rain had slowed to a drizzle.

44. ICE AGE / BOOK 1 (1953)

She had stolen her dinner from the market. No one had noticed her. She strode through the little back streets of the eighteenth arrondissement. All at once, she was standing in front of the Sacré-Cœur, staring up at it. She tried to feel something. The cathedral remained cold and indifferent.

Her hair was starting to grow back, and she didn't stand out as much as she had before, when she was bald as a leper. The revolution had come here, to the holy mountain; the revolution had beheaded the monks who were hiding here; blood had flowed on the holy mountain. Both were silent, the basilica and the bald woman.

Autumn was nearing its end. The building resisted all winds and scorned the bald woman, as if wanting to bury her beneath itself, with all her angry thoughts.

She went inside.

All the tormented souls and martyrs looked down at her. It was cool in the empty church. An old woman was sitting in the back row of pews, muttering to herself.

Tantalus, you god of all gods, she thought, you devourer of children. Gods who eat children. Suddenly she couldn't help but laugh, a loud, contemptuous laugh. The old woman looked around. It was quieter without her babble, quieter even than it had been before. These masochists. She fled the building and started running.

Will anyone remember how many we were? How many *I* was? Will anyone remember my cold fingertips? She ran through the streets.

In a shop window, she saw a doll in a wedding dress. The doll looked lifeless and abandoned, and yet it had on this ceremonial wedding dress.

She felt immensely sorry for it. She stopped and tried to look the large doll in the eye. Its eyes were painted blue, with false lashes. There was no life in it, there wasn't even death in it: only unbearable emptiness. She pressed her face against the cold glass and stared at the emptiness. She started to cry. The tears felt unreal. The emptiness gave no answer.

In the window, she saw her own body. The whiteness of her skin. Her small, sagging breasts and her arms, rather too long, dangling limply at her sides. The grazed knee, red and raw. She saw her ribs, frighteningly visible through her skin. The flat stomach, the undefined waist; the legs, long, white, and shapeless. The face. So stiff and so alien. So shockingly alien. The little nose. The lips, no blood in them, no life. The high cheekbones, the coarse chin, and pointed ears. The broad forehead and the eyes, deep and dark, marsh green.

I AM ALONE.

AND I CANNOT.

I'M AFRAID.

THE DRAGONS GET TANGLED IN MY HAIR, THEY BREATHE FIRE AND I BURN UP. BURN UP FROM STANDING STILL.

45. APIDAPI (2004)

She stopped on the corner. She spent forever searching for a parking space, and finally squeezed in between two mopeds. One of them tipped over. At first, she intended to right it, but then just walked away with a childish sense of schadenfreude.

It was noisy in the third arrondissement, but few tourists ever set foot in this neighbourhood. The street lamps were doing their best: flies, moths, and small insects were laying siege to what little light the old lanterns were managing to give off.

It was still too early. She'd said she would be there at 9 pm. She lit a cigarette. A gay couple walked past and threw her a friendly smile, and she felt slightly self-conscious. Rue Eugène Spuller. Inner courtyards and bars.

A little girl came galloping down the street carrying a huge wine bottle, her ponytail bouncing on her back. Laura thought of her little niece. What must she look like now? Lina was simply untouchable, but she had never really warmed to her younger niece. Sometimes Laura thought that there just wasn't room in her heart for more than one person. Child, husband, or sister, it didn't matter. It was a very monogamous heart, a very eccentric heart.

There was sure to be a storm, and she didn't want to arrive wet and dirty. She clutched her bag tightly to her chest and hurried up the street. And there, in an old, renovated, whitewashed courtyard at the back of an apartment building, she found the bell: 'Leavit.' Handwritten.

It didn't take long; the entry buzzer was pressed and the door sprang open. She climbed the stairs slowly.

On the third floor, the door stood open. It was a large, bright apartment with high ceilings. She stopped in the hallway, which was furnished in a rather austere style. She waited, her bag still clutched to her chest.

'*Salut* … Come in,' said someone in a very French-accented English.

Laura had learned French at school in Jakarta, though she'd never really got on with the language. She'd always found it too saccharine and indirect. So she was glad that the voice from the other room had gone to the trouble of choosing a neutral language for their conversation.

Laura entered a very spacious living room, just as austere as the hall. The door to the balcony was open and an oversized candle was burning in a corner. Outside, the sky had darkened. Inside, the smell of something burning. In another corner was an old, unvarnished wooden table and a lot of books. Opposite, two armchairs from the seventies, beside a fireplace that looked like it hadn't been used in a long time.

'I'll be right there — *pardon*,' called the voice, this time from a completely different direction.

A large photo hung on the wall. Laura pushed her narrow glasses up her nose and squinted at it. It was an African scene: three Black children in barren surroundings, bare trees in the background, dry earth. How sad that clichés were true. With a little more effort, Laura could probably have heard animals and the singing of some exotic tribe.

A very tall woman stepped through the white curtains and let out a laugh. She switched on a table lamp and shook Laura's hand.

'I'm sorry. My milk boiled over. Please have a seat.'

She seemed to speak almost perfect English, but still with that comical accent.

She gestured towards an armchair, and Laura sat down. The woman must have been in her mid-forties. She was wearing a white men's shirt and blue jeans, and her feet were bare. Quite powerfully built, but with that typically French physique that always looked elegant. Was that a terrible cliché too, Laura wondered. She had light brown, shoulder-length hair, with a few white strands shimmering in it. She wasn't beautiful, exactly, but she had an air of tranquillity about her. Her nose and chin were a little too coarse, almost masculine, but she also had wonderful, full lips. A kissable mouth, thought Laura. And very lovely, golden-brown eyes.

'Can I offer you something? I've got coffee and tea, but … Ah, let's have a glass of wine. There's probably no hope for that milk now. I hope you like Sauvignon Blanc? They say the Dutch are picky — funny, I've never known a Dutch person before.'

Laura was caught off-guard by this woman's casual manner. Particularly because, on the phone, Madame Leavit had hesitated a long time and Laura even thought she'd heard one of two swear words. Now, all of a sudden, she seemed quite soft and affable.

'Well, now you know a genuine Dutch woman.' The word 'genuine' felt like a lie to Laura. She looked about for an ashtray. 'May I smoke?'

'Yes.'

'Thank you for letting me come to see you.'

'Yes, please forgive my initial hesitation. I just didn't want to see any more journalists. At the time, they only made everything worse. No one has shown any interest in it all for nearly ten years now. And then two people get in touch with me at the same moment …'

'Two people?'

'Yes, someone else called before you. A woman from Sydney, no? That in itself was a surprise, but what she said was very confused. I didn't really grasp what she wanted. Though perhaps that was me not understanding Australian English.'

'I see.'

This had piqued Laura's curiosity. She didn't like it when someone else muscled in on work she'd decided to do herself. But she didn't want to appear hot-headed.

'I'm afraid I don't know anything about that. But let me start again from the beginning … It's a research project, really, but perhaps …'

'Oh no, no publicity, please. This fucking book's done enough damage already.' Now Laura was certain she'd heard Madame Leavit swear over the phone when they had first spoken. 'Talking about it again in public just re-advertises the whole business. It starts all over again, and that can't be allowed to happen.' Her voice suddenly had a hard edge to it. She leaned back and sipped her wine.

'I understand, but I wasn't talking about the press. I just think it's an interesting phenomenon to research for literary reasons. People need their myths, yes; even in the twenty-first century they want them. And this cheap little book seems to have provided these myths, at least to some people. But the book itself is just the medium. This is about the myth of the lonely girl who wants to destroy the world and instead kills herself. Supposedly kills herself.'

The French woman pulled a face before putting down her glass abruptly and opening her lips as if to say something. Then she hissed: 'What do you mean, supposedly?'

'Listen, I've been here for ten days and I've used every means at my disposal, searched through everything it's possible to search in relation to this, and I haven't found a birth or death certificate. No reports about this young woman's suicide. No newspaper clippings. Nothing.'

'What do you mean?'

'I thought you had also …'

'No, no … I left it alone, after Olga, after …'

'Of course, it might be a pseudonym — that would be one explanation. But since this whole tragedy is so bound up with the author herself, her symbiosis with her work, it's important to know who she was. I've been to the Gendarmerie archives — and between 1950 and 1955, no female of seventeen or eighteen threw herself in front of a train in Paris. In the whole of Paris. There are records for two old men, three young men, an old lady, two students, but no girl. There are also records of people who were never identified, but none of them fit Jeanne Saré's case.'

The French woman's face twisted again. Laura watched her. She had mentioned the name Olga. Emphatically. So it was more than just the name of a magazine. How close, how important, how painful was that name to her?

Nadine got to her feet and fetched the bottle of wine, refilled her glass. Paced back and forth, sat down again and stared at her hands, which were now folded in her lap. Then she looked up. 'You suspect Jeanne Saré didn't exist?'

'Yes, exactly. I'd like to start looking at the handwriting next; that might provide some clues.'

'Oh, *mon dieu* …' Nadine turned her face away again. Laura felt grubby. Why awaken these ghosts? What right did she have to interfere in a stranger's life?

'Forgive me ...' Nadine left the room.

Laura lit another cigarette. A message notification popped up on her phone. It was the Freak: 'I've got the address. The guy doesn't want to talk. But I've got the address. We should go tomorrow! Are you making progress?' Laura was bothered by the exclamation mark. That energetic tone. Masculine, urgent.

Progress. What did that mean? Pulling the rug out from under people who'd been hurt enough already?

Nadine came back. She was red in the face, but composed. She sat down. 'I didn't want to know. I wanted to forget the whole business. The only thing I did was try to stop any new editions being printed. I didn't want to advertise death. And in my articles criticising the book I never spoke openly; the things I said were encrypted, if you see what I mean. Eventually the furore died down. That was good. I didn't have the strength to carry on.'

Olga must have meant a lot to her. More than Laura had guessed. 'It's hard to believe, but all the same, someone must have written it. Someone who was really good at playing the part of being seventeen and sick and insane.'

The storm broke.

'What do you want to know?' Nadine asked, calmly.

'Everything. Everything that happened.' Laura pressed on, against all her misgivings. 'Everything about Olga.'

Nadine fell silent. Looked at her for a long time. Laura had spent her whole life researching, and she loved nothing more than digging up old stories. But those old stories were in the distant past — they were dead — they had left no one behind. Here, there *were* people left behind. This story was still living.

'Olga would have turned twenty-four that October. In September, she killed herself. It was the day I came back from Provence.' Nadine was standing with her back to Laura. The rain was pounding on the tiles of the balcony, but it was still strangely quiet. Laura didn't look at Nadine.

'I was heavily involved in women's rights back then. At the time, I was having real problems with Olga and I was very upset by it all, so I went off to a demo. It was something to do, an escape. But even on my way there, I was missing her, and I wrote her a postcard, trying to explain myself. Olga had withdrawn: she'd stopped going to lectures, and all that summer there had been a change taking place in her. She was studying to be a teacher. In the spring she'd bought this book and read the whole thing in a day, and that night she came to see me and raved about the book and insisted that I read it. I didn't — I just skimmed through and found it rather unpleasant. I thought it was just a phase. Olga could be very temperamental. She often started off liking things and then changed her mind. But that was beautiful; it meant she was incredibly open to everything that was happening around her. When things got more serious, I didn't believe it was all the fault of that book ... I came back that day and my train went to the Gare de l'Est, not the Gare du Nord; the Gare du Nord was closed, they said.'

She swallowed and paused for a few seconds.

'I thought about Olga all the way back. Then I came home and saw police officers outside my building and thought — oh, I don't know what I thought ... And then I saw Lydia with this awful collar round her neck, this roll of paper, and at once I knew what had happened. Even before the cop came over and asked me if I was Nadine Leavit. And before he could say anything else, I collapsed. They carried me into the flat. And suddenly I also knew why I'd had to get off at the Gare de l'Est. I felt I had to take her dog in. But Lydia barely ate after Olga's death; she died that December. And now ... now you're saying she never existed ...'

She didn't cry, though Laura had expected her to.

'I loved her, very much, and I never told her, not really.'

'Would you like to be alone? I can ...'

'No, it's fine. I've internalised the story. I have it in my head.'

'I'm sorry for saying "sorry", but I can't find any other words.'

'It's all right. I live with it.'

'Why did you sell the magazine?'

'I wanted to start living in the present again, to be with my son.'

'You have a son?'

'He lives with his father. He's nine.'

'Oh.'

'Do you have children?'

'No, not really.'

'Not really?'

'The baby was stillborn.'

'Shit.'

Laura froze. Nadine hadn't said 'I'm sorry', but 'shit'. That was more honest.

'There were a lot of other victims besides Olga, who killed themselves in the same or similar ways.'

'I know. I've spoken to four families. Quite soon after Olga's death, her mother had a stroke. She couldn't comprehend that her daughter had … No one could comprehend it. I think in the beginning, I was just angry. Olga had had a lover in the final days of her life — he saw her on the day she died. Him, not me — I couldn't understand it. Michel. I hated him, but he was actually a nice guy … I think it really affected him as well, but we could never share our love for Olga. He always avoided me. He's an academic now, I think. I lost track of him.'

'What did Olga leave behind? What reason did she give?'

'The reason? Ah, the reason … Is there ever a reason? I don't believe so. I think it's always everything. She left me her manuscript of the book; she copied the whole thing out and made notes on it. But the notes don't make any sense; they're completely in thrall to the style of the original prose. And covered in question marks. Olga was unstable and very sensitive; she felt rather than understood the book. She left me a note, some practical instructions for the dog and the flat, and there was a note on Lydia's collar, too. It said that she was very happy. She must have written it at the station. Then she jumped in front of a train … Those words have never left me. The fact that she wrote them specifically to me. It's cruel. The old Olga would never have done that.'

They sat in the living room until three in the morning. They were on their third bottle of wine, and Laura was chain-smoking and listening — she wasn't making notes, wasn't thinking about that anymore.

Eventually Nadine brought her two photos. One of her son: a sweet, slightly chubby boy with a very serious expression, taken in a school playground — and then an older photo. Nadine with short hair and pink lipstick, and Olga. A very beautiful woman, very young, exactly as she should be remembered. Taken three months before her death. How could anyone look so wonderful when they were planning to die?

Laura thought of her dead baby, of the shouts: 'He's not breathing, he's not breathing.' She hadn't been able to look.

'I went to Ethiopia. Wanting to help, all that idealism, so terrible … I can't let it go, either: I still think you can change things, improve things.'

'You can, Nadine.' Laura was calling her by her first name now.

'Oh, stop it … it's just a strategy for giving your life some meaning. I miss her so much … I've been silent for so long.'

Laura's phone was now showing four messages from the Freak. She wrote asking him to get a cab over and drive them both back to the hotel; she was too drunk.

Ten minutes later, her phone rang.

'I assume you'll be in touch again,' said Nadine, as she walked Laura to the door.

'Yes, you won't get rid of me that easily. Thank you, Madame Leavit. Thank …'

'I thought we were on first-name terms. I'll wait. I feel like I need to think, to consider.'

The Freak was waiting in the courtyard, leaning against the wall.

'Thank you,' murmured Laura again. They walked to the car, drove away. Laura sat back, closed her eyes, and began to weep quietly. 'Laura's terrible crying,' her sister had called it.

The Freak pulled up at the side of the road and turned to her. Laura saw that he had a grown-up, wise face.

'What's wrong?' he asked, too loudly. His hands were trembling.

'I just want to cry …'

He hesitated. Then he leaned over to the passenger seat and wrapped his arms around her. At first, Laura tried to free herself, but eventually she yielded.

46. ME (2005)

So I am going home, to what I am currently calling home. I think I need to get there urgently, after this pointless day of lattes and empty conversations.

Today I decided to throw off my vulnerability, to shrug it off like a carnival costume.

I decided I need a change of scene. I need to go somewhere else. To a country I don't know, to a city I've never visited, where I know nobody.

This is not the way to achieve peace of mind. This is not the way to stand up to the unhappy girl; in the end, she'll get me too, like all the others. In the end I am the unhappy girl myself. I need to go somewhere else so that I can finish writing it.

And so in a few days I will leave for another country. A country even worse than all the countries before it, and yet I want to go.

I could launch a paper boat; it could float to your shore and then you could remember me with a tender smile.

You shattered on me like a little glass animal; you fell and broke. Where should I look for the shards, and what good would it do?

I know it's over.

47. FREAK (2004)

'You are stubborn, no?' She spoke a broken English, but not as bad as he'd feared. 'I didn't have much to do with it. You are from Amsterdam?'

'Yes. It's just for a research project, nothing public.'

'My brother won't talk; he has not talked about it for years.'

'I understand, and I'm not trying to use you to get to him, please don't misunderstand me ...'

'Yes, but then how can I help you? I will not talk about my brother.'

'I get that, and I don't want to force you into anything ...'

'You cannot force me into anything. I am dog-tired, and I am cross that I came to this meeting and that I waste my time.'

'Just listen to me for a minute, that's all I want.'

'What *do* you want?'

They had met in an out-of-the-way café, hidden down one of the countless back streets. It had taken him an hour to find the place, and now they were sitting here.

This bleach-blonde woman and him. In his head, he was trying to follow all Laura's advice. But the woman seemed an even more difficult nut to crack than they'd thought. She had a slightly vulgar face with bright red lips and a Roman nose that had something very insistent about it. That way she had of gesturing with her hands as she spoke, as if she were using sign language at the same time, was something he found hugely irritating. This is how you would imagine a French woman if you were prejudiced against French people, he thought. Laura had told him it was better to deploy a man to speak to women when trying to gain information 'in these instances' — and a woman to speak to the men. But this didn't seem to be the most feminine of women, exactly.

He mustn't fail. He thought of Laura's words: 'You say you'll do any-thing to make progress. So get in the sack with her and give her the best orgasms of her life if you have to.'

The idea seemed even more distasteful to him now. But when he'd got used to this woman's manner, it might be enjoyable to simply observe her.

'It's about the book.'

'Yes, you said.'

'We're now convinced that the author never existed. That the book was written by someone else, male or female. And that your brother might know more about who the real author is.'

'Sorry? What do you mean? Jeanne Saré is a cult figure ...'

'Yes, but she never existed, at least not under the name Jeanne Saré.'

'Are you kidding me? I know the story well enough. What, there is no ...'

The woman rolled a cigarette and started biting her fingernails. She was over fifty, but she behaved like a twenty-year-old. She was the sort of person who would be embarrassing after a few drinks, he thought to himself, and just as he was thinking it, she ordered a whisky on the rocks. Then she suddenly leapt to her feet and hurried into the café. She returned a few minutes later, looking even paler, but a little calmer.

Laura had gone to the Bibliothèque nationale to go over the works of Anne Duchamp's brother with a fine-toothed comb. She had been like a different person since her evening with Nadine Leavit. Not that she'd said much about it.

'Have you checked variations of that name?' the French woman said. 'Sarye or ... maybe she used a pseudonym, I mean ...'

'Like I said, in the early fifties there was — '

'Are you *sure* about that?'

Laura had been right: this was the trump card. The afternoon was quiet and the café down at heel and almost empty. For a moment he felt a need to comfort this woman, but he quickly dismissed the idea as silly.

She drew on the cigarette that had gone out, relit it, sipped her whisky, and avoided looking him in the eye. The wind began to get up, and the tablecloth fluttered.

'I'm surprised no one thought to look into this before now.' The Freak smiled.

'Hey, stop, you have no idea, eh? This is madness, what you are telling me. It cannot be. Lives have been ruined by it. I still remember it like it was today, when the book was published. It was sheer madness. And now you waltz in here and announce to the world that the book did not exist?'

'I'm not talking about the book, just the author.'

'It is the same ... Hey, stop kidding me, it cannot be ...'

'It's a fact.' He watched her as she started on her nails again.

'I think I need to be alone a little while. Can I telephone you?'

'Of course. I'll wait for your call.'

'And you are sure?'

'One hundred per cent.'

'*Merde* ... I will telephone you tomorrow or the day after. Give me the number again, I did not write it last time — I did not plan to telephone you back.' She saved his number in her phone. She refused to let him pay for her drinks, and so he paid his own bill and left. He knew the woman would call.

48. ANNE (2004)

In the heavy traffic, it had taken Anne over an hour to reach Chatou. Her hands were trembling as she parked her old VW outside the large house and hurried towards the front courtyard. The gate was open, and Garibaldi barked a welcome. She could scarcely stand; all that whisky on an empty stomach was having an effect. She stroked the dog and then headed purposefully towards the converted barn. But she didn't find her brother there. She had to gather all her strength and call for him.

'Brother!' she shouted. She hadn't done that for years. She knew it would make him jump. It was vulgar to shout like that, but Anne wanted to hurt him — Anne wanted to hurt him so very much.

The house and its grounds radiated peace. The enormous garden that stretched away behind the barn and the tall apple trees and the covered thing that was once supposed to become a swimming pool — even that seemed perfectly integrated into the landscape.

Garibaldi wagged his tail, refusing to let Anne out of his sight. This fucking idyll, she thought. It was all a lie.

Suddenly he was standing behind her; he'd been in the garden. She had never got used to the way he appeared so unexpectedly. Always. That day she'd wanted to taste Jules' penis; suddenly, there he was. And turning up at Mother's funeral. Mone had screamed when he materialised beside her without any warning. She despised him for it, for this shadowy existence.

'What was that for?' he boomed. She gave a start. He'd become an old man, she realised now. The grey hair and the ancient jeans and the lines on his forehead and those eyes, so sunken and so tired. Without saying a word, Anne walked towards the house.

'What was that for, I said.' He followed her.

There was something unearthly about him. A broken man who hardly left his home and lived like a hermit, sealed off in this world of make-believe, with Garibaldi and the silly ducks in the pond. She had never liked this house. It was too big, too empty, too rural ...

She went into the kitchen and began to roll herself a cigarette. Her hands were still shaking. Garibaldi had followed her.

'It was you ... It was you, you bastard ... It was you, it's your fault ...' she roared, unable to hold herself together any longer.

He lit her cigarette with a steady hand. 'What exactly did you come here for?' His breathing had grown audible; the cigarillos had taken their toll on his lungs. He wheezed, reached for a chair, sat down slowly, and tried to take the absolutely neutral tone he always adopted when he didn't like something.

She felt ill; she needed alcohol and she knew he always had plenty of wine in the cellar. She went down there and picked up a bottle of the white wine he had bought for her. In the kitchen, she uncorked it and sat down with him.

'What's wrong?' he asked calmly, taking a beer from the fridge. Why was he keeping up that pretence? And what difference did it make, ultimately, whether you needed two bottles of wine a day or twelve bottles of beer?

He ran a tender hand over Garibaldi's head.

'I can't understand it ...' she was drinking straight from the bottle.

'You're drunk, Anne. Again. And now you march in here, apparently wanting something from me. Well, all right, but what is it? What do you want?' He smiled.

'You wrote it, didn't you? It didn't arrive in the post from some anonymous sender ... There was no concierge ... You wrote that book yourself and you never had the courage ... and Marie ... Oh God, I feel sick.'

He stayed still, his attention focused on the dog, as if he hadn't heard.

'You're so *small*.' The white wine was helping, for now. 'I idolised you, and even after Marie, I was there ... Everyone admired you. You're such a bastard, I'm ashamed to be your sister.'

He didn't look at her. 'What are you talking about, Anne?'

It was a good thing Maman was dead, a good thing it was all over. And yet, as hateful as he was, she couldn't imagine ever freeing herself from that feeling that bound her to him, to this broken man who was too frightened to leave his house.

He sat there, calmly drinking his beer with a smile on his face. Even death seemed cultivated and restrained in this house. She would cry, if she weren't trapped in this brick prison, and already beyond all sadness.

'I'm talking about Jeanne Saré, Patrice.'

'What?' He got up, and stood there for a minute, at a loss, before going to the fridge and getting out some cheese.

'Patrice, I'm not drunk. I just had a little whisky in some bar with a student, and he told me there was never any girl named Jeanne Saré. We had quite an interesting conversation. I want some answers, Patrice, and I expect you to provide them.'

'Anne ...'

It hurt her to hurt him. She remembered him the summer after he graduated, when Mother had come to Paris but didn't want to see Anne, and he had played the mediator. Or the way he'd always picked Mone up from the station and mothered her, taking over Maman's role when they were in Paris, while Mone wept over her 'lost little sister'. And how it had been to have his steady voice on the phone when she needed him. She'd spent many weeks here, summer and winter, in this house with her brother and his wife, thinking that nothing was wrong.

'Is that true?'

'Who is this student?'

'Patrice — answer me!'

'You don't understand.' He sat back down, lit a cigarillo. The stench of it, which Anne couldn't stand, was so familiar ...

'I'm asking for my own sake, Patrice. Mine.' She drank quickly and breathlessly, sucking at the bottle.

'There's a lot I would have to explain to you — and I can't, and I won't.'

'But why? I don't understand it. Why? Did Marie know? I loved that book ...'

'You never liked it, never!'

'No, I just never told you … and why should I have? It would have looked like fawning. Oh, shit, I need to get out of here. I'm moving back to Marennes!'

'Marie knew.'

'Oh, God …'

'What?'

'Now you're actually admitting it.'

They both fell silent.

'Do you really want to go back to Marennes?'

'Yes, I have to.'

'Why? That's not your life anymore.'

'Why did you never tell me?'

'I don't know.' He got up and walked out of the kitchen, taking his beer with him. Garibaldi, who had been lying at his feet, gave her a puzzled look.

Anne stood up and was about to leave when she realised just how drunk she was and remembered that she had only recently got her driving licence back. She went outside; it had started to rain, and suddenly this idyll seemed wonderful. Anne stumbled over to the pond, lay down in the damp grass, and let the rain wash away her cares.

Then she thought of Marie. Garibaldi came and stood by her for a moment before running off again. Soon after, Patrice appeared and sat down. He was just as sodden as she was.

'I never wanted to lie to anyone, Anne.'

'I can't believe you —'

'Please.'

'My God, it hurts.'

'Oh, Anne.'

'Be quiet. Just be quiet. Shut your fucking mouth and stop going on like that: "Oh, Anne. Oh, Anne. Oh, Anne,"' she mimicked him.

'This is the wine talking again … I wish you wouldn't … please. I'm losing you.'

'Stop it, we never belonged together anyway.'

'Don't lie, you bloody … Don't lie!'

'Forgive me.'

'Anne?'

'Yes?'

'Marie … I didn't want that. It's my fault. She knew. She knew from the beginning and she hated the book. I invented Saré in Marennes. I was eighteen or nineteen. And then I …'

'I'll kip here tonight.'

'All right. Are you hungry?'

'Yes, why don't you cook something.'

He walked away, with the wet dog, who had suddenly appeared again, following him as usual. Was there anything more pitiful in the world than a rain-soaked old man with a dog at his heels, going back to his house — a house with eleven rooms and only one occupied? Anne closed her eyes.

49. WOMAN (2004)

'It's three in the morning, Leo.'

'I know, I'm sorry. I had to call. Will you tell me what you're doing in Paris?'

'I ... I ... Fuck, I need a cigarette.'

'Fran?'

'Yes?'

'What are you doing in Paris? I mean, be honest, what are you up to there?'

'I bought a book and read it. I actually just came for a holiday. And this book, uh, well, it was kind of about me. And I'm looking for someone who knows about it and can help me to find out more about the author. It's by a girl who killed herself. And then ... then other women killed themselves because of the book.'

'That sounds insane, Fran.'

'Yes, I know.'

'Is everything all right?'

'There's no need to act so worried, I'm just doing something that interests me.'

'I'm not acting. I *am* worried. I've been thinking about you.'

'Oh, Leo. I'm thinking about a lot of things, too, so what? It's three in the morning and we don't actually have that much to say to each other.'

'Have you been drinking?'

'I'm drinking right now.'

'Fran, I want to see you.'

'There's no sense in that.'

'Tell me something …'

'Are you feeling like shit because your wife left you, is that it?'

'Fran, please …'

'Hey, I just want to be left alone.'

'That's unfair.'

'Doesn't matter, so are a lot of things. Fucking life is unfair, Leo.'

'I mean, you're being unfair.'

'So?'

'Fran, what the hell are you doing in Paris?'

'I thought I told you that already.'

'But that's not … that can't be the real reason, surely?'

'Oh yes, it is, Leo.'

'I can come to Paris. It's been five years since we last saw each other.'

'Hmm.'

'I can take some time off.'

'No. I don't want to see you. I don't want any past in my present.'

'But I want to see you.'

'Enough, all right? Just because I asked you for a favour, doesn't mean that …'

'What?'

'Nothing.'

'You think it was my fault? You think it was because of me?'

'Stop it …'

'No, it's been five years and five years are five years … What's this about? Being open? Drinking? Okay, I'll make myself a gin and tonic and then we can talk all night, if that's the way you want it, Fran …'

'I'm hanging up.'

'No, you're not! Do you think it was jealousy? I don't think so. I think Frank had problems and I think there's no *why* about it …'

'I don't want to do this now, I'm hanging up.'

'I want to see you. I want to come to Paris and tell you all this to your face. I don't think we'll find an answer, but I also think it doesn't make sense to keep trying to apportion blame.'

'Fuck blame. He was my son and he was my husband.'

'All right, this is good, Fran. At last you're talking to me.'

'And fuck your sympathy, too. Frank loved you, you know … You were special to him, you know that, you shithead, and now you're telling me that …'

'No, I'm not trying to tell you anything, I just want to talk. And to be allowed to talk.'

'Fuck off.'

'Come on, Fran, this is a good thing … So what if we slept together? And Frank found out. That all happened nine months before the …'

'Shut up.'

'I loved you, and I … I told Frank that, back when we were twenty-two, when we, when … He knew it all his life. He lived with it, he married you knowing it, he had the children knowing it, knowing that fact.'

'I don't want to — '

'And I really tried … No, I don't really care that my wife left me. We were together for nearly six years, but I don't really care and do you want to know why, Fran? Do you? Because I didn't desire my wife, because I could never bring myself to desire her.'

'Stop it!'

'No love, then — as far as I'm concerned, let's say love can go to hell. As far as I'm concerned it isn't that important. What's more important is that right now, you're getting blind drunk again.'

'Fuck that. What did you all expect from me? That I'd go on being the good little history lecturer, looking after students, netting myself a new husband so Lynn would have a substitute father … Did you think we'd get together then?'

'No, I didn't.'

'It was my family, Leo, it was my life.'

'Frank *knew*, he knew we'd had sex, he knew months before.'

'Oh, leave me alone … What's all this in aid of? I wanted to ask you a favour, that was all. I asked for your help, you got me the information, and now I want to be left alone.'

'What are you wearing, Fran? What do you look like? How are you?'

'What?'

'How …'

'I'm dead. Deader than Frank or Max. I'm ugly, I'm old, and tired and too weak to go and too tired to stay. That's how I am.'

'Don't cry, please ... I've never been able to bear it. Please.'

'All this is idiotic. It's not going to get us anywhere.'

'I love you, Fran.'

'But I don't love you, Leo.'

'Yes, I know, of course I know that ... but even that isn't important now, right?'

'Yes, that's true.'

'Look, I want to see you, even if it's just for a couple of hours. Please allow me to do that.'

'No.'

'You've got years of life ahead of you. Not many, if you carry on like this, but still. What do you want to do with them?'

'Be left alone.'

'It wasn't because we had sex, Fran. It was down to him. Frank gave up on everything. It wasn't your fault.'

'What do you know about it?'

'I know you think it was your fault, that there was something you didn't do that Frank expected of you, something Frank believed in. I know a lot of things.'

'Please don't call me again.'

'I've given you enough time. I got married, I got divorced, I went to another country ... I gave you time. I've given you enough time.'

'I want to be alone.'

'How many whiskies have you had?'

'Leave me in peace.'

She hung up. He would call back; she knew it.

MAX, ARE YOU DEAD BECAUSE OF ME? MAX, IS IT MY FAULT YOUR LIFE WAS CUT SHORT, YOUR FUTURE STOLEN BECAUSE OF ME? I REMEMBER WHAT YOU LOOKED LIKE, AS A DEAD CHILD. YOUR EYES. WHAT WAS YOUR LAST THOUGHT, MY SON? FORGIVE ME. HOW CAN I LET YOU GO? PLEASE TELL ME ...

50. APIDAPI (2004)

'I'm going out this evening, do you want to come?' She took a sip of her morning coffee.

'You'd like to go out?'

'Yes. I'll leave the car here and go and have some fun. It's Saturday.'

'I know.' They were sitting in the courtyard of the hotel, the only guests there. Exactly two weeks had passed since they'd first arrived in Paris.

The previous night, he had given her a detailed report of his meeting with Anne Duchamp, and she had merely rubbed her hands in satisfaction.

'I've made a reservation at the Cabaret Club, you can come if you like.'

'Yes, why not?'

'It's not a date.'

'I know.'

'And how do you know that?'

'Well, I assume it. You're not the type of woman to take me out.'

They fell silent and Laura finished her coffee. The previous night, she had dreamed about her ex-husband. She was churned up inside and had been frightened she'd start thinking about him again. That was why she had decided to go out that evening.

The Freak really wasn't the ideal companion, but he was familiar and easy to be around. He stared at his empty cup. The speed at which he could drink hot liquids without burning his mouth was incredible.

A warm morning that seemed to hold promise. Laura was wearing a pair of oversized sunglasses she had bought in Canada, white linen trousers, a touch of lipstick, and large earrings. It was a day you could make something of.

She went back to her room one more time and leafed through her notes. 1986. Olga Colert, Gare du Nord. 'Very close friends with N.L.' she had noted in the margin. What did that mean? Laura hadn't made any notes on Nadine. 1987. Simone Belle, Gare du Nord. Her family lived in Brittany and refused to give interviews or speak to anyone.

She went over and over the list of women who had died by suicide. Then she scrawled the name Patrice Duchamp on a hotel serviette and read through his brief biography again, pausing at the name of his wife. Marie Bessonville. It had a lovely ring to it.

She fired up her laptop and went online. There was nothing new to be found about Simone Belle, except for one hit listing her among the 'Ice Age suicides', and saying that she had studied medicine.

Marie Bessonville. There were several pages that mentioned her name. Laura clicked on the first one. She put on some Neil Young as she read, and stretched her back.

'Born 1946 in Le Pecq, near Paris … publisher, essayist, co-founder of Liberacion Press … dedicated campaigner in the women's movement of the late '60s and '70s … member of the Communist Party since 19 … left in 19 … Married to high-profile science-fiction author and publisher Patrice Duchamp … died 1992 by suicide.'

*

'I'll be outside the Cabaret Club at 9 pm. Place du Palais Royal. If I'm late, go on in, there's a reservation in my name. I just need to find something out. But am definitely coming. So wait for me. I will have some news. Laura.'

She left the message for the Freak at reception and took the car. She had marked the route to Chatou on the map with a kohl pencil.

She reached the village in thirty minutes. Was now standing in front of a closed black metal gate. An old-fashioned bell with a lion's head on it, and the name Duchamp elegantly engraved beside it. She rang the bell. She heard a man's deep voice in the distance: 'Oui?'

'My name's Laura van den Ende. I'm researching *Ice Age*.'

'Go away,' the voice came back in a disconcerting English.

'You have to talk to me. It's about Marie …'

'Go away … I don't give interviews.'

'Your sister has already spoken to my colleague.' The word 'colleague' sounded peculiar.

The gate opened and Laura stepped into a broad, green yard. There was a huge garden behind the house, and a dog was barking in the distance. Laura stood still. How quiet it was. Just a few kilometres from Paris was another planet, green as a picture postcard.

A large, black German shepherd ran up to Laura and sniffed her, wagging its tail. Laura wasn't afraid of animals; she had a deep-seated trust in them. Animals had been a natural part of her childhood. Soon a tall, older man appeared, wearing a green shirt and a black hat.

'What the devil do you want?' He stopped a couple of metres from where Laura was standing.

'I want to talk.'

'Well, I don't.' He gave her a mocking, superior look.

'Did you write the book?'

'Leave me alone.'

'I'm not after an interview, I'm not from the press. I'm an art historian. I just have a few questions. Marie, your wife …'

'These questions, always these questions, as if I were God himself. No one has bothered me for the last ten years. I thought it was over. Then all of a sudden, you and the boy … What is this?'

They were still standing facing one another. Laura suddenly felt sorry for him. She didn't want to bother this old man any longer. 'I'll leave you in peace … I'm sorry. I'll leave my number, and …' she placed her business card on the grass in front of her, aware of how absurd this move was. She was just desperate to escape. 'I'm sorry,' she murmured. Then she walked back to the road.

Her hands were trembling. She had to pull off the motorway and smoke a cigarette. She felt grubby. Laura leaned back and switched the radio on. The man had watched her go, seeming surprised that she wasn't more persistent. And yet Laura knew only one word had made him open the gate: Marie. She had realised it back in the hotel: Marie was the last person on the long list of dead women, she was sure of it. The fifteenth.

'Don't let me down, don't let me down ...' issued from the radio.

Her cigarette trembled along with her hand; she looked at herself in the mirror, purple lips and glassy eyes behind fogged spectacles. The phone. She dialled a number automatically. Digits that her brain had long since repressed, but her fingers still knew by heart.

It rang. Laura waited. Then the voice — the phone fell from her hand, and as she searched wildly for it in the footwell, she heard another 'Hello?' She hastily ended the call.

It was only now that she realised she'd been holding her breath all this time. She turned the key in the ignition and stepped on the gas, wanting to get away at once. A few minutes later, her phone rang. Now the numbers on the screen looked so familiar. She accepted the call, but didn't dare say anything. Someone raced past her on her right-hand side, a hair's breadth from clipping her car. She swore loudly.

Laura sounded the horn, but the idiot was already gone.

'Laura? Fuckssake, say something, I know it's you.'

'I'm sorry.' In a flash, she had regained her composure and was now thinking clearly. 'I just dialled your number, sorry, I ...' She couldn't come up with a lie that sounded any better than the truth.

'Laura ... what's all that noise, where are you?'

'I'm fine, really, sorry ... I didn't mean to call.'

'Laura, stop it. I called you, too, but you weren't there. You're not in Amsterdam?'

'No, I'm not at home. I'm ... away. Can't talk now, I'm on the motorway, I need to ... Sorry, Daniel.'

'Laura ... this is crazy.'

'Forget it, please.' She was getting angry. She needed that voice to be out of her ear immediately.

'I wanted to talk to you ...'

'Got to go, Daniel, sorry.' She hung up on him.

★

The Freak had got the note and left the hotel at about five. Laura took a shower and lay down on the bed, naked, her hair still wet. It was bright outside and distant sounds filtered into the room. Laura kept her eyes closed. How long had it been since anyone had touched her? She hadn't been able to bear it, since ...

She got dressed, put on some make-up and perfume, and went out.

Just after nine she was outside the club, looking around for the Freak. She couldn't see him anywhere, so she went in alone. The futuristic room was bustling and lit in red. Prettily made-up Parisian women were eating at round tables and chatting animatedly.

Suddenly, he was walking towards her. He was wearing black trousers, a black shirt, and had swapped his beaten-up trainers for plain leather shoes. Did he imagine this was a date after all?

Attractive girls in white t-shirts walked gracefully around the room, flirting as they took orders. She asked for a martini. So did he.

'You look very ... I don't know, different.'

'Yes, well, I made an effort.'

She was waiting for a compliment from him, but none came; the Freak was not to be coaxed into pleasantries.

'I think there are a few things you should tell me ...' He smiled, and the smile puzzled her. She reached for a fresh cigarette to mask her embarrassment.

'Well, I thought I'd have more to report, but I was wrong.'

'Laura?' He very rarely called her by her name.

'Yes?'

'Tell me!'

'I don't know anything at all, I still don't know anything.' He stared at her. 'All right, then ... I went to see Duchamp today.'

'That's what I thought. And?'

'And nothing. He doesn't want to talk.'

'But why did you drive out there? That wasn't part of the plan ... You must have had a reason.'

'Well ... oh, it's all just speculation.'

'Come on, Laura. That's silly. The last few days you've been acting so ... well, like this! And being so secretive all the time. I feel like you're shutting me out.'

'This afternoon I went through the list of suicides again. The last one was Simone Belle, as you know. Year of death, 1987. I did a bit of digging online and didn't find anything about her. And eventually I came across the name Marie Bessonville, Duchamp's wife. She took her own life in 1992. A curious coincidence, don't you think? They were married for twenty-two years. Then a thought crossed my mind and I went out to Chatou to see Duchamp. It was only when I linked Bessonville to the book that he let me in. He didn't say anything, but I'm sure Marie Bessonville's death has something to do with it. The strange thing is that she was with him for twenty-two years and it was only after all that time ... Maybe she discovered something that made her do it. She was an energetic woman, very active, very dedicated to various causes.'

'I still don't quite understand.'

'I can't explain it to you. Not yet. We still don't have the facts. But maybe soon. I have to get him to talk. I left him my number.'

'But he doesn't talk to anyone, you know that.'

'He will. I'm sure he will.'

'Do you believe ...'

'Oh, let's forget the bloody book for one evening. I want to enjoy myself.'

They had three more martinis. He seemed thoughtful and was monosyllabic. There was no more real conversation between them. Laura asked him to dance with her. He politely declined, and she went onto the dancefloor alone.

A tall man in his early thirties began flirting with Laura. Laura smiled at him. Eventually the Freak got up, came over, and asked if it would be okay if he left. She patted his cheek and nodded and felt incredibly stupid even as she was doing it. The Freak walked away, and Laura went on dancing. It was two in the morning. Before leaving, he'd spent around two hours sitting there and watching her dance with various sweaty men. She was letting go.

She'd certainly had one too many martinis, but Laura was feeling good.

The tall man, whose name she hadn't heard over the loud music, undressed her and said something to her in French. She saw baby photos on the walls, in a loft somewhere in Paris. Laura lay down on a strange bed. It was good to rummage around in strangers' lives when you had lost your own. A stranger's life might one day be able to return yours to you.

On the man's back she read the name 'Mathilde' — a tattoo. Where was this Mathilde right now, and who was she thinking of? You engrave unassailable values on your body, only to then betray them. Perhaps Mathilde didn't care that he was cheating on her. Perhaps she'd given him the boot long ago. Perhaps the tattoo was just a memory. An old story.

He penetrated her, and for a moment there was a little rebellion, somewhere inside her. A renewed, recurring grief at the loss of her innocence.

51. NADINE (2004)

THAT WAS WHEN YOU INVITED ME OVER FOR THE FIRST TIME. YOU OPENED THE DOOR AND KISSED ME ON THE CHEEK. YOU'D NEVER TOUCHED ME BEFORE AND YOU LOOKED AT ME AND I SAW YOUR EYES, FULL OF LIFE, AND I THOUGHT TO MYSELF I HAD NEVER SEEN ANYTHING IN THE WORLD MORE BEAUTIFUL THAN YOUR EYES. AND WE STOOD THERE, IN THE NARROW HALLWAY, AND WERE EMBARRASSED, AND THEN YOU INVITED ME IN AND YOU STROKED LYDIA, WHO BARKED AT ME, AND THEN YOU SAID: NO, LYDIA, THAT'S NADINE, OUR NADINE. AND I TURNED RED.

THEN WE SAT IN THE KITCHEN AND DRANK TEA, AND YOU HAD BAKED A CAKE, IT LOOKED TERRIBLE BUT I LIKED IT. AND YOU SAID SORRY A HUNDRED TIMES, AND IT MADE US LAUGH. YOU TOLD ME A LOT ABOUT YOURSELF THAT EVENING.

AND AT SOME POINT YOU SAID YOU WOULD LEAVE PARIS ONE OF THESE DAYS, HEAD FOR BORDEAUX, AND THEN YOU'D BE NEAR THE SEA, AND YOU WOULD MARRY SOMEONE AND GET FAT AND BE A BORING TEACHER. WE LAUGHED. YOU STROKED MY HAND AND TOLD ME YOU WERE AFRAID OF LIFE …

I REPROACHED YOU, BUT I WAS JUST TRYING TO SAY THAT I WANTED TO FIGHT FOR YOU, THAT I WANTED TO BE THERE FOR YOU AND DEFEND YOUR DREAMS, BUT YOU NEVER REVEALED THOSE DREAMS TO ME, YOU NEVER …

I WAS SO JEALOUS OF THOSE DREAMS.

SOMETIMES I HATED YOU, OLGA, FOR YOUR LIES, FOR YOUR ABSENCE, FOR YOUR LISTLESSNESS. THE WAY YOU LOOKED AT ME WHEN I TOLD YOU ABOUT THE DEMOS, THE AMBIVALENCE IN YOUR EYES.

THE WAY YOU WERE ALWAYS BITING YOUR FINGERNAILS AND THE WAY YOU WOULD EAT AN ICE CREAM LIKE YOU WERE SOME BLOODY LOLITA.

I WONDER IF I WOULD EVER HAVE DARED TO TOUCH YOU. PERHAPS IN MY LUST I WOULD HAVE MADE YOU EARTHLY, AND I COULD NEVER HAVE ENDURED THAT …

YOU MADE ME DISAPPEAR.

52. ICE AGE / BOOK 1 (1953)

'Monsieur, Monsieur, my heart is as soft as a stone the sea has been licking for years. One day it will become invisible. Please do something to stop it.' She pleads with a grey-haired old gentleman on a bridge. The man gives her a baffled look and tries to walk past her, but she blocks his path. He coughs, embarrassed, nods, and tries to move on. She doesn't let him. Now he is starting to get annoyed.

'Please love me, Monsieur, please,' she whines.

He tries to push her aside with one arm. She sticks a foot out; he trips and falls to the ground. She steps over him. He yells.

She has lost interest in him.

53. ME (2005)

The television is promising me eternal happiness if I sign up to this dating site. You can choose men and women between the ages of 18 and 99. 99, is that how long we can expect to live? And eighteen, is that the age when love begins?

I vomit.

I've already packed my bags and am hoping to reach the foreign country with the little money I have.

Fear lies on me, heavy as lead.

Did I invent you, you unhappy girl, my little Jeanne? Or are you inventing me? Are you inventing me so that things will go on like this forever? I'll find some way, just wait; let me go out into the new desert, and there I'll find some way of standing up to you.

54. BROTHER (2004)

It would rain again that afternoon, he knew it. He loved the smell of rain. He had made coffee and asked Madame Sour, the housekeeper, to bring some cake when she came. Now the doorbell rang and Garibaldi ran barking to the door. He got up, stubbed out his cigarillo, and let the woman in. She was attractive. Had an air of impressive doggedness about her. He'd called because he liked her. He hadn't liked anyone for years.

She held out her hand. 'Thank you for phoning. I was very surprised.'

'Have a seat. I hope you drink coffee?'

'Sure.'

He poured the strong, black coffee into two large mugs. It smelled glorious. She didn't want milk or sugar.

'What exactly are you researching?' he asked.

'I came across the story by chance, really — through Jan, one of my students, and he convinced me, so to speak …'

'You're a literature expert?'

'No, an art historian.'

He was finding it difficult to revive his weak English. Sometimes he used French words, which she seemed to understand. 'Ah, right.'

'To put it simply, the facts indicate that Jeanne Saré never existed. No death certificate, no birth certificate, no suicide that fits her story, no newspaper reports. I've spoken to people. It's astonishing that no one noticed these quite obvious gaps before. I spoke to a friend of one of the women who died by suicide, a Nadine Leavit …'

'Yes, go on.' He smiled benignly.

'And so I started to think that maybe you …'

'You don't go questioning a myth. That's why it's a myth, you know.'
Garibaldi lay down at his feet.

She went on talking, not allowing the dog to put her off. 'I went through all the names and came across Madame Bessonville and it was only then that I discovered you were her husband.'

'So what now? The story and the book have been forgotten, and very few people want to dig all that up again. Going public won't get you anywhere. It will annoy some people. But only because their idol's being taken away from them. They won't actually believe you. You'll just cause some disappointment, that's all. And some surprise at what else I'm supposed to have written. It won't bring fame and glory.'

'So it *was* you?' Her words had a clear, considered quality that he liked.

'What are you hoping to get out of this? It's over and done with, once and for all. It's been nearly ten years since anyone came asking questions. The whole business has been forgotten and apart from a few freaks ...'

'Freaks?'

'Yes, freaks — everyone has lost interest in it! I want to leave the book be, as well. I haven't permitted any reprints; after what Nadine Leavit, whom you mentioned, put in her magazine, there was practically no demand anyway. It was a small book. It has disappeared.'

'You wrote a book, and in response fifteen people took their own lives, including your own wife. Come on! I know it's none of my business ... But don't the people who lost friends and family members have a right to know that the whole thing was a lie?'

'It isn't a lie!' he cried out. Garibaldi woke and looked at his master in surprise. 'You have no idea at all — you come here wanting to play detective, but you don't understand anything, anything at all. And Marie — Marie had nothing to do with it. And the bastards that claimed she did ...'

'Are the lives of those other people worth so little to you, then?'

'Don't play the moraliser here. I've had to live with this my whole life ...'

'Why didn't you reveal the lie before? It might have prevented some of the suicides.'

'Come now, you don't even believe that yourself. I told a story, that was all. I never intended to publish *Ice Age*. I wrote under a pseudonym. Under her name. It got into circulation. And after that I had no control over it. It took on a life of its own. And then suddenly the madness started, you can't imagine what it was like. I mean, it was a different time, there was a kind of general spirit of renewal. So I published the book in my little press in an attempt to regain control. And not long afterwards, two people killed themselves. I was frozen in shock. I didn't reprint it, but people were doing that themselves in cellars and things, printing it illegally. Translating it. I could allow it or prohibit it, that didn't matter, I no longer had control. Marie and I were horrified. Do you think it would have done any good if I'd claimed that Saré never existed? People believe what they want to believe. You know that! I hate this book; it ruined my life ... I would be the first to destroy it; only, I'm afraid what's done can't be undone.'

'All the same, you must have some explanation for why the book unleashed such madness? I have to tell you honestly that from a literary point of view, I think your other works are better than Saré's writings. It's adolescent stuff. Apocalypse? We're a long way beyond that. And why was it only women who killed themselves? And why is Saré a woman in the first place?'

'Why only women? All I have are suppositions, too.'

'But Marie, your wife? She must have known that you ...'

'Do I have to answer that? I don't feel any guilt about these women, though you might think me inhuman for that; I think they wanted Saré. I have no better explanation — Saré always existed, and sometimes I think she invented me and not the other way around. Marie — Marie's death — that's nobody else's business.'

'But it seems obvious to link her death with Saré, doesn't it? I can't be the first person to have thought it had something to do with ...'

'She slit her wrists, she didn't ... Shortly before her death, she wrote the word "distraction" on the wall. That was enough evidence ... And so at the start, yes, there were rumours. The hardcore *Ice Age* fans used the word as a kind of sign among themselves. Almost all the women who died left that word behind somewhere ...' He suddenly fell silent and looked her in the eye.

'I'm sorry. About your wife.'

'It was eleven years ago. In November, it'll be twelve. I survived. I let my wife go, just because I couldn't stop, just because I ...'

'What do you mean, you couldn't stop?'

'I carried on working on Saré. There's nothing I hate more than the name Jeanne Saré, but ... I think it's how a drug addict feels.'

'There are more writings by Saré?'

'I'm not going to answer that. It's private.'

'So Saré is your private business?'

'You misunderstand me.'

'I'm trying to follow ... Fifteen people kill themselves and you're saying it's something you had no control over?'

'Yes, that is what I'm saying. If you make all this public, they'll do it again, and then ... then maybe you'll understand me. You have my full approval. Reveal it: I'm not a writer anymore. I've stopped writing and it doesn't matter to me what people say, but ... do it, and then come and see me again. Then we can talk.'

'I don't intend to hurt anyone ...'

'Oh, I know, I know ... you mean well. Do what you like. You won't be able to hurt anyone. It's over; for most people it's over. And I believe that one day, it will be over for me, too.'

'I'm not trying to attack you. I know I can't prove it, but I think that even for just one person — for Nadine Leavit, say — it's important for her to know why the woman she loved died.'

'And would the reason be clear if Madame Leavit knew I was the author? Do you think these women were so naive that they simply fell for an idea? Would they be alive today if it wasn't for my book? Why don't you try looking a little deeper?'

'That's why I'm here.'

'I'm no teller of fairy tales! I've searched for answers, but I can't answer your questions; you need to make more effort. If people want to portray me as some evil bastard, then let them. I've already lost everything I had to lose — but I don't think I have the answers to all your questions.'

She finished her coffee. For a while they sat facing one another in silence. She was flushed; he was strangely calm. He cut the cake into small pieces.

'I'm sorry, I don't want to give the impression that I'm trying to lay the blame at your door — I've just found myself mixed up in this business and I'm trying …'

'I like you. It's a long time since I've liked anyone, and I'm talking to you for that reason and that reason alone. You don't scare me, and the press doesn't scare me. I have my answers, and you'll find yours. Go ahead and look for them!'

'I will look for them! Why "distraction"?'

'In *Ice Age*, there's a little reference to her flat. 42 rue Bonaparte, in the rear building, that's where she lived. The book doesn't say so specifically, but the area is described in quite a lot of detail, and so a few people who knew Paris well worked out the address. And at some point, one of the first women who died by suicide went to find the building, and saw the word scratched into the wall. Apparently, a young girl lived there between 1952 and 1953, and she had carved the word. The concierge supposedly confirmed it. Go and look. I certainly didn't write anything on that wall. And certainly not in 1953. I was very, very young then and living in Marennes. I only went there after Marie died. I wanted to see that bloody word with my own eyes. I wanted to know how it could be true. You don't believe me, and you don't have to — I don't believe in ghosts, either. It could all be rumours, of course. But it was the building I had in my mind's eye as I was writing, and …'

'You're surely not saying …'

'Saré existed. I'm not superstitious, but I didn't invent Saré; I simply wrote down her thoughts. That's what happened. And I'm not just saying it to try and escape any kind of responsibility.'

She looked at him in astonishment, not knowing what to say. 'Could I see some pictures of Marie? Photos, I mean?' she asked, awkwardly.

He hesitated before going upstairs; Garibaldi stayed with the stranger. That was odd; he never stayed with strangers, he always followed Patrice. He brought back three photos, all of them black and white.

Marie was still very young in the first photo; it wasn't long after they'd first met, and she had just moved to the seventeenth arrondissement. She was sitting on the floor in the kitchen surrounded by countless empty bottles, smoking, her arms wrapped around her knees, looking straight into the lens with a languid expression. Her dark hair up and her lips painted a dark colour.

The second picture: they were already married, and he'd earned his first big advance for his debut novel published by Satyricon Press. They were thinking about buying a house. Marie was sitting on the sofa in the Paris flat, and in the background was Anne, who was probably living with them at the time, going through one of her difficult periods. He couldn't remember exactly. Marie had a book in her hand. She looked very beautiful and relaxed. She was in the middle of writing her dissertation on *Madame Bovary*. He loved that dissertation.

The third picture was the last one of Marie, taken by Anne. That alone was reason to love his sister. Marie in the garden, here in Chatou; she had planted tomatoes and was wearing wellies and a pair of his old denim shorts. She seemed tired, and her dyed-black hair made her face look older. Anne appeared to have taken her by surprise. Marie hadn't had time to hide, as she usually did when she sensed a camera nearby.

The stranger looked at the photos, her eyes lingering on the final picture. 'A very beautiful woman,' she said suddenly, giving him a searching look.

'Yes, she was the most beautiful woman I'd ever seen, and that didn't change in all the years we were married.'

'May I ask why you don't have children?'

'May you, may you — I don't know, just ask ... Marie didn't want them. Why is something you may not ask.' He laughed and poured himself another cup of coffee, offered her some, but she didn't want any more. The coffee in the pot was now lukewarm. She was still staring at the final picture of Marie. He wished she'd seen her in real life. All at once, he realised why he liked this woman. Why he'd liked her as soon as he'd opened the gate to her. She reminded him of his late wife.

That frightened him. The longer he thought about it, the more this vague feeling grew. It was desire. He could feel his palms growing damp with the tension, and was disgusted at himself and his body. He looked away.

She must have sensed something, and contemplated his face with a questioning look in her eyes.

'Let's take a walk around the garden, it's nice outside.'

Laura got up without saying a word and followed him, and so did Garibaldi. They walked all the way around the outside of the house. She asked him how long he'd lived here.

'It's a huge property!'

'Yes, I'd earned a fair bit of money, and Marie worked a lot, as well. Then we started the publishing house; she built it from the ground up and published anthologies. They were mostly very successful, they sold better than my own books did. She took care of all the operational stuff. The press was hers, really, and when she told me she wanted to sell it, I couldn't understand it at first.'

'But it must have been pretty lonely out here … I mean …'

'That's the way I wanted it. I haven't been able to bear people … since … well.'

She lit a cigarette.

This time, the silence had an ominous quality. Suddenly, he no longer felt so old and tired. It frightened him. He thought of Marie's body, of the countless nights and days spent with her, all that time but it still hadn't been enough. He thought of a particular night in the garden, out here, not far from the pond. Marie leaning against a tree and taking her trousers down, a cigarette in her hand, looking provocative. Offering herself to him, selling herself to him, to her husband. And afterwards running away and screaming at him: 'Well? Was I like her? Is that how you imagined it, you pig?'

'Sorry?' Laura had said something he hadn't heard.

'I was asking if you loved Jeanne Saré, as a woman, I mean, as …'

He was shocked; no one had ever put that question to him, no one. And Marie hadn't needed to ask. 'How do you mean?'

'I mean it as I said it.'

'It just sounds really — I don't know, how should I put it — absurd.'

'No more absurd than this business is already.'

'I don't know.' He looked her in the eye, and Laura held his gaze, her eyes cold. 'What else do you want?' he asked gruffly, staring at her white throat, the most vulnerable part of this woman's body.

'What do *you* want?' She simply returned the question.

Marie had cheated on him many times. She'd always come back, and he'd always known. Always forgiven her. It was like a law of nature: she cheated and then she came back to him. And he'd known why she did it, too. What she was taking her revenge for.

'I think you must have guessed what I want.' The words came out before he could stop himself.

At once, the stranger leaned forward and kissed him; the kiss was cold and calculating, but it was a kiss all the same and he grasped her wrists and held her there.

Then they walked to the barn in silence. She followed him and he led her by her cool hand. In the barn, the woman began to undress. He watched her, observing each movement. She had wonderful breasts. Heavy and full. She took off her black bra with one hand and stood there in her jeans. He didn't move. Then he went to her and knelt down; he licked her stomach and undid her trousers. The woman lost her coolness and became pliable. She was more toned and angular than his wife, but there was something so familiar about her. Her body was sensitive and adaptable … He took off her trousers as she undressed him, hastily pulling off his clothes.

She kissed him. This kiss was softer and wetter than the first. She lay down on the floor. He cradled her head in his hands, and with every movement her head and his hands hit the bare, cool floor. It was so easy to endure.

55. APIDAPI (2004)

So that was how desire was awakened ... Laura lay naked on her hotel bed. She had spent two hours in the bathroom, scrubbing and washing herself, but the desire refused to leave her body. She had tried to quench the burning with cold water.

Laura was suddenly afraid, afraid of her own body, which in the space of a few hours seemed to have developed a life of its own. Her body dared to defy her.

She thought about APIDAPI, and the protection afforded by these wonderful, childish letters. She thought about going back to Amsterdam, calling a halt to all of this, ceasing to sniff around in other people's lives. But she couldn't go back, not yet, there was something here she needed to understand; it was very close now, within her reach, just a little longer, a tiny bit further, and she would grasp it.

The older man had reawakened the frightening desire that had destroyed so much and had brought forth a dead child from her belly. She took the book and began to read the highlighted passages:

I open my legs and allow my brain to be raped, and as I do I think about revenge and yet I stay cold, and yet my heart is made of stone ... I intoxicate myself on others' intoxication and I despise them for it. Someone else's sweat clinging to my body. Do you know me? Do you know me? I let you swim through me, let you pierce your way to my heart, so that you will discover the silver dagger there and bore through my heart with it, disappointed and humiliated ... Go on, have no fear ... You will never see me again, I will wipe away all trace of myself, wipe my blood from your body. I stay clinging to no one. Go on, come in ... I am endless.

Laura suddenly became aware of how sad the person who wrote those lines must have been, whoever they were. She reached for her phone.

'Hello?'

'Nadine? It's Laura.'

'Oh, I've been waiting for you to call.'

'I'd like to see you, it's important.'

'I'm at home, come over.'

She drove to the third arrondissement without looking at the map.

Nadine was looking younger and fresher. She placed an ashtray in front of Laura as if it was the natural thing to do.

'I spoke to Duchamp,' said Laura. 'Spoke' sounded wrong to her. How much of this story could she tell?

'That bastard ... Did he admit it?'

'Marie, Marie Bessonville, his wife, killed herself. She was the last of the *Ice Age* victims.'

'Marie Bessonville ... That name sounds familiar. Wasn't she the publisher?'

'Yes, and the fact that she was his wife is seldom mentioned. I don't know why, probably to avoid even more misunderstandings. But people knew they were married, of course. The whole thing was so obvious that everyone overlooked it.'

'It's funny, since you were last here, I haven't been able to stop thinking about it all. I wanted to ask if I could help you in any way. Marcel is going away with his father for two weeks. I was thinking I'd go to Provence, but I'd rather stay, I want to ...'

'Duchamp said some strange things. What I want to know, first of all ...'

'Yes?'

'You have Olga's writings, don't you? May I see them?'

'Yes, well, I can show them to you, but they're pretty much identical to the original. She just copied out the words and added the odd comment, but those are mainly questions about the text.'

'Do you remember seeing the word "distraction" there? Did it come up in Olga's notes? Does the word appear in the book, as well? Does it have any kind of symbolism?'

'Olga mentions the word a few times. I noticed because she wrote it into the book in several places. It doesn't appear in *Ice Age* itself. Why do you ask?'

'Are you sure it doesn't?'

'Yes, I've studied that book very, very closely. Believe me.'

Laura told her the story of the building on the rue Bonaparte.

'But that could just be a lie …'

'But Olga? Even if Duchamp wrote that graffiti, why does it appear in Olga's writing?'

'She might have seen it on the wall of that building, but …'

'Yes, exactly: but. Somehow the whole thing doesn't hang together. I'm convinced he did write *Ice Age*, but maybe he took the idea from someone else? Could you go and look at the wall and find out? Do you know anyone who's good with handwriting? I mean …'

'Yes, I have someone in mind.'

'Okay, I'll get hold of a sample of Duchamp's handwriting, and we can ask an expert. I'm sure the word is there. I'll go myself, tomorrow.'

'I'll do it. I'll call Michel …'

Laura leapt up, embraced Nadine, and ran down the stairs. She wanted to go. And she knew why.

She drove back to the hotel; she needed to see the Freak and apologise.

After a year and a half of abstinence she had, in less than forty-eight hours, slept with two different men. The thought haunted her.

She knocked on the door of his room. He opened it right away and stared at her in surprise. She walked in without asking permission.

'I wanted to say sorry, Jan. I think I behaved a bit oddly last night.'

'It's fine.'

'No, that's not really my point.'

'You weren't here last night, were you?'

'No …' They were standing in the hotel room; it could have been anywhere in the world. She went to the Freak and hugged him. His body was weak and silky.

'I want to know what you know,' he said, as she was hugging him.

'I'll be at de Flore tomorrow at twelve on the dot, and then we'll talk about everything, okay?'

'Yes, I think you owe me that, Laura.'

'Be there at twelve, I'll meet you there.'

'Yes. Okay.'

She kissed him lightly on the cheek and left his room in a hurry. She was so tired that she wondered whether she was still in a fit state to drive. But she opened the car door and by the time the clock on the radio said 22:49 she was back in Chatou.

The gate was slightly ajar; she parked the car right in front of it and ran across the front yard. She had been running all evening, without knowing why or where to.

Lights were on downstairs. And she could see dim candlelight coming from the window of the barn. He was there. It was so quiet.

She stopped outside the door, her heart pounding, and then called his name.

She heard his quick footsteps. And suddenly he was standing before her. His hair, thick and almost white, was tousled. The dog appeared at his side and greeted her with a bark, before licking her hand. Only then did it occur to her that he hadn't barked when she came through the gate. As if she was familiar.

She didn't know what to say. She looked at the man. Then she simply took his hand and kissed it, kissed his fingertips, staring at him all the while.

He took her into his study. Three large candles were burning and an old typewriter stood on the desk, with paper piled beside it. The room was filled with books, notebooks, and loose sheets of paper; it smelled like a library.

She looked at him, looked at his face: that perfect handsome nose, the deep grey eyes with their heavy shadows, and the turned-down corners of his mouth.

He undressed her very slowly and she let it happen, as if she were sixteen and wanted nothing but to be in love. He knew why she'd come. He'd been waiting for her; she knew that.

She was naked, and still scented from the shower. Perhaps she was so eager for his body because then he might reveal his secrets without meaning to. Perhaps she could tease them out of him.

He satisfied her with his hand, pressing her up against the desk and looking into her face. Desire. Distraction. Desire. Distraction. Desire ... Laura cried out and clung to the man, who had been watching her throughout.

'You can stay the night here, if you like.' He left the room.

She lit a cigarette and put her knickers back on. The dog was outside; perhaps he wasn't allowed in? Perhaps this was the wise man's realm and his alone? She wandered around the room.

There was a framed photo on the wall. A very old picture. Two teenaged girls: one a little older than the other and lost in her insecurity, and the other rather more assertive, strong, and defiant. They were sitting on a flight of steps, in front of the door to a brick house. Both girls were looking into the camera. The smaller one had red hair and a snub nose, and was wearing a boilersuit, completely wrong for her age and at least two sizes too big, since the sleeves and trouser legs were rolled up. The other looked shy and quiet. She was wearing a narrow pair of glasses and a checked dress that also didn't suit her; it looked too childish and naive for her age.

The room was filled with books; one bookcase held his own works, and the rest were a mixture of all genres. There was no order to them. A lot of science fiction and classic horror, with *War and Peace* and poems by Verlaine shelved alongside them. She went back to the desk and for a moment she couldn't help but smile at the thought that a few minutes ago, she'd been standing there with her bare backside pressed up against it.

A full ashtray, two coffee cups (both half-finished), and a cocktail glass that looked as though it had been left there for some time.

There was a painting leaning up against the desk lamp. It depicted a man who looked like a tortoise. In the bottom corner, a scrawled 'M'. She bent over the typewriter, which was scratched and battered, the letters worn off most of its keys. She ran her hand lightly over the keys and felt a kind of familiarity. Then she flicked through a sheaf of paper that was lying next to it in a folder, the only orderly-looking thing in the room. The sheets were handwritten. In a very small, very sober hand. And the sentences were ... it was Saré.

She put the folder down as if it were poisonous. She quickly put on her bra and slipped into her jeans.

He returned carrying a tray. The dog barked outside, and he called out a few words to him in French. He had brought a baguette, butter, and cheese, and two bottles of beer.

'I was a little hungry, and I thought that …'

'Oh, thank you. Is the dog not allowed in here?'

'No, he isn't. Here, I need my peace and quiet.' Laura ate a piece of cheese and sucked at the beer bottle.

'Patrice?' As she said it, she thought this was a name she might learn to love.

'Yes?' He was sitting on the sofa and eating with great concentration, enjoying the food.

'I took a look at the folder.' She was standing with her back to him.

'Yes?'

'That folder, there.' She pointed to it.

'What about it?' He seemed to be concentrated entirely on his food.

'I mean, she still exists.' She didn't dare look at him.

'Oh, God. Laura … This is all too much for me, not now, not now …'

'I want to read it.'

'No!' he shouted, his piece of bread falling from his hand.

They looked at one another.

56. WOMAN (2004)

WHO ARE YOU? I DON'T KNOW YOU AND YET YOU HAVE STOLEN MY DREAMS FROM ME. I WANT THEM BACK. WHO AM I WITHOUT THEM?

I WAS SO SCARED, LYNN, SOMETIMES WHEN I LOOKED AT YOU AND WONDERED WHO YOU WERE, HOW WAS IT THAT YOUR FATHER AND I MADE YOU — THOUGH YOU DON'T CALL HIM FATHER AND THAT'S OKAY — YOU DON'T HAVE TO, IT'S A GOOD THING YOU DON'T … ONCE YOU LOOKED AT ME AND ASKED ME IF THERE WAS A GOD AND IF MAX WAS WITH HIM AND I SAID YES, BUT I WAS LYING. AND THEN YOU ASKED ME ABOUT FRANK, IF HE WAS THERE TOO, AND I SAID NO, AND THEN YOU DIDN'T KNOW WHAT TO SAY AND THEN YOU ASKED IF HE WAS WITH THE DEVIL, AND I SAID NO, HE JUST DOESN'T EXIST ANYMORE. BUT I WAS LYING ABOUT THAT, TOO, LYNN. AND REALLY, I BELIEVE THAT MAX DOESN'T EXIST ANYMORE, EITHER, BUT THAT'S TERRIBLE AND I DON'T WANT IT TO BE TRUE! I WANT TO FIND MAX … I WANT TO FIND A PLACE WHERE MAX — PERHAPS EVEN FRANK, TOO — COULD STILL EXIST, DO YOU UNDERSTAND, LYNN? I BETRAYED YOU. I'M SO SORRY, LYNN, FOR LEAVING YOU ALONE. AND NOW I FEEL SO …

She searched through her notebook and found a crumpled sheet with a number on it in Lynn's handwriting. It said 'Camp' — typical Lynn, only ever providing the information that was strictly necessary. She dialled the immensely long number.

She might be in luck — Lynn might have stayed on a bit longer, might still be at camp and not back at home with Granny yet. It was the craziest time to be calling the outback, but she had to do it. Finally a deep, tired man's voice answered.

'Hello? This is Francesca Lowell, I'm Lynn Lowell's mother. I'd like to speak to her, please. It's important.'

'Sorry, say again, who is this?'

'I'm looking for Lynn Victoria Lowell. I'm her mother.'

'Just a sec, I'll go and look.'

Francesca was anxious, beads of sweat appearing on her forehead. She waited a long time, an eternity, and was afraid Lynn might have left, but then suddenly there was her voice, that wonderful, familiar voice, and she saw her daughter before her, boyish, reluctant to accept her sex, the divided Lynn with her unfinished features.

'Mum?' the word barked, urgent. 'What's happened?' Her voice didn't sound sleepy at all.

'Lynn, sweetheart … I'm so glad …'

'Oh, Mum, what's happened?'

'Everything's fine, don't worry, nothing has happened. Are you okay to talk?'

'Yeah, sure. Where are you?'

'I'm in Paris, Lynn. In France. I stayed here and I'm going to be here for a while longer. I didn't go to Athens, I found something here — I'll explain it to you, later, not now. I just wanted to hear your voice, I wanted us to stop — I mean …'

'Mum, are you drunk?'

'No, Lynn, no I'm not. Just trust me for a second, okay? Just for this one conversation — I know you don't, but I'm asking you to now. I want us to stop — stop pretending to ourselves, I mean. I want to tell you that I love you so much, and that I'm sorry for having lied to you so often, for neglecting you, for not being there so many times, but I want to tell you that I want to change. I want that, Lynn, for you and for us. I believe in you so much, Lynn. I'm sorry for getting on your nerves and for saying "Lynn" all the time, but that's what I cling to, you know? Your name is the only fixed point in my life, and I have to keep repeating it, so I can feel it — and then I'm all right. I love you, Lynn!'

'Oh, Mum …' her voice was shaky.

Tears welled up in Francesca's eyes. 'Darling … I didn't love Max more than you. I know that's what you think, but it isn't true. It's just … when you lose people, then you overlook the ones who are left, in your grief, you know? Sometimes you forget that the people you love just as much are still there. And I want your forgiveness.'

'Mum …' Lynn was crying.

Francesca tried to recall when she'd last seen her daughter cry. Lynn almost never cried. All the same, she could see her daughter's face very clearly in her mind's eye, the silent sobbing. 'Lynn … please.'

'I … was scared. I thought you'd … gone.'

'Lynn, forgive me … I'll come back to you and we'll do everything different, all right? I don't want to lose you, Lynn. I wouldn't survive it.'

'I don't want to lose you either, Mum.' Now she could hear a tender smile mixed in with the tears. How wonderful she was, and how wonderful that she didn't even know it.

'Is it good there? When are you going home?'

'It's great … I'm having fun. I've got one more day and then Granny's coming to get me. She didn't want to let me travel alone, you know what she's like. But Mum — Paris — that sounds exciting. What are you doing there?' Something was different about Lynn; she sounded more mature, more receptive.

'I'm researching something. It's a long, complicated story, I'll tell you about it some other time. But the city *is* exciting — you'd like it, we must come here together sometime, okay?'

'Okay. Mum?'

'Yes?'

'There's something I want to tell you … I …'

'What's wrong?'

'Nothing, nothing, you don't have to be so … worried. I've, well, I've met …'

'Lynn?'

'There's this boy ...'

'Whaaat? Who is he? Oh my God — Lynn!'

'I like him a lot ... You don't know him, he's seventeen, he goes to St Helens High, you know? His name's Jim.'

'Lynn ... That's awesome.'

'Did you just say "awesome"?'

'Yes, I did.'

'Mum, what is going on with you?'

'I'm shocked ... I ... I'm delighted that you've told me. I want you to be happy.'

'I think I am, now.'

'I love you, Lynn.'

'I ... love you too.'

'I want to meet this Jim when I get back.'

'Don't go planning a wedding though, okay?'

'Okay. I promise.'

Lynn's voice was still echoing in Francesca's head long after she put the receiver down. She was excited to imagine Lynn with this Jim. She pictured him as a lanky boy with freckles, who made an effort to look cool. So she had met a boy, good girl Lynn, and told her about it as well — just a few weeks ago she would never have told her, never.

The sky was grey and heavy with rain. She stood in front of her suitcase, which she was still using as a wardrobe. She took out all the clothes, folded them carefully, and put them in a large plastic bag. She went into the bathroom, took a shower, then picked up her nail scissors and cut off her soft, shoulder-length hair; the cut was crooked, but that didn't matter. She put on a flowery summer dress, one she had bought last year with Jen. Then she went out.

She took the plastic bag with her and left it on top of a wheelie bin in the backyard of the *pension*. Her hair, short and wet, gave her a sense of liberation.

She had nothing else — she hadn't even taken her small handbag with her — just a few crumpled banknotes clutched in her fist.

People didn't seem to be interested in her. It wasn't bad, it was actually reassuring. Sometimes she thought she knew the answers already ...

Perhaps he just hadn't known how to forgive? Not even leaving behind the idea of a love in silence — she'd turned away from him, from the man with crystal-clear blue eyes.

She walked on, and her head began to empty itself.

THE WORLD IS TURNING TO THE OTHER SIDE.

THE SKY IS FULL OF DUST. WE WERE ALL THERE: MAX, LYNN, FRANK, AND ME. WE EXISTED.

57. ICE AGE / BOOK 1 (1953)

As I am, I cannot be.

It is great, my dream; it is great, my palace of ice. And I have refused entry to everyone. I have resisted everyone.

I no longer want to come to you, Achilles. I have become self-sufficient.

I write down every destruction meticulously on the pages of time. It will be noticed, that much is inevitable.

Behind me I leave full ashtrays, I leave beads of sweat, thousands of kilometres of loneliness and gaping wounds, I leave stains of fear and war, and I leave the images of love destroyed. I will come, Achilles, I will open myself up to you, you rapist, you; will you be fair to me? Do you have the greatness for it?

I spread myself out and I let you swim through me, all the Niagara Falls in me, but you won't get far. At the end of the tunnel you will find an axe and you will split your skull open, since your last dream will be ended, your last hope of freedom destroyed — and shall I tell you why you have failed — shall I? You expected to.

★

The candle beside the bed has almost burned down, the electricity has been off for days, the rent paid with stolen money. The girl — wrapped in a raincoat, emaciated, with her bald head, half-naked in a naked flat. A table bought at the flea market, the mattress too old, too torn and filthy, harbouring a thousand stories and a thousand stains. The girl with dead fish eyes, bordering on ugliness. The girl has opium; a man with a long moustache — a war veteran — got it for her. She did him a favour; she masturbated him.

She has barricaded herself in and is smoking opium from a piece of foil. The night is dark and windy; soon winter will come and close everything up, and the world will turn to silence and death. The girl has dirty feet and reddened, raw knees. The girl is starting to lose consciousness, and loneliness eats into every pore. The girl is a little afraid, but only a little. Her squared-paper notebook is almost filled with her girlish handwriting; soon everything will have reached its end.

The end is white and glorious. She knows what has to be done.

The smoke rises into her brain, her eyes grow heavy, and the empty space expands; colours grow clearer and more intense. At that moment she loves the opium man, perhaps the only person in the world she does love, and is glad of this brief happiness she has been granted.

Someone enters her world: a woman, a beautiful woman, though a little pale, and wearing a polka-dotted dress over her bare skin. Her flesh, vulgar, cries out for lust. The girl puts out a hand towards her and laughs; the young woman comes and sits on her lap. She smiles.

'I'm Olga, I couldn't come until now. The times didn't fit together, do you see?' she says, stroking the girl's cold hands. She leans forward and kisses her on the neck.

'The times?'

'Yes. I know you. You were dead when I was alive.'

The girl laughs, at once all her self-control and her cold exterior has given way. 'Oh, I see …'

The young woman with the Russian name and the dark hair stares at the girl, as if she knows her, and then she kisses her on the lips, a wonderful kiss.

The girl has returned to her senses and undoes the zip of the pretty dress. The dress looks strange; it isn't right, somehow.

'I know you. The times didn't fit, do you see? I waited so long …'

'Oh, I understand …' says the girl as she watches the woman take off her dress. She stands in front of the girl, naked and beautiful. She has large, dark blue eyes and full, moist lips; she runs her tongue over them and the girl has to get up and move closer, much closer to her.

Then she takes the woman in her arms and they dance ... the whole bare flat has been waiting for their dance. It has always been waiting and she just didn't know it. Now the room is filled.

'I've been waiting for you, and I've done everything you wanted ... and yet I was never happy: really, the times didn't fit, do you see?' the woman says again.

And the girl wants to weep. The room is filled with their intimacy. The girl is fascinated by the beauty of it, then she closes her eyes and cries out: 'Are you dead?'

'Yes, and yet I am still very young, too young for you ...' the woman replies. They fall silent and go on dancing. They stroke one another's bald heads.

'Did I kill you?' the girl asks, suddenly kneeling down. The woman says nothing, merely touches her collarbone.

When the girl wakes the next morning, feeling nauseous, she is alone, but she has a secret that she doesn't want to share with the world ...

58. ME (2005)

I have arrived in the country, the country of strangers. I am living on the twelfth floor of a tower block. I wandered around the shopping centre today: which costume will I have? Which self will I choose today, I wondered, until my head ached. I float above myself.

The city, large and mendacious, mysterious and full of stories drunk on blood, weighs down my eyelashes; every blink is filled with the breath of this city and the sad thing about it is that I have so little use for it, because I know neither the beginning nor the end.

Last night your spirit came knocking here. At least, that was how it seemed to me, and I was ready to open the door. Today I wouldn't open it, not in daylight. Stop pretending to yourself! I cannot handle disappointment. Have I ever told you that?

I drink the best wine in the world, wine from the wine country, which almost tastes better here than in the place it comes from. My phone never rings; few people know the digits that would let them glide in here, down the cable into my shadow world. Tea with honey, lying naked on the bed, sometimes giving my body to strangers' hands to satisfy, drinking wine and cough mixture. Watching black-and-white films, thinking about friends, letting the future fly away, looking into the empty fridge, glumly eating a tomato salad, sleeping through the afternoons — exhausted from the wakeful nights, sometimes checking the virtual post, which is not post at all, and feeling nothing.

I am reading all the books in the world to find you, searching every corner, but you are nowhere now. Perhaps I secretly love a dead seventeen-year-old girl?

Here I sit, thinking that I won't move from this place until I've tracked down the unhappy girl to bid her a proper farewell!

59. NADINE (2004)

DO YOU KNOW WHO I MET TODAY? MICHEL. HE'S HARDLY CHANGED, JUST GROWN THINNER AND SOMEHOW MORE EARNEST. HE WAS SURPRISED WHEN I CALLED. AND WHEN I TOLD HIM EVERYTHING, IT HIT HIM HARD … HE'S DIVORCED, NO CHILDREN. I THOUGHT HE'D HAVE CHILDREN — IT WOULD SUIT HIM. DID YOU LOVE HIM? WHAT DID HE GIVE YOU? I MET YOUR LOVER AND TALKED ABOUT THAT BLOODY WORD AND HE LOOKED AT ME AND THOUGHT I'D GONE MAD. WE NEVER ESPECIALLY LIKED ONE ANOTHER AND BACK THEN, AT THE FUNERAL, WE JUST STOOD THERE STUPIDLY IN OUR GRIEF. AND I HATED HIM FOR NOT STOPPING YOU. DID YOU KNOW I WAS THE ONLY ONE WHO SAW YOUR BODY? I HAD TO IDENTIFY YOU. YOUR PARENTS COULDN'T; THEY DIDN'T WANT TO, AND THEY COULDN'T. I TOOK THAT UPON MYSELF.

HAVE YOU HEARD, OLGA, THAT YOUR DEATH WAS A FUCKING LIE? HOW COULD YOU FIRST HAVE SEX AND THEN THROW YOURSELF UNDER A TRAIN?

AND NOW HERE I WAS SITTING WITH MICHEL, WHO IS DIVORCED AND CHILDLESS … HE WANTS TO TAKE A LOOK AT THAT FUCKING WORD. HOW DO I DEFINE MY OWN LIFE WITHOUT YOURS?

★

There were toys lying everywhere, the room just as the boy had left it, chaotic and cosy. She had delivered the baby by caesarean and felt she had lost out; she would have liked to have felt pain for him, didn't want to be anaesthetised when a new life was beginning ...

She stared at the blank wall, inhaling the boy's scent. He was away now with his father. She loved that man, whom she had never loved, for being a good father. He deserved to have this child, was better able to love him than she was ... She smiled and buried her face in the boy's t-shirt, sweaty and dirty. She felt a rush of warmth. Then she got up and opened the window.

60. BROTHER (2004)

He had driven the Jeep into town and done the shopping. He was wearing a black trench coat. The woman's smell was still on him.

Anne had called and 'threatened' to come over; she always 'threatened' before she came over. Madame Sour had cooked and cleaned. He decided to forgo Madame Sour's roast chicken and made himself some onion soup.

It was a lovely evening and he considered lighting the fire, though it wasn't really cold enough. Garibaldi seemed to have picked up on his master's good mood and was continually wagging his tail.

He laid the table, went to the cellar to fetch wine, uncorked the bottle, and sat down. The food tasted wonderful, with black bread, and two ripe tomatoes from the garden. He always ate when he wanted to; he never waited.

Not long after, Anne arrived. She was wearing leggings and a long, striped jumper, her hair up, her eyes ringed with black kohl. He had always found her clothes tasteless and yet, despite all her mistakes, her revolts, she was a beautiful woman.

He watched her: the haphazard way she rolled a cigarette, her bitten fingernails. Perhaps this combination of the attractive and the repellent was the reason men grew so attached to her. Why all the ex-lovers would come knocking on her door again sooner or later. She would always let them back into her flat and her bed for a few nights. This woman was a kind of leftover from a past age.

He was glad Anne had come. She was the person who linked them all: him and Marie, him and his mother and Mone. And maybe their anger at one another was greater and more enduring than any normal love between siblings could have been.

She rolled herself a joint and put it to one side. Then she took a sip of the Spanish red wine he'd opened for her. She picked up a piece of Madame Sour's chicken and ate. Turned on the ancient radio. The presenter was reading the latest news, a bus accident in Caracas, thirty-one dead. Unrest in Ukraine. A French director wanted to make a film about Che Guevara. Then came a frothy saxophone melody, adverts.

He put the dirty crockery in the sink and ran some cold water. Then he sat down again and watched Anne's pretty, slender fingers lighting the joint. He took a cigarillo from the pocket of his shirt and they smoked in silence, a familiar ritual — 'pacification' as Anne always liked to say.

'I called Mone earlier, I think I'll go in October — are you listening? I've taken time off work, and I'll stay down there for a while. I'm going to enjoy Marennes. I'll have the house. Mone told me that would be absolutely fine. I can have the upper floor. And — '

'Come off it, you'll go out of your mind there, Anne. You'll last two days at most, and then …'

'No, I've given notice on my flat here, and I don't care, I really don't. I'll enjoy it, it's absolutely fine. I think …'

'What good is it going to do?'

'What good does going home do?'

'I don't know. I thought *this* was your home.'

'Ah …' Her eyes grew heavy, sad. 'I'll stay here tonight,' she announced, before getting up and walking slowly to the door. He followed, not knowing why. And suddenly she saw the picture of Marie, the last picture, the one she'd taken herself here in this garden; he had forgotten to put it back after showing it to Laura. The picture of Marie that had served as a bridge to the stranger's body …

Anne stopped and picked up the photo, taking a long look at its surface with vacant eyes. Then she dropped it abruptly and walked out. At the door to the cellar she put on the old pair of wellies that had belonged to Marie and went out into the grounds; Garibaldi barked, and Patrice grabbed his coat and followed his sister, the dog running ahead of him.

'There's this woman, you know … she comes here, sometimes …' the instant he had uttered the words, he felt ashamed to have put it like that.

'What woman?' She seemed to have no objection to him accompanying her on her walk.

'The woman who came to France with the guy you met.'

'Oh. Sometimes?'

'She's doing research. I'm letting her, I don't mind, she isn't from the press. I like her.'

'You mean you're fucking her?' She stopped walking.

'That's not what I said.'

'It's what you meant.'

'Well, all right, if that's how you want to put it.'

'Well, well, brother mine … this is something altogether new.'

'Anne. Are you angry with me?'

'You've made me sad, Patrice, that's all.' She called Garibaldi, stroked him, walked slowly towards the pond.

'I feel the same, Anne. I want you to forgive me.'

'No, no, forget it … doesn't matter anyway.'

'Don't be like that, not now, please …'

'Patrice, you let it happen! In the last few days I've got out all the books, and I've been reading, trying to relate every sentence to you, you and Marie.'

Anne had adored Marie; sometimes he'd actually been jealous of the two of them, they got on so well. And after all the complications in Anne's life, she had always come back to her, to Marie. Marie loved Anne. Marie had developed feelings for Anne that were almost maternal. Sometimes he believed that Marie was the only reason Anne hadn't cut all ties with him.

'I've tried to put myself in your shoes, to understand, but I can't! That you could have brought yourself to lie so brazenly all these years … When did you start? Why? I was crazy about Saré, everyone was crazy, and I can't forgive Marie for never telling me either, goddammit!'

'Don't exaggerate, Anne.'

'Exaggerate? Me? Do you *realise* what you've done?'

'Just look at me if you want to know that.'

They sat down on Marie's bench, which still stood by the pond. The large, black dog lay at their feet.

'This woman reminded me of ... That might be the only reason I let her in.'

'Patrice, these are our lives you're jeopardising here! If word gets out that it was you, they won't forgive you. And they'll turn Marie into number fifteen for certain. They'll kick your door down and ...'

'No, they won't. No one will want to believe it. They want to believe in Saré. If they even still remember who she was. I'm not afraid, you know that.'

'Not afraid? What about us, me, and all the others who, for all those years ... Forget it!'

He laid an arm around her shoulders and pulled her to him. He thought of that evening in Marennes, years ago, when they had stood on the balcony smoking. That old cow Madeleine had been there; Anne had smoked in secret and painted her lips red.

At first Anne refused to yield to him, but soon she gave in and sank into his arms. Her head rested on his lap and she curled up on the bench. He wasn't sure whether she was crying.

All her life she had lived for others, refusing to accept help though she was always in need of it. All her miscarriages, when she had so longed to have children. Eventually she'd told him, as if it were a throwaway remark, that she saw it as a kind of punishment. For what, exactly, she didn't know. He'd had to shut his eyes to rein in his sympathy.

'Sometimes I have the sense that we've both lived the same life, Anne. You've just approached it from a different side to me. But it was still the same ...'

Anne said nothing. She got up and went back to the house. He and Garibaldi trudged slowly after her.

She finished the wine in front of the television, in the living room with the stone floor and the rug from Istanbul. Suddenly she called out to him; he stopped in the doorway and looked at her, lying on the sofa with her head hanging over the arm.

'Did you want Marie to be like *her*? Did you want to make her the same?'

'No, no.'

'You did, Patrice. I'm not judging you. I will try … to forgive you. I'll try to change things. Enough of this.'

'Anne …' He was about to say something, but then he fell silent, turned round, and walked quickly out of the living room.

He went into the study and sat down at the desk. He lowered his head; saw the picture that Marie had painted when she was twenty-six. 'A man like a tortoise,' Marie had called it.

61. APIDAPI (2004)

Empty cigarette packets were scattered around. The sun was rising. She had woken up, and the black and red digital clock in the hotel room read 5:36. That was no time to be doing anything, thought Laura.

She sat up, drank some water, and looked out of the window. It made her think back to when she was writing her thesis — on Bacon's image of the pope after Velasquez — and suffering from panic attacks. She couldn't look at the pope paintings now, having spent months studying and researching them. Even the thought of the screaming pope made her anxious. It was a terrible image, and yet she couldn't help but be fascinated by it.

She stood at the window in her black knickers, the curtain pulled a little to one side. It wasn't yet completely light. People were sleeping.

Nadine had called; she'd had someone check the writing in the rue Bonaparte. Laura and the Freak had also been to the address the previous day to look at the word. A chimera. But Nadine told her that the apartment building's oldest resident, who'd lived there since 1948, had confirmed that the word had been there ever since he could remember. He also said that a girl had actually lived on the attic floor in the 1950s, and had then disappeared. Nadine had considered trying to verify these things, but they made no sense, there was no possible rational explanation for any of this. Laura felt overwhelmed.

The Freak had studied her with a strange look on his face as she was telling him about her encounters with Duchamp. She thought she saw scorn in his eyes.

She lit a cigarette and picked up the book, along with Olga Colert's squared exercise book, which Nadine had given her, and sat on the bed to start comparing the texts. She flicked through the anthologies that Marie Bessonville had edited in the years 1985, 1987, and 1988. Mostly erotic stories or avant-garde, unknown authors, selected with style and taste, with clever introductions. Somewhere in there, between the lines, she would surely find something. Laura's eyes stung. She massaged her temples and let out a groan. Her back hurt and she was so tense she could barely move.

Laura switched the television on; there was an opera playing, *Madame Butterfly*. She turned up the volume and tried to concentrate on the music. It was devastating.

There was a knock on the door, though it wasn't yet seven o'clock. She threw on her kimono and went to see who it was. The older man stood before her. He had been lured out of his cage, out of his hiding place. Puccini came flooding out into the sleepy corridor. Patrice was wearing a raincoat and a black hat, and she thought he looked wonderful. She didn't say anything; he stepped into her room, holding two paper cups.

He looked around: the disorder, the full ashtrays, a dry half-eaten sandwich from the day before, her underwear draped over the chair. He put the cups on the glass coffee table, which was covered in books and notebooks. Then he sat down on the edge of the bed and picked up one of the anthologies, put it down again, reached for his coffee, and took the first sip. She drank the coffee he'd brought for her.

'She felt guilty because she'd urged me to publish *Ice Age*. She'd thought it great fun to come up with a biography for the mad girl.' He looked into his paper cup. 'I was thinking about you — I couldn't sleep. My sister is at my house. We talked for a long time, in a way we haven't done for years. I ...' He took some sheets of paper from the inside pocket of his coat and put them down among the books. ' ... brought a few pages with me, from the folder.' He paused, looked at her, and said: 'I would like to make love to you.'

She took off her knickers as she was sitting beside him, then opened the kimono, and planted herself in front of him. Perhaps she desired him because he seemed just as empty as she was.

'Did you look for *her* in your wife? And is that why you're here, too? Am I to be like her? Is that what this is about?' She stood naked before him, waiting for his hands.

He undressed slowly, carefully, staring at her all the while. He took her hand in his and drew her down onto the bed. Then he got on top of her, sought and found, and thrust into her. She trembled; he held her by the hair. He pressed her face into the pillow. She struggled and pressed her fingertips into his eye sockets. Her hair was sticking to his throat. She fell. She lay on the floor and he lay down beside her, her back pressed against his belly. She felt his hands on her buttocks, he rubbed himself against her back, her hands clawed at his ribs. She no longer felt any pain. She cried out, turned around, straddled him and began to choke him, and he offered no resistance. It frightened her; she couldn't stop, took his head in her hands, banged it against the floor, bit his shoulder.

All at once she felt something warm and wet. She was bleeding — blood was running down the inside of her thigh — and she rolled off him. He sat up suddenly and held her legs apart, then wiped away the blood as she screamed at him to take his hands off her.

Now he was stroking her back gently, as if there had been no pain and no blood. She wanted him to leave her alone, but at the same time she felt herself yearning for his touch, despite everything, despite her disgust at having his hands on her again.

He got up abruptly and began to put his clothes back on. She had crawled onto the bed and was lying curled up there. Her whole body ached. He leaned over her and smiled. She wanted to spit at him, but instead she offered up her lips. He kissed her, brushing away the strands of hair that were stuck to her face.

'I can't bear Paris for more than three hours at a time,' he said, before leaving the room.

62. WOMAN (2004)

Her hair was about three millimetres long, and she was wearing a new t-shirt and a new pair of linen trousers. She had spent the last three days in the Bibliothèque nationale, searching for meaning. She walked through the streets, sensing everything, smelling everything, seeing everything, as if she had been numb to it all before, and was suddenly perceiving the world with sharpened senses.

The dreams had stopped, too. She had time. She went on studying the book. Studying someone else's thoughts that had once been hers, too. She contemplated her tall frame in the mirror; her body looked starved and dried out, but no longer lifeless.

Sometimes she would go for a stroll, eat at a café, drink, read, or stare at people. She bought an old record player at a flea market and lugged it back to her room at the *pension*. She listened to the blues and drank whisky. Sometimes she called Leo and talked herself hoarse; his genius seemed ridiculous to her now.

She bought roses and distributed them all around the shabby room. She read a lot, wherever she was: in the bath, in cafés, on staircases, in parks, at restaurants in the evening. Everywhere she saw lines of text that looked like signposts.

She ran a hand over her body, over her skull, feeling herself. Sometimes, but not often, she drank to excess. Those were the evenings when she felt lonely. She noted down new names, tried to understand connections — Nadine Leavit, Patrice Duchamp, those who had been left behind.

Three times a week she went to a jazz bar near Saint-Germain and ordered cocktails. The tightness in her chest had almost gone. She was feeling her way towards herself, tentatively moving forwards. She usually fell asleep at dawn and woke around midday.

Eventually she told Leo he mustn't think she blamed him. He didn't reply, but she knew he was grateful for those words. She told him he shouldn't blame himself, either. She knew how he felt, she said; she had seen it in his eyes on the day of the funeral. They both knew she should have left Frank, but inertia and comfort meant that she had let it come to this. In the last years of their life together, she hadn't wanted anything more to do with him. From the first time she announced she had a migraine and didn't want sex. And of course, none of that justified what Frank did later. But she had let it come to that, hadn't stopped him falling apart inside. She did know him better than anyone, after all.

She told Leo that maybe one day she'd be ready to meet up with him, to talk to him about everything that had happened, but not now. She was sorry, she said on the phone, about his wife. In the future, she was sure a lot of things would change. Leo said that 'the future' was an ironic concept when the present had been lost. She told him the present could never be lost.

Suddenly Leo began to weep, and his sobbing travelled down the line, tears surging kilometre after kilometre, to the other end, to her. He murmured something through his tears.

'What did you say, Leo? Are you still there?'

'I told him. I told him you were with me.'

'What?'

'Yes. I was angry with him, because of the project. It was our baby, we'd spent years working on it and all of a sudden he just wanted money, and he left me behind. He should never have done that! I needed him! We had big plans, and then he betrayed me! And then you and me, that night … What did he need all that money for? That night, that night, Fran, it was so precious to me, so … I didn't intend to destroy anything.'

'You …'

'I went to see him, I needed his help, I was desperate to get this funding, I wanted my project to keep going, I needed his help and then … he just left me in the lurch. I didn't know he wasn't well, I didn't know he had problems.'

'He didn't have problems.'

'No, no, Fran, he had big problems. I asked him to stay, to keep focused, he'd already got everything he wanted ... And he said: "no, no. No." I couldn't do it on my own, and when he turned to leave, I told him. I don't know why. I didn't plan to. It just slipped out and ...'

'I see.'

'No, no, Fran, wait ...'

'I want to be on my own now. That's all.' She hung up. She had freed herself from him, too.

She walked the streets; the city left her cold. The gods had fallen from their thrones, otherwise she might have prayed ... perhaps.

She took the train out to Chatou. She wanted to leave her own marks on the map.

63. ICE AGE / BOOK 1 (1953)

Time was a watchful, tender, subtle fox. She went walking in the cemetery, marching through the army of graves in order to touch life.

She had injured herself; in the night, she had shattered a glass with her fist, a glass stolen from a café weeks earlier. Her right hand was cut to ribbons and smeared with blood. The night when the beautiful woman had come to visit her still clung to her skin: in the form of a soft, barely perceptible scent.

All she needed were a few small supports, no more than that, crutches on which she could lean, just a little longer, just a little longer, then the exercise book would be full, just a few more notes. Just behead the fear, just a few seconds longer …

All the false priestesses were dead, and she didn't want to be one.

Her head hurt. She was hungry. The graves seemed so happy.

She lay down on one. She stretched. The stone reached out to feel her bones, pressed against her ribs, her rump. She sniffed the dead flowers, which smelled of autumn, and gently stroked the stone. What lay beneath it? What did it know? She pressed her cheek against the gravestone. No reply, not even an echo. It remained as it had been: lifeless and discreet.

She got up, let out a laugh, threw back her head. Her hair had begun to grow again. Nature thirsted for life. It probably never got enough. She opened her arms and embraced the wind, then she began to dance with it, a waltz in the autumn, a waltz for the dead. Everything danced with her: the stones, the wilted flowers, the statues, the old trees. And everything was so peaceful, so beautiful … she felt a little stab in her heart at all the beauty. Her laughter danced with her. A waltz of ghosts, played for ghosts.

The place so perfect in its self-sufficiency.

On the way into the city, back into life, she happened across a funfair. She plunged into the crowd, got lost, re-emerged. The people — all eager for a little bit of joy, standing in a queue that seemed to have no end — ignored her.

She hurried away. As she darted through the crowd, she'd snatched a purse.

She took out the notes and coins and threw the thing itself into a bin. Then she went to a stall, bought three crêpes and ate them one after another. After that, she treated herself to a glass of punch.

Having warmed her belly, she walked over to the large roller coaster. Boys thronged around it, their trousers threadbare at the knees, gawking strangely. She stuck her tongue out at one of them, and the boy giggled. He was sixteen at most and had freckles and pretty blue eyes. She pushed her way through the throng, he followed her, and they reached the ticket kiosk at the same time. Without speaking a word, he took a seat beside her and the ride set off.

The world sped up. She closed her eyes and joined the general shriek-ing. The boy was silent, clinging to the bar. She let go theatrically and waved her arms in the air, and the boy copied her. She lifted herself as far as she could out of her seat, leaning forward as if she wanted to fall; he hesitated, but then copied her. She liked that. They stood for the rest of the ride, her legs aching with the effort. The ride slowed, and when she got off, he followed her.

'Do you want an ice cream?' he asked. It was too cold for an ice cream, but she wanted one all the same; she wanted everything. She nodded. She bought one for him, too — he didn't seem to have much money. They mingled with the crowds. Later, after three rides on the carousel, they sat on a bench drinking fruit punch, and she smoked. Now she owned an entire packet of cigarettes.

'You're not from round here, are you?' she asked him.

He said he wasn't. 'I'm from Toulouse. Started an apprenticeship here three weeks ago.'

'How old are you?'

'Seventeen.'

'Where do you live?'

'With relatives. A bit out of town.'

'Fun, isn't it?'

'What, this here?' His demeanour was far too serious for his youthful looks. He was slender and frail-looking, though he had a handsome face, delicate and aristocratic. His speech was coarse, and he used dialect. 'It's all right. I've seen bigger carousels.'

They fell silent, watching all the people around them. Suddenly he snatched the old cap off her head and looked at her. 'Your hair is so short. I thought …'

'What did you think? Give my hat back.'

'It looks funny.'

'Give it to me!' She took the hat from him and put it back on.

His eyes were wide with alarm. 'I thought .,.'

'Shut up!'

She walked away and he followed her. Darkness was falling; she left the fairground and ran. He stayed with her, though she hissed at him, swore, ran again. She couldn't shake him off.

'What do you want? Go away!'

'What's your name?'

'Leave me alone, are you deaf?'

'Mine's Paul.'

'I don't care. Go away!'

She walked to the bus stop. It was dark now, the street lamps giving off a dim light, and it seemed hard to believe that the funfair was still in full swing nearby. The two of them sat down on the wooden bench and waited. She smoked greedily, one cigarette after another.

'I'm Saré,' she said eventually.

He didn't ask what kind of a name that was. She wondered what he wanted. Money, perhaps — he looked so down at heel. And so hungry.

'Why is your hair so short?'

'Because that's how I like it.'

'I think it's strange.'

'So?'

The bus took them away. They got out at the boulevard du Montparnasse. The pavements were not yet empty; artists and street vendors were still hanging around. She bought a cigarette holder, just like that, and yet more cigarettes. She thought about the afternoon and her waltz and giggled to herself. The boy walked beside her, his hands in his trouser pockets, with a vacant expression. His presence had stopped bothering her; he hardly said a word.

'What kind of apprenticeship are you doing?' she asked eventually, out of boredom.

'Carpentry.'

'Carpentry,' she repeated.

They walked aimlessly, at some point sitting down in an unfamiliar café and ordering a salad with cheese. She had a glass of lemonade as well.

He watched her, and then all at once he lowered his eyes and asked, staring at her fingers: 'I've got ten francs saved up, will you do it for ten francs?'

She choked on her food. 'I'm not a whore.' She looked him in the eye.

He froze, got to his feet for a moment, sat back down, blushed, and began to breathe faster. 'I … I thought …'

'I know you did. But I'm not. I just have short hair, because I like it that way, you understand?'

'I … I didn't mean to …'

'It's fine.'

He got up and slunk away, his head bowed in shame. Confused, lonely, and silent.

64. ME (2005)

Every night I hear this strange sound, like fireworks, but I can't pin it down to any particular event, can't even tell where it's coming from; there are no colours in the sky to go with the sound.

I buy poetry books and begin to find the general unfriendliness here amusing. I listen to ballads and nestle my body against other bodies when I dance and drink vodka or beer — drinks that I hate.

I am starting to learn not to care, and I no longer find it frightening. 'Be with me, my little dove,' someone is singing on the radio as I stare out of the bus window. I am discovering the city, and I thank it for granting me such anonymous asylum.

As I am punching in the code to unlock the huge metal door, as if it were the entrance to a high-security prison, I lose my name, my face. In the dirty blue corridors I finally forget everything, and I arrive at the stained door of the flat as a nobody.

I love this city because it has swallowed me up, because it hides me and lets me stare idly at its monumental buildings. Did I come here to flay myself?

I am like a spectator of my own life. Eating popcorn.

I take the metro, smell strangers' sweat, buy beer and bread from the same woman, watch people fucking on television, and think that my NON-EXISTENCE is making me so light that I could spread my arms and fly off into the darkness. I am building walls so that no one will disturb my isolation.

I forgo all the sights, deliberately walk the more deserted streets on my way home, and don't pack a street map to ensure I will get lost. I am performing a ritual of purification. I go out onto the crooked balcony and stare at the monstrous buildings whose roofs press into the sky.

I write. I remember only rarely, and when I do, all I remember is that I should be writing. I write my name in the books I have bought and feel silly doing it. I lose the urge for ownership and would think it a fine thing to have just one pair of trousers and one shirt, but I find that elitist, too. And so I don't do it.

My neck stiff, my joints cricked. I will have to start all over again, if I should ever abandon my walls. For the first time, I weigh up the possibility that I may have unlearned love. Strangers phone me. The people I was in love with have different phone numbers now. I don't try to reanimate old affairs. Could I?

Am I hurting YOU by not doing any more than this? Good.

Was that pathetic, now? Fuck it. I admit, I often cry in the cinema.

65. BROTHER (2004)

YOU WILL NEVER BE ABLE TO PUT AN END TO IT. YOU
WILL ALWAYS GO ON LIKE THIS. I WILL NEVER BE ENOUGH
FOR YOU, NO ONE WILL EVER BE ENOUGH FOR YOU. I HAVE
SERVED UP MY LIFE TO YOU ON A SILVER PLATTER. AND YOU
ONLY SNIFFED AT IT NOW AND THEN, WHEN SHE'D LET YOU
DOWN. DO YOU NOT REALISE THAT SHE'S A CORPSE? YOU'VE
POISONED MY LIFE. I LOVED YOU. I SHOULD HAVE KNOWN
IT. YOU WILL NEVER CHANGE, NEVER. THEN GO TO HER,
FIND HER. YOU WANTED TO TURN ME INTO HER. BUT — IT'S
ME, MARIE, IT'S ME, MARIE, MARIE. I DON'T KNOW WHO I AM
MYSELF ANY MORE. YOU MADE ME FORGET. LOOK AT ME AND
TELL ME WHO I AM! TELL ME! YOU COWARD. GIVE ME MY LIFE
BACK. DO YOU THINK YOU CAN GO ON LIKE THIS? DO YOU
THINK NONE OF IT WILL CATCH UP WITH YOU, MY BELOVED?

She had said these words three weeks before her death. They were sitting in the kitchen; he was cutting bread, and she launched into this speech
out of nowhere.

Three days after she died, in his bid to devour the pain, he had searched
through her things, aimlessly; had sniffed her clothes, which still held the
last scent of her life. Then he'd leafed through her notebooks and torn
pages out of them. They said things like: 'When you look at me, do you
still see how I burned? How much senselessly wasted lust there was in
me? How hungry I have been? When you look at me, do you see it in my
ageing, wilted features? How much wasted life there was in me? When you
look at me, what do you see?'

Four pages further on, he found another note: 'S. makes imperious demands. We have lost ourselves. We make love at night; afterwards I am in pain, but I can't stop, his flesh is my one final connection to what life I have left. By day he lives with me. I can't sleep. This silence drives me crazy. Sometimes, gardening. Sometimes playing with the cats. I planted tomatoes and then cried for no reason. I'm isolating myself. No more phone calls.'

He had torn the pages out and eaten them, then vomited.

Anne had driven into town. He sat by the pond, listening to the evening around him. Garibaldi lay lazily staring at the ducks, refusing to let them out of his sight, though he knew he'd never catch one — the dog's tenacity was admirable. He contemplated the large, handsome animal; he was old and tired, too …

Suddenly Garibaldi leapt up and ran towards the front yard, barking — it must be Anne, though he hadn't heard a car. He'd left the gate open. Perhaps it was the foreign woman for whom he was waiting with such longing.

That morning in her hotel room, when he had almost died of desire, he realised it wasn't Marie who the woman reminded him of. Her body, her stubbornness, and her lust made him think of *her*, of Saré.

But it wasn't the foreign woman. Someone had arrived on foot; he saw an unfamiliar silhouette and stopped where he was, staring intently. It was a woman with very short hair, dressed in dark, baggy clothes. Tall and shapely. She spotted him, walked towards him.

'*Bonjour*, my name is Francesca Lowell. I came because of the book. Could you spare me a few minutes?' She was speaking English. He waved a vague hand, hoping to send her away. But she remained standing there stiffly, looking at him.

He was puzzled, annoyed, disappointed. 'I want to be left alone. Are you from the press?'

'No, I'm not. I'm here for personal reasons. Just listen to me for five minutes, that's all I need. I just want to tell you something. I'm not intending to take advantage of this whole thing.'

'Oh, God, I'm tired!' he muttered in French, walking slowly towards the house. She followed. He led her into the kitchen, switched on the little table lamp, and studied her face. She was a very beautiful woman, with clear, delicate features, large, blue eyes, and skin as smooth as a baby's. She was long-limbed and fine-boned; she put him in mind of an elf who had grown a little too tall. There was a feverish glint in her eyes, and for some reason that sheen made her look older. She seemed a little jaded. He mulled over her accent. He offered coffee; she declined.

'I'm from Sydney. I was passing through Paris, a few weeks ago, and I happened across this book, and since then I've been doing a lot of reading, a lot of research. I've had a hard time over the last few years and ... well, things haven't been great, you know? So, I read the book. And I know it sounds weird, but those are *my* thoughts. That book — it's me. Somehow. I realise that sounds mad. I've thought things, felt things that are in there, word for word — some of it, anyway. And I came to you because you published it. Can you help me? My life is on the line here ... I can find out hardly anything about the author, and I need to know ...'

Her eyes had been fixed on him the whole time, and he kept having to look away. The gleam in them was unhealthy.

He thought for a moment, considered the folder in the barn — then an image came to him: the naked body of the foreign woman in the hotel and the blood on her thighs; he saw Marie's face buried in the pillows; he saw Anne and her cold despair when she had learned of Marie's death; he saw Garibaldi lying there asleep, heard a buzzing in his head, felt a shudder run through him. 'She never existed. I wrote the book.'

'What?'

'Yes, I'm sorry. It's a long story and soon more of it will be made public.' He didn't doubt for a second that Laura would go to the press, once she was certain about it all, and had followed up every line of enquiry. 'I'm telling the truth.'

'I ... I don't understand.'

'You know, this isn't really a good time. I can't say anything more than that. There are some people working on this story already ... Maybe you should just talk to them. Forget the book, forget Jeanne Saré: the whole thing is just nonsense, and it's over now, once and for all. I'll give you a phone number for a lady who'll be able to tell you more. I must ask you to leave now. Forgive me ...' He wrote down the hotel address and phone number, held out the slip of paper.

She got up.

He looked the woman in the eye and saw that she had turned pale.

'Are you feeling all right? Do sit down ... What's wrong?'

'I ... I'll go ... it's fine.'

She didn't move. There was a sudden noise outside, and Garibaldi woke up and ran out. The woman seemed rooted to the spot.

'But, but ...' she murmured.

'What is it?'

'I ... was ... That's my life. Those are my words.' She put a hand on the table to steady herself.

Anne came in with Garibaldi behind her. She brought cool air with her from outside, and was a little puzzled to see the woman there. It had always been just her and her brother in Chatou, since Marie's death.

He saw the question on her face.

Suddenly, as if she had awoken from a deep sleep, the woman shook her head and hurried to the door.

'I didn't mean to disturb you,' Anne said pointedly, moving out of her way.

He threw an angry glance at his sister and walked the woman to the gate.

She looked at him one last time before disappearing into the darkness. He stayed in the yard for a while and lit a cigarillo. Then he went into his study, switched on the old computer, which he had taken so long to get used to, and waited for the shrill beep. Online, he typed 'FRANCESCA LOWELL' into the search engine and found eighteen links. Twenty minutes later, he knew her story. He shut down the computer and banged his fist on the desk.

Then he opened the folder; the letters swam before his eyes, and he had to press the black pen firmly into the paper before it would obey him.

66. APIDAPI (2004)

The Freak and her. She had told him what she knew. She'd told him that the writing in the rue Bonaparte wasn't identical to Duchamp's. She'd told him that the oldest tenant there had spoken of a girl who lived in the building in the fifties. Just for a short while; she had disappeared, the man said, but she'd had short hair, worn a hat. Laura talked about Olga Colert's notes. Her visions. And she spoke of Marie Bessonville and her 'Distraction'. It was all absurd, she said. She told him she didn't believe in neat resolutions.

He seemed agitated, he needed answers and asked her for money, saying he was broke, he would pay her back. She said no; he nodded. It was a silent battle. He went and bought cigarettes for her, because she was too stiff to move.

'What do you want to do, then?' He took a sip of his beer. He was always drinking different things, as if he hadn't yet found the right drink for him.

'I don't know. I don't believe Jeanne Saré existed. I'll write about Monsieur Duchamp, but that's not the real point, is it? I'd like to know what *you* want to do. We've been here longer than we planned ... I don't know what's next, Jan.'

That evening, in that café, he didn't look as lost as usual. What did she know about him? Who were they to one another? Strangers.

'To have your heart I cannot slake my lust:
I crave your kisses' lambent blaze outpoured:
I crave as Christian yearns for Saviour Christ
To feast upon the body of my Lord.
You are my hallowed Godhead: this I crave:

Your blood and body in my flesh to hide.
Yours, the sweet flesh I hunger to receive,
Till you in me, and I in you, have died.'
He looked at her. 'Remember?'
Laura froze. 'What was that for?'
'I wanted to remind you.'
'Of what?'
'Those lines.'
'What about them?'
'Think about it! Why are we here? This isn't about Saré, it's about us.
That's always the way.'
    'What are you talking about? What on earth do you want, Jan?'
She felt powerless. She suddenly saw her father's face in front of her,
the house, her childhood — the poem held all that and so many other sweet
promises. Those lines contained the beginning. Was that what this was about?
    'I think we're here to find a fragment of the truth. And that truth relates
to a woman who, if you ask me, wasn't a real person, so why must we — '
    'Stop being so pathetic! It's incredibly annoying!' She was getting angry.
    He fell silent, shocked. He drank his beer, breathing louder and faster
than usual. 'I'm going to stay in Paris,' he said finally, and looked up at
her, his lips pressed firmly together. This face made him seem older and
unapproachable.
    'Look … I didn't mean to attack you, Jan. I'm not indifferent to this
business, either, but I'm not reaching any conclusions here. This isn't a
typical research project: we're not studying an art object, we're exploring
the lives of people who died.'
    'Why are they dead?' he asked, with a naivety that disarmed Laura
entirely.
    'I … don't know. I think they were looking for a way out and they
found one in this book. I don't have any answers, Jan.'
    'Why does someone kill themselves? Because they've given up?
Because there's always a distance between you and life? Those are simplis-
tic reasons, and I can't accept them!' He was suddenly quite worked up and
red in the face, literally panting.

Laura didn't know what else to do. 'I think ten more days, and then that's it. I don't want to stay any longer, and I can't, either, Jan. You look for your answers, I'll look for mine. In ten days, we leave. I don't want to spend half my life here, searching. Do you understand? It's not doing me any good ... I'll stay another few days, but then ... I'm going home. I don't want to feel guilty because I couldn't bring the dead back to life.'

'It's not about the dead, you know that.'

'I'm going to go now.'

'It means so much to me, it means so much, Laura.' He looked away, but she could hear something in his voice. Laura leaned forward and touched his cold hand. Then she paid the bill and went out to the car.

★

They made love, in the study, in the dark. It hurt. She scratched at his face, not holding back. He held her so tight she could scarcely breathe. And yet she would not shrink from the pain. She had gone to see him because she wanted to feel like herself.

They made love on the desk, on the floor, against the wall. Laura twisted and turned under his weight, groaned, the lust causing pain, the pain causing lust. He didn't let go, he wasn't satisfied. He began again, holding her legs apart. Laura tried not to cry. She was helpless in the face of this desire.

He nodded off as it was getting light. She crept half-naked from the room, not wanting to wake up beside him. She was grazed and bruised. She got dressed in the car and set off towards Paris, but had to stop on the way because she could no longer see through the tears. It took her nearly an hour to reach the hotel.

In the lobby, as she was getting out her key, she heard someone calling her name. A voice she didn't recognise. It was just before six. She turned around slowly.

'Laura van den Ende? Francesca Lowell. Patrice Duchamp gave me this address. I really need to talk to you; I've been waiting here since ten o'clock. It's really very urgent ...'

'Patrice?'

The tall, attractive woman was staring intently at her, studying Laura's face for so long that it began to feel uncomfortable.

'Yes.'

'It's very late. What's this about?'

'Jeanne Saré.'

'Uh-huh. What do you want?'

The inquisitive porter was gawping at the two women. Laura went to the lift, beckoned the woman to follow her, and flashed a brazen smile at the disappointed porter.

Then the two of them were facing one another in the lift. Laura saw that this woman was beautiful and that in comparison, especially right now, she must be crushingly ugly ...

She took the woman up to her room. Her underwear, shirts, and jeans were lying on the bed, folded by the chambermaid. The woman stopped beside the glass coffee table. Laura opened the fridge and took out the little whisky bottles. The woman looked slightly taken aback, but then nodded. Laura sat on the edge of the bed and took a small sip. The woman sat there looking cowed, waiting.

'All right then, tell me: what's this about?'

'It's about me.'

Laura was cross with Duchamp for sending people to her just to get them off his back.

'I don't really understand. You come here at dawn, completely out of the blue, wanting to talk about Saré, and all you can say is: it's about me?'

'You know ...' the woman seemed to be pulling herself together. 'I found out today that Jeanne Saré never existed, and Patrice Duchamp was the one who told me. He refused to give me any explanation — he just handed me your address. And here I am, looking like a total idiot, letting strangers humiliate me, just to find out the truth. Whatever it is, I need to know. My life is at stake here.'

'I'm sorry, I can't hear the word "truth" any longer ... Who are you, anyway?'

'I'm Francesca, Francesca Lowell, like I said. I'm from Sydney and

I used to work at the university. Ancient history. My area of research, I mean. But ... well. I discovered this book as I was passing through Paris, a while ago now ... I was actually supposed to be in Athens, and then ...' The woman told her story in detail.

Laura listened attentively and at once, she no longer felt tired. 'Why do you have such a burning interest in it? This book, the whole ...'

'I have this feeling that they're my words. Please don't make that face, this is difficult enough as it is. I have been and maybe still am in crisis, but I'm not mad. When I discovered Saré, it was as if I'd been turned to stone. That was *me*. I mean, those thoughts, I'd ...'

It struck Laura that every lucid idea they'd had over the last few weeks had been wasted. Nothing made sense. And suddenly, she felt the need to talk. Laura told this woman what she knew. She even considered mentioning her relationship with Duchamp, but she stopped short of that, not wanting to shock her too much.

'And now?' the woman asked, an eternity after Laura's voice had fallen silent.

'I don't know, either. I don't know. I've said ten more days, and that has to be an end to it.' Laura had picked up another little whisky bottle, and it was only now that the other woman opened hers and took a large, eager swallow.

She must be on familiar terms with alcohol — unlike Nadine Leavit, who although she always drank when she was with Laura, clearly didn't seek any enjoyment in it, more a kind of stasis.

'It's crazy, why did no one hit on this idea before, why did no one check? No one! Why did so many people have to die?' the woman whispered, hanging her head.

Laura flopped onto the bed. They went on drinking, emptying the fridge of everything alcoholic. It was light now. Laura had the feeling that the woman had always been there. She closed her eyes. 'I'm going to make it public. And then my job is done.'

The woman shrugged. 'My husband killed himself and my five-year-old son. I've never got over it. We had no problems; his mental health was fine, or so we all thought. And then, when I read the book, when I

... Well, I couldn't believe it: I was sure that was me, word for word. It's ridiculous, I know. And so I was shocked when I heard she never existed. Maybe Duchamp wrote it, maybe not. I don't believe in ghosts, but I see them everywhere, and you might think I'm mad, but that doesn't matter now. I've let everything go, I'd like to know just one thing and ... then get back to my daughter. She's all that's important now. It isn't self-pity; I've been feeling sorry for myself for years, but this isn't my self-pity. I just want to know who I am — if I really was Saré, and if I still am. It always comes down to that. I take up other people's stories in order to find my own, that's all I can say. I used to think these stories were like clothes that we could put on and take off. But it was only when I read that book that I realised how wrong I was. Now I think stories are the only things that can connect people. I mean, the only way to find our identities. Maybe we can write a story together that makes sense, in which each of us has a place, a purpose. It was never about Jeanne Saré. She was a phantom, and that's the only reason that people were able to help themselves to her story. People who had lost their own place in the great book. I've devoted my whole life to history, and never grasped what lay at the heart of it, isn't that shocking? And only here and now am I starting to grasp it. Think about déjà vu, or the moments you share with people, when those people are feeling the same thing as you. Some people call it love, some call it faith — for me, it's stories. I'm convinced of it. You won't find any answer to why women killed themselves after reading a book that no one wrote. But you can investigate their stories and you'll find a pattern, there will be points of connection, central points, do you see? And Jeanne Saré will be one of them. Because Jeanne Saré can be everything you're looking for.'

When Laura woke up, it was late afternoon and the woman had gone. On the glass coffee table, beside a lot of little empty bottles, lay a note: 'Thank you for last night. I'm not going to apologise for it. Here's my number: you might need me; but if not, that's fine, too. I'll be in Paris for a few more days. All the best, Francesca.'

67. NADINE (2004)

Nadine Leavit was a good judge of character. She came from a working-class background and had managed to get 'an education', which gave her a special position in her family. And she was robust, having grown up with three brothers. Her parents had been loving — not very academic, but honest, good-hearted people, who had toiled their whole lives to give their children 'a life'.

Nadine Leavit came from the suburbs. That was significant. And alongside all these qualities, she had ideas and courage in her convictions. She was proud of that.

When she was fourteen, she once got into a playground fist fight with some boys two years above her because they'd been tormenting a weaker child. And of course she got beaten up. She came home with a black eye, but no one told her off; in fact, they praised her for it. A few days later, she went into the playground with her three brothers, and by the end of that afternoon five tenth-grade boys, battered and crying, whimpered their apologies. That was the birth of Nadine's first idea. The idea of justice.

At fifteen she took part in a demonstration against animal cruelty, and her parents liked that, too. While all her friends were meeting up with boys in secret, Nadine was writing incandescent letters to various companies that polluted the environment. Once, she even got arrested, and her father had to pay a fine. Her brothers were proud of her.

Nadine had reinvented herself. By the time she came to Paris at nineteen and enrolled at the university, she had a life filled with convictions, but few people she trusted (with the exception of her family, of course). But Nadine didn't give up. The more she fought, the more there was to fight against.

And so she began where she saw the greatest need: with her own gender. She started a women's group at the university. She fully believed in the work she was doing. But after two years in Paris she had still found no way of building a real relationship with anyone, no time to take a break, nowhere she could relax. She sometimes felt alone, but she fought her fear by constantly doing things that scared her. Nadine met men, went out with them, and it always ended badly.

At eighteen, still living with her parents, she'd felt like she was in love for the first time. It was a boy who also campaigned for animal rights, and whom she thought was wonderful for that reason. They went to the cinema, kissed, and then he took her home, introduced her to his mother. After three weeks, she stayed the night with him. His mother was out of town and they were alone. She was excited, even putting on red lipstick like the girls in her class. But the boy just took what he wanted and fell asleep beside her, satisfied. Nadine crept out of the house at dawn, weeping as she walked, and went into a park, where she sat thinking until midday. That was the end of her longing. The wound left by that night took a very long time to heal.

She felt the echo of that night all the time ... until one day, in the cafeteria, she met Olga. A slender girl who stood quietly in the queue, letting everyone who asked go ahead of her, and looking at the floor as if contemplating something. Nadine spoke to her, hoping to cheer her up a bit. The girl looked at her, said nothing for a long time and then smiled, and it was the most beautiful smile Nadine Leavit had seen in all her twenty-two years.

After Olga's death, Nadine stopped eating. She was signed off sick for months, and left Paris, unable to bear the city any longer. She went back to live with her parents. She made a fresh start, but something in her had died. After seven months, Nadine was an old person.

She finished her degree and kept on demonstrating against the injustices of the world, but with less conviction — because she hadn't been able to prevent the greatest injustice in her life. She got a job at a magazine and worked her way up. She started meeting people again, going out, slept with men and women, until she realised that neither gave her any satisfaction.

She started her own magazine, pursued her ideas and earned money. Then one day, she gave it all up and travelled to Ethiopia as a volunteer with an aid organisation. There, she finally ended up in the arms of a doctor, who got her pregnant. She came home. Exhausted, pregnant, and anxious. She tried to enjoy the pregnancy, but never really managed it. The baby's father returned to Paris for the birth. They had a beautiful, healthy boy and Nadine tried to focus her ideas on the child. When he was three, she left him with his father, who was now working at a hospital as a surgeon. He was a good father. She hated herself, went away again, came back. And sometimes at night, she would think about her youth and about Olga. She remembered how she'd felt.

And now something had happened; someone had come to talk to her about Olga. Nadine had woken up. She started searching again. Not for Olga, not for her past, but for something like an idea.

In all the years after Olga's death, she had never ceased to exist, never completely vanished from Nadine's life. Her scent, her smile, the way she moved, the way she frowned, or wrinkled her nose when she was uncertain about something — it was all still present for Nadine. But Nadine realised that the saddest thing about the death of someone you love is the disregard for your own life that follows it. She started to take an interest in her ideas again.

68. ME (2005)

My story was always foreign to me. I didn't want to make this story my own, so I started to write. I wanted another life, another history, other outlines, but it never worked. I crept like a thief through foreign cities, on the hunt for other ways of living. But it wasn't that easy to slough my story from my body.

And then, one day, I stopped in front of myself and looked.

Not in the mirror.

I saw myself.

69. ICE AGE / BOOK 1 (1953)

Her thoughts have no power now, no colour.

She goes under, and is glad to have received her faithful night-time companion from the opium man — she did him another good turn, and he patted her cheek. For a moment she wanted to hit him, but then she had to suppress the impulse. The anticipation of a little opium makes everything easier.

Loneliness spread with the onset of the cold weather. She stole a man's hat, to ward off the cold. Recently, she had simply been doing things she liked. And so she usually had some money in her pocket, too. She used to steal only when she could no longer bear the hunger, but now she didn't care. She felt no shame. Her hands had become masters at it.

The winter made her skin raw and her nose run. Sometimes she sat in the park and watched people; she'd never found the time for that before. Now her thoughts became intolerable, and she tried to banish the whispering in her head.

She had stopped smoking filterless cigarettes and moved on to cigarillos from a fancy box she had bought at the tobacconist. It felt good. She'd paid the rent, too, putting the money in an envelope and sliding it under the concierge's door. Sometimes she didn't write at all. She missed it less than she thought she would. She let her hair grow, and it now covered her ears.

One night, she dreamed of Paul. Of the fragile little creature who had been assigned the male sex by chance and didn't know what to do with it. The dream had been fun. She regretted not doing what he'd wanted. Being a whore for a man who was not a man at all. She would think of him when she took her remedy, late at night in the bare flat.

She stole a bike and rode it through the streets, then abandoned it somewhere, and strolled towards the Latin Quarter.

She walked into the courtyard and saw the word she had scratched into the wall and gone over with charcoal: Distraction. That was her mark, the only message she would leave for the world.

She entered the dark, shabby stairwell. The small hole where the fat concierge sat was illuminated by a greenish light. She scurried past. The apartment house was always silent, neglected, and dirty. It smelled of decay and dog shit, but it was the temple, and this was where she became untouchable.

The wind wolf-whistled as she slammed the door behind her. She got undressed, filled the bathtub with lukewarm water, closed all the windows. The darkness enveloped her. She lay in the bath, thought about her games with the chubby little Eros, and caressed her legs. A warm, painful bliss rose through her body like steam as she dug her short fingernails into her flesh, on the inside of her thigh.

It was time … She took the silver foil, lit it, pressed it hard against her mouth and smoked … smoked … smoked.

She was in a desert in the middle of nowhere, and the desert had no beginning and no end. Then she lay down in the hot sand and burrowed herself into it, her hands digging quickly and skilfully until even her head disappeared.

And then she saw the beautiful, strange woman with the foreign name again and she smiled. The woman came through the door, took off her polka-dot dress and climbed, slow and smiling, into the bathtub, but she couldn't touch her.

'Where were you?' she asked, reaching out for her.

'I'm here.'

'But where were you?'

'I went away.'

'I see. Why can't I feel you?'

'Oh, but you can. Here, here I am.'

She couldn't. 'Do you still love me?'

'Yes. You know that. It's just that the times didn't fit, do you see?'

'Yes, I see.'

'I missed you. Now it's BEFORE.'

'I see.' She stretched out to reach her, but the body seemed intangible.

'The times didn't fit, you see?'

'Stop *saying* that!' She cried out and banged her head against the yellowing edge of the bath. Then it got dark and she vomited. She crawled out of the bathtub, naked, wet, and the cold air pounced on her and gnawed its way into her bones.

The woman had gone.

She crawled to her eiderdown, which was lying on the floor. Her knees hurt; the floor was hard and she was always slipping over. Somewhere, a car horn sounded. She rubbed her eyes, wiped her mouth with her hand, reached for the eiderdown and wrapped herself in it, lay down, curled up in a foetal position, and pressed her head against the cold floor. The dreams had been so brief this time.

'Jeanne … Jeanne …' she whispered suddenly, closing her eyes, it was so cold, so terribly cold. 'My little Jeanne, my little girl … It's me, do you remember me? It's me, my Jeanne. I'm here with you. I won't leave you, I know it's bad, my little dove, but I'm here, come, I'll stroke you, I'll pick you up, I'll take you back home, shall I? Shall I, my poor little Jeanne?' She whispered louder, stroking her head. Stroking her face, her ears, her neck, her cheeks. 'My Jeanne. Come, let's go home, you've done enough. Now we need to sleep, to rest. I'll lie down with you, I'll warm you, I'll give you my most beautiful stories, so you'll never need to talk again. Yes? Do you want that, Jeanne? I'll tell you where to go, I'll make your food, I'll cook onion soup for you, you like a good old onion soup, don't you? Or a crêpe filled with melted cheese, you like that, too. And then I'll take you to bed and stroke your hands, your cold, lovely, white hands. Oh, my little Jeanne. What on earth has happened to you? What has happened to you? To your face? I'm here, come, my sunshine, come, my little dove, I'll hold you very, very tight, so that no one can hurt you … We're going home.'

70. BROTHER (2004)

She asked him about Francesca Lowell. She asked why he had told her he'd written the book.

He looked at her expectantly.

She said: 'Well, maybe it isn't true.'

That confused him and he sat up; his wife had believed him unconditionally.

He was with her in her hotel room, and they had fucked. He didn't like the word, but his wife had always used it.

Laura had shouted as they were having sex. This was all sick, she'd shouted. She didn't want this. He caressed her then and she relented once more and came. And as she did, her face grew very, very rigid, as if she was no longer conscious of what she was doing. He looked at her all the while and eventually she gave a little start, as if trying to shake everything off, as if ashamed of her lust.

She was getting dressed now.

He saw her bruises and was puzzled that he didn't feel any guilt over them. She moved like a gazelle. She put on black underwear, as usual.

He asked what she had meant.

She shrugged and paid him no further attention. He was standing right behind her. Then he touched her back lightly.

'Perhaps ultimately, we can't invent anything. Perhaps we're always the ones who are invented … Patrice …'

'Laura, what do you mean by that?'

'Nothing, nothing at all. I was just thinking about what you told me. I went to the rue Bonaparte, and had the writing checked. Not the same. The graffiti really could be from the fifties. I'm just spinning a little yarn here, spinning out your thoughts, Patrice.'

He had gone around the armchair and was now holding her by her wrists.

She didn't try to free herself. 'I mean, these women. I found some things out, Patrice. Do you know what I realised? All the people who picked up this book were a little bit Jeanne Saré themselves, weren't they? That's right, Patrice, isn't it? And then ask yourself the question: who are we? Who was your wife? Who are you? Sometimes I wonder if you've ever really known who you were ... Maybe you wanted to be like her? Primitive, uncompromising. There's something in you, and you know it: the way you take hold of me, for instance. Is that what made you think it all up, made you want it all? And sometimes, Patrice, I wonder what you want from me. Could it be the same thing you wanted from Marie?'

He let go of her. He studied her for a minute, then took a few steps back, and turned his eyes away. 'Who are you, Laura? An intelligent art historian with a lot of prizes to her name? An interesting woman with an exotic childhood? Or a lost, unhappy lover? And an even unhappier mother?'

'How ... how ...'

'Oh, Laura ... So, tell me: who are you?'

'I'm a nobody. To you, at least.'

'Exactly, you're right: a nobody.'

'You don't seem diabolical, Patrice, if that's the effect you're going for. I'm not afraid of you.'

'And you don't seem very experienced.'

She dropped her cigarette, ran at him, and slapped him so hard he felt dizzy for a moment, then she rammed her right knee into his stomach — though without much force, since he had shrunk away from her. She grabbed his hair and pulled it, he threw her off; she fell to the floor, he hit her in the face and she seemed to lose consciousness for a second. He was surprised she was so quiet, not uttering a single sound. She crawled back, her nose bleeding. She reached for a black high-heeled shoe and hit him with it, hauled herself to her feet, and kept at him with the heel. He let out a brief laugh and grasped her hand, twisting it. She dropped the shoe, he forced her to her knees and pushed her back, and she fell to the floor beside the bed.

'She's dead. She's finally dead,' he said, straddling her hips, holding her still. She spat in his face, and he just smiled, leaned forward, and planted a kiss on her forehead. She bit his lower jaw and he jerked his head back; she tried to throw him off but he rested his whole weight on her and held her hair with one hand, keeping her on the floor. He loved her at that moment. He loved her. He could feel every muscle in his body, and he felt young again. Then he pulled up her jumper, unbuttoned her trousers, took off his shirt — she had given in and was now lying motionless, her eyes turned away from him, staring at the edge of the bed. He pulled her legs apart, kicked off his trousers, and threw them aside. Fell on her, penetrating her almost effortlessly. He took her face in his hand and turned it towards him, the other hand feeling in the pockets of his jeans on the floor beside him and taking out a pen knife as he thrust deeper and deeper into her. She looked up at him, her face blood-smeared and stony. He felt no sympathy; he pressed the handle of the knife into her hand and leaned down to her.

'I'm hurting you. So do what you have to do …'

'You don't know me …'

He gripped her throat and squeezed hard. She flinched slightly, struggling to breathe. He clasped the knife more firmly in her hand but she tried to shake it off.

'Is that what you wanted from Marie? Was that the reason …' she panted as soon as he let go of her throat.

'Shhh …' He kissed her lightly on the lips. He was raping her, and yet he kissed her on the lips more tenderly than he had ever kissed anyone before.

'It doesn't make any difference if she dies now, it's too late …' she said. She wasn't crying.

He banged her head against the floor as he came, then took her hand and pressed the handle of the knife into it again. 'You do want to hurt me. Go ahead …'

But she just threw him off her, and he crumpled. She leapt up, flung the folded knife at his chest, picked his shirt up off the floor and wiped her face with it, then went into the bathroom.

He heard the water running. She was washing herself. All at once he had an image of Anne, in Marennes, in Anne and Mone's bedroom on the first floor, the door ajar, and then the man's bare legs, Anne's face so close to them. He'd never been able to forget that image and he suddenly became aware that what he'd felt back then was simply a humiliating, shameful sense of loss. It was loss. He had lost Anne then: her innocence, her uniqueness, her wilful affection for him.

He stared at the knife lying on his belly, then picked it up and tossed it into the bin in the corner with disgust. He dressed himself, smoothed his hair back with his hand and scribbled a few words on the hotel notepad: 'Forgive me. You have changed so many things, Laura. She is dead. I thank you for that. Please don't turn away. P.' Then he opened the white wooden door and was gone.

71. WOMAN (2004)

Francesca had a new face; Francesca had a new head. She was sitting in a café drinking a cappuccino. Her head felt lovely, round, and free. She had a new pair of shoes, simple black moccasins.

She had called Lynn, who was back at school now. Francesca's mother refused to speak to her on the phone and had come silently to Sydney to look after her 'little girl'. Lynn told her she was in love and that she was waiting for her, and was pleased she was feeling better. 'You sound good.' Francesca had smiled.

She had called Leo, too. He'd said he would give anything to see her. She told him she needed time.

IT ISN'T HARD TO FIND YOU. AS IF YOU WERE NOT — WELL, GONE AT ALL — AS IF YOU WERE HERE WITH ME AND MAYBE THAT'S HOW IT IS. I HAVE COME SUCH A LONG WAY. DO YOU REMEMBER THAT AFTERNOON AT THE ZOO? YOU AND ME. YOU WOULDN'T LET ME TELL YOU ANYTHING ABOUT THE ANIMALS; YOU WANTED TO FIND IT ALL OUT FOR YOURSELF ... THAT'S WHAT YOU WERE LIKE, YES. SO INDEPENDENT. I'M NOT AFRAID ANYMORE. DO YOU KNOW WHAT I DECIDED, MAX? I DECIDED I'M GOING TO TAKE LYNN TO THE DOLPHINARIUM. TO THE DOLPHIN SHOW — THEY STILL DO IT. FOR THE THREE OF US! THE DOLPHINS WILL DANCE FOR YOU. I'M SURE OF IT. THEY'LL KNOW ... AND THE THREE OF US WILL KNOW IT TOO, OKAY?

Francesca smiled and suddenly realised something in her was changing: she felt a little stab somewhere near her heart and then ... peace.

She paid and left. It was windy and cool, but she felt hot. She was very weak, too; she stood still for a moment, closed her eyes, and tried to listen to the feeling — she didn't yet know exactly what it was, but it was there. She hailed a cab and went back to the *pension*. A message was waiting for her there: 'I am very keen to see you again, and talk to you. And I would like to thank you. Please call me as soon as you can. I'm waiting. Laura van den Ende.'

Francesca went straight to the phone and dialled the mobile number. The voice on the other end sounded agitated. Francesca said she could be there in an hour. No matter where. Laura suggested a particular bar, and hung up.

Laura van den Ende, the fine lady who Francesca had somehow remembered as being very majestic, was wearing a pair of oversized sunglasses. This time, she looked tired. On closer inspection, there was a little cut on her lip, and her nose looked slightly swollen. Francesca shook her hand and took a seat opposite her. The waiter soon brought a glass of champagne, which Laura must have ordered before she arrived. Slowly, she took off the glasses, and Francesca saw a bruise under her right eye. Her whole face looked a little unsettling, but Francesca didn't want to pry.

'Thank you for coming.'

'Is there a particular reason?' Francesca smiled.

'Maybe. At least, I hope so.'

'Go on then …'

'I'd like to talk to you. After we spoke, a lot of things became clear to me. And anyway, er, as you can see, there's been a little incident … But I'll tell you about that later. I wanted to talk about Saré. I get the feeling that, of all the people I've met here who know about her, you're the one who has really grasped what lies at the heart of this madness. I'm going back to Amsterdam on Saturday, and that's an end to the matter for me, so I wanted to tell you everything, because I think you have a right to know …'

'I'm all ears.'

'Thank you. Let's have a drink first.'

They drank a Moët that worked miracles, and were silent for a moment. 'There's this picture by Mikhail Vrubel, a Russian painter,' Laura

began. 'It hangs in the Tretyakov Gallery in Moscow. There are several
different versions of this painting, but the most famous one is *The Demon
Seated*. That picture broke the artist and he went mad, but I think it's one
of the best paintings in the world. I went to Moscow once specifically to
see it, and spent hours sitting in front of it. That was five years ago. It's
painted in the Impressionist style: a handsome, bare-chested young man
sits on a mountaintop, looking out at a vague, distant view. His long, dark
hair is tousled and his lips are pressed firmly together. There's a strange
apathy to the way his muscular arms are hanging down, but what is most
beautiful and most terrible in that painting are his eyes. They're wild, sad,
cruel, red, fiery, violent, and filled with this fathomless grief. I always liked
that picture, I gave lectures about it, and then, one day, I realised what it
was that fascinated me about the painting. It's about changeability, the fact
that it's possible to see in it whatever you yourself are feeling. The picture
itself gives nothing away, and that's its strength. I think it was this quality
that tipped the painter himself over the edge. The picture never made any
statement. You had to give yourself over to your feelings, to your own state
of mind, and transfer it to the picture. And that's the essential truth of it. I
mean … this whole business, this story that has so many people caught up
in it, isn't much different. The story itself tells you nothing, but it allows
you to find yourself in it. I don't want to be in the book anymore. I don't
want to make a home for myself there. Regardless of whether it was Saré or
Duchamp who wrote it — the book exists. It's done enough damage! I'm
finished with it. Even if Duchamp is lying and he didn't write it — though
that seems quite unlikely to me — even if there was a prototype, a real
person, that isn't important now … after you left my room, I thought about
what you'd said — that we could have been caught by it, that you or I could
have been the women who … But then I realised we wouldn't have been. I
withstood it. So did you. That's why we're the antipodes of this story, and
that's a good thing. We're the antidote to the poison. And yes, you're right,
we live in a state of constant loss, but in the midst of that there is also life.
There's an awakening. And that's what I'd like for myself. And it's what I
hope for you, too, Francesca …'

She took a sip of champagne.

'I think I've always tried very hard to live on my own terms. My urge to do that was so strong that it was often to my own detriment. And then, one day, after my baby was stillborn, after I separated from the baby's father, I saw how ridiculous that feeling had been! That belief in control! How little of my life, ultimately, had been lived on my own terms. Perhaps that's my version of the story.'

She looked for a cigarette, found one, and lit it.

'I've been in touch with a journalist I know. He's going to write about all this. Then it will be over.'

'It won't change anything, Laura. If not Duchamp, then one day someone else will write something, or paint another "Demon".'

'Yes, but that's not my concern now. I want to stop chasing ghosts.'

Laura recalled the painting in Moscow and how she had felt in front of it. She hadn't been standing there alone; her husband had been with her. They had both looked at the picture and then they had kissed. Kept kissing until a museum attendant had disturbed them. A few years later, when she came across the picture in a book, she felt only hatred and anger when she saw the demon's crazed red eyes.

Francesca and Laura finished the bottle. They didn't have much more to say to one another. Laura's whole body still ached, but the pain was no longer at the forefront of her mind.

As they walked out into the street, tipsy and tired, Laura tried to hail a taxi.

'When's your flight?'

'I haven't booked one yet. I don't think I'll stay much longer. I miss Lynn.'

'Your daughter?'

'Yes.'

A taxi finally pulled up; Laura opened the door and persuaded Francesca to get in, she wanted to walk a little further. Francesca thanked her and disappeared into the car.

72. APIDAPI (2004)

Laura watched the taxi pull away. The night felt good. She began to walk slowly, aimlessly.

On a corner, under a street lamp, she saw a familiar figure. It was the Freak, and he was talking to a girl, evidently a sex worker. The girl kept shaking her head and waving her hands; the Freak was trying to convince her of something.

Laura was surprised to see him there and couldn't look away. She watched the faceless young man. She suddenly realised that he, too, was an empty space. The thought frightened her. She contemplated walking away, but just then the Freak turned away from the girl and strode off across the street. He spotted Laura, and stopped in the middle of the roadway. Then he came running over. She saw aggression in his strides.

'What are you doing here?'

'I just came out of a bar … and … then I saw … I'm sorry for not walking away at once.'

'Doesn't matter. It's nothing bad. I don't have any secrets.' He seemed to be ignoring her black eye. 'I know that girl … She calls herself Georgette. A prostitute. I asked her to read Saré and give me her impression.'

'Why?'

'Because I think prostitutes don't have a lot of prejudices.'

'You shouldn't go telling people to read that book, it isn't right. Go home and …'

'That's unfair, it's completely idiotic … So far we've got nothing, nothing at all.'

'No, Jan, we have.' That morning at the breakfast table she had tried to outline her view of things to him, but he had resisted, refused to accept what she was telling him, had got up, and left.

Laura instantly felt clear-headed. She was gripped by a sudden, astonishing rage. His stubbornness and his exaggerated zeal were driving her crazy. His whole little-lamb demeanour had vanished in the last ten days, and instead he had become blinkered in a way that made her uncomfortable.

'Let me be, will you? We were so close to a breakthrough, and then you embarked on this bloody affair and let everything slide.'

Laura was wrong-footed by his words. She considered what to say. Of course he had known about it all this time …

'It's none of your business, Jan. I don't have to hold myself accountable to you.'

'I thought this was *our* thing! I'm sure I wouldn't have got this far without you, but suddenly, when we're more than halfway there, you want to call a halt to the whole — '

'There's nothing more to find out!' Laura shouted, now incandescent with anger.

'Of course there is: just think … the writing on the wall and my research, they lead us to … You don't seriously believe this idiot made it all up? Just because you're sleeping with him doesn't mean you have to take leave of your critical faculties!'

Laura stared at his insolent, desperate face. He looked so lost that she suddenly felt sorry for him.

'What did you say?'

'Oh, Laura, come on …'

'Shut up.' The words just slipped out; they had crossed a line and she could see he was startled. 'I want to tell you something … For some reason that you are keeping from me, you refuse to accept the facts. I have no idea why you dug this whole business up again in the first place. I think your reasons are personal ones. That doesn't matter. Jeanne Saré doesn't exist, and if she ever did, then in my opinion — if you really want to think of it that way — she's dead now. That's the reality! We need to wise up and realise that we have to live our lives and not follow Jeanne Saré or whoever else to the station. And we should try to share that realisation with others

... There's no great truth to be discovered here. When you can accept that, you'll accept that this here isn't all there is. And that there's another story as well: your own.' It was doing Laura good to speak Dutch again.

A look of surprise came over the Freak's face, which then twisted into a grimace. He put his hands over his eyes and made a strange sound, then he sat down right there, on the pavement, and wept.

Laura, now completely out of her depth, knelt down beside him. He wept silently, in great, heaving sobs.

'I'm sorry ...' he said after a while, running a hand over his forehead.

'You don't have to be sorry.'

'I'm sorry I was rude to you.'

'You don't need to worry about offending me. I might have been a little abrupt as well.'

'No, it's fine. I probably deserved it. I should ... thank ... you.'

'Are you okay?'

'My mother ... my mother ... hanged herself when I was thirteen. I found her. And afterwards, I went looking ... for reasons, answers. I didn't find anything. And then a few years later, I discovered the book in a crate in the attic. *Ice Age*. My mother loved romance novels, tales of chivalry, tear-jerkers, but not that kind of thing. I thought I'd found the reason for her death. I *wanted* to believe it. I was so afraid that this book might just have come from a flea market ... the book gave her death meaning.'

Suddenly he got up and walked off, almost ran, without saying anything else.

Laura didn't go after him; she knew he'd come back.

73. ME (2005)

The trip is nearing its end. There was a party last night. With the few friends I have here, throwing caution to the wind. But last night, something else happened, too. I don't like it at all, but ... so, that's what it feels like, that's exactly what it feels like ... growing up. There comes a moment when you lose the right to suffer. The night made something click in my head.

74. ICE AGE / BOOK 1 (1953)

The exercise book was full. It no longer meant anything. She sat on the floor in her room and stared at herself in the mirror, a small thing that had belonged to her mother. She stared at herself; she had no 'remedy' for the coming night. Perhaps she should go out, steal, murder, get hold of this magic potion, go to the opium man, sell her soul to him. But she felt lethargic. She had got her old clothes out of the suitcase. When had she come here? Where had she been before? Did this checked school skirt really belong to her? And the ribbon for tying up long, dark, unruly hair as well? She had put on the skirt and the white blouse; had even found a pair of fine stockings, and rolled them carefully up over her shapeless, white legs.

She sat there on the cold floor, looking at herself in the mirror … She had applied some stolen rouge to her cheeks. The only thing missing was the hair, the long, brown hair that used to hang in a plait down her back. She tried to imagine it, but couldn't. Then she took the man's hat and put it on; the hat was familiar, but it didn't go with the rest of her clothes.

The face in the mirror was pale and strange. Nothing fitted together, somehow; the nose was a separate entity, so were the eyes. Everything seemed to have a life of its own. And the look in her eyes was expressionless. It gave nothing away, it fixed on nothing. She had found a small amount of rum, in a paper bag; the bottle seemed to have been lying around for a long time, she couldn't remember where it had come from.

Her lips were dry and colourless. She tried to dab some rouge onto them as well; she didn't have anything else.

She paid no attention to the thin exercise book. It was no longer important.

She stared at herself. She stared at her face and the longer she looked, the less she saw. There were no secrets. Nor was there any place for anger now, everything was calm. Nothing spoke to her. Even her own face ... And so she closed her eyes and took a slug of rum that burned her throat, in an attempt to feel something.

★

'I WILL LEAVE NO TRACE BEHIND. I VANISH NOISELESSLY. I VANISH WITHOUT ENGRAVING A NAME. ONE DAY, WHEN I HAVE TURNED TO WIND AND DUST, I WILL WHISPER TO ALL EMBRYOS WHO ARE NOT YET BORN, NOT YET CURSED. IN THEIR SLEEP I WILL WHISPER TO THEM AND MAKE THEM DREAM, SO THAT THEY NEVER WAKE. I WILL KISS ALL THE PRINCESSES IN THEIR POISONED SLEEP DEEPER STILL INTO FORGETTING. THEN PERHAPS I CAN BE DIFFERENT, AND THEN YOU WILL COME AND TAKE ME WITH YOU. THE WORLD IS NOT ENOUGH WITHOUT YOU.'

★

She pressed harder, and harder still. The little mirror shattered in her hand; the shards pierced her skin; the pain was her one sign of life in the realm of the dead. The blood was a reminder of life. It felt good. She took a shard and brought it up to her face. She cut into her cheek and then drew the shard up towards her eye. Before she reached her eye socket, she paused. Her whole face was a gaping wound. The cut was quite deep. Now she took the blood-smeared shard, wiped it on her white blouse, and looked into it. And smiled to see herself. She caressed her face with her left hand and smeared the red liquid around. Until her whole face was red. She smiled.

75. BROTHER (2004)

He was losing sleep and had spent the last few nights at his desk. He'd started daydreaming and couldn't think any longer, could hardly even eat. He was frightened, and sometimes overcome by shuddering. He stared at Marie's pictures, searched through old things, turned the pages of his books, even looked at the post he'd stopped opening several months ago. He found dull, official letters: invitations to readings, an offer to give a seminar at the university, bills. Nothing to interest him in the slightest. He thought about that day in the hotel, thought about the woman who had made him feel alive.

And so he sat there. The stranger had come and offered herself to him, and life had opened up to him just a crack, only to close again afterwards more firmly than ever.

He stared at his bookcase, saw the eleven books he'd published. And could hardly recall when and how he'd written them. Most recently science fiction novels, which he'd come to in the seventies, with a 'whiff of philosophy and metaphysics' about them. When and why had he written them?

Loneliness was a tender companion; she lured him in, caressed him, kissed him, and rocked him to sleep — but in the night she, too, had left him. He looked at the old photo of Anne and Mone on the front steps of their parents' house, looked at the two little girls. Anne so cheeky, so proud even then, her head full of mad ideas — and quiet, taciturn Mone, who never revealed her longings, who took over their mother's role without a word of protest. He felt so close to them, suddenly. But where was he? Why was he not sitting on the steps with them when that photo was taken? Where had he been? Why had he given up his place between the two of them? He longed for nothing more ardently than to turn back time and have his photograph taken with them ...

Garibaldi barked outside; it wasn't yet nine o'clock, but he'd lost all sense of time. Someone was pulling up in a car, but he didn't get up; he stayed sitting there, motionless. A couple of minutes later, there was a knock at the door. He opened it at once and stood there, holding his breath.

She had a small scar on her lip and a black eye. She was wearing no make-up; he'd never seen her like that. There was a large, bulky cloth bag slung over her shoulder. She came in. He avoided meeting her eye.

'I wanted to say goodbye, Patrice. I'm going back tomorrow.'

'I'm happy you came. It's more than I can hope for, but still, I'd like to ask for your forgiveness.'

'I don't despise you. Somehow, I sensed this is how it would be. I allowed things to go that far.' She looked him in the eye and fiddled with her lighter.

He was standing leaning on the desk, unshaven, wearing an old Breton-striped shirt and washed-out jeans. He was ashamed. 'I'm asking you to forgive me.'

'Yes, all right.'

'Would you like something to drink?'

'No, I don't want to stay long.'

'Is it finished, then? The research project?'

'Please don't. Sarcasm doesn't suit you.'

'I'm sorry. I hate these conversations.'

'And I hate it when people don't take me seriously.'

'Laura, I didn't mean it like that. Laura.' He was intoxicated by the sound of her name.

'I'll send you everything I get from the press. A few people might turn up here, but I don't think that will be a big deal for you, will it? Just keep the gate closed.'

'No; after all, I did know this was coming.'

'Oh, now that's where you're wrong, Patrice: you didn't know it. But you wanted it ... And ultimately, so did I ...'

He shrugged. Lit a cigarillo, coughed, rubbed his forehead. 'I'm going to stop writing.'

'I hope so, Patrice. Not because of the book, or the dead women, or your late wife, but for your own sake.'

'What will you do?'

'Me? I'll go back. Home. I'm in a good mood — strange, isn't it? I must be the only happy person in this whole story. No, that's not quite true. I don't believe I'm entirely alone in that.'

'Do you mean the Australian?'

'Francesca, yes. I had a long talk with her.'

'Well, at least two people are happy, then.'

'Yes, it's good, Patrice. You should be glad. This suffering — doesn't it strike you as silly now? It must be so stressful to have to live with it, day in, day out ...' Her eyes were glowing; she looked slightly nervous.

He couldn't keep a little smile from his face. The way her fingertips danced, the way she grinned, her head tilted to the left, her frantic smoking — suddenly it all amused him.

'It isn't the suffering, Laura. It really isn't the suffering. You really shouldn't think that.'

'What is it then, Patrice?'

'It's the love ...'

She got up and seemed about to say something, but then thought better of it and sat back down, only to stand up again at once and come over to him. She stood there, smiling. They didn't touch, and for the first time it was all right not to. A wonderful woman, he thought. They smiled, and their smiles soon spilled over into hearty, uninhibited laughter; they were laughing at themselves.

'"Love" ... the way you said that, the look on your face ...' They laughed until they could take no more.

'Can I see you again? Sometime?'

'I don't know. I really don't know, Patrice. For now, let's just leave things as they are. You can call me. You might find yourself in Amsterdam one day, and then you can get in touch ... But first I want to go back to my life. Alone.'

'I guess I'll have to respect your decision.'

'And what will you do?'

'I'll stay here ...'

'Is that all?'

'Maybe I should try writing a romance novel — take you, us, as my inspiration ...'

'Oh, stop it.'

'No, seriously.'

'Then do it. I give you my blessing.'

She kissed him, softly, tenderly. Then she opened her bag, took out the pages that he'd left in her room and put them back on the desk. She pulled out an English edition of *Ice Age* as well, and placed it on top of them.

He stood there a while longer, watching as she walked out to her car and drove away, and then he went back to the house with the dog and drank some of Anne's 'very healthy' herbal tea, which tasted revolting.

He waited for Anne; he'd promised to take her to the station the next morning, to catch the train to Marennes.

★

Anne arrived in Chatou late that night. She sat down in front of the television with a box of biscuits on her lap.

'Stay here — I mean, don't go to Marennes.'

'What?' she asked with her mouth full, putting on an expression of exaggerated surprise.

'What indeed? There's plenty to do here, for both of us. Things that Marie and I wanted to do, that you wanted to do. All of that.'

'I don't know. I mean ...'

'Shout at me, tell me off, do something — but stay!'

'I want to go back first.'

'All right, do it — you'll end up here again in four days anyway, horrified — I know you.'

'And there's a lot going on here, you say?'

'We can change that. You can. Aren't there things you always wanted to do?' He fell silent for a few minutes. Then he said: 'Tell me something.'

'What?'

'The photo of you and Mone, on the steps, at home, the one that Uncle Jules took. Where was I? Why didn't you call me like you usually did when someone was taking those stupid photos?'

'Oh, I know the one you mean. We did call you — don't you remember? It was Maman's birthday, and it was Uncle Pierre, not Jules; the whole house was full, one of those dreadful Duchamp family parties.'

'And?' He had sat down beside her and was now reaching into the biscuit tin.

'Well … we called you. Uncle Pierre and Mone fetched you, having searched everywhere for you — I remember that, too — and then you came outside and Mone pleaded with you, like she always did. And you were annoyed and went back in and slammed the door. Then we took it without you. What made you think of that stupid photo?'

'It isn't a stupid photo, it's a wonderful photo. A really wonderful photo.'

They sat for a while longer, until all the biscuits were gone, and Anne eventually went to get ready for bed. She called back to him from the hallway:

'I'll think about it … But if I do stay, there are a few things we really need to change around here.' He didn't respond, just smiled to himself as he ate the last crumbs from the tin.

76. WOMAN (2004)

She bought a bright red jumper and a denim jacket, now that the weather had turned cool. She bought a pretty, overpriced bag for Lynn, and a black beret for Jen, and took a taxi to the airport. Her only luggage was a large plastic bag. It was a lovely, liberating feeling. She left the book at the hotel; it seemed wrong to throw it away.

She had two hours until her flight from Charles de Gaulle, and she waited in an uncomfortable airport café. It was a beautiful, slightly cloudy October day. She leafed through a British newspaper and bought a few silly souvenirs. Her scalp drew curious glances from strangers.

77. ICE AGE / BOOK 1 (1953)

One day you will dream of me and you will go to my grave, if you should find it, and we will bear the pain together, yours and mine. One day you will write my name on a fogged window, one December evening, when the world is frozen. I won't be there. Very far away, in your memory, that's where I'll be waiting. You won't know the look in my eyes, and you won't know how I smoke and cry and breathe and what I look like asleep. It will be you *now, not* her. *But somewhere, sometime — we will see and recognise one another.*

I was in my grave by the time you were born, but that doesn't matter. I will be the autumn of your life.

I will drive out all the ghosts, take my place on the throne in your soul, right beside your lungs. I don't want you to bring me to life, but to recognise me! In the afternoon sun, when the autumn is putting the last sunbeams in its pockets, greedy, scornful, mean: that's when you will leave the prison that surrounds you, and you will chase the wind, a long, long way, into the land of eternal snow. You will find my palace and come to me.

I will be there — I will be your bridge. Don't doubt it. We will drink time down to the dregs. We will form new words, out of mud, out of clay, never again use a full stop, never pause.

You will read me between every line, your pen will pursue me. You will never be rid of me and you will grow on my dead soul, until you die or I live. Balance out time, do you hear?

You will create me in your image so that you can love.

First camels, then fish, then dragons, they carry us away. Home. What more do you want?

My heart is a scaffold of bones. Am I already dead, and you not yet born?

But kiss my knee. Then I can walk again.

Do nothing, you won't do it. Everyone is going to bed; do nothing, I won't do it.

78. APIDAPI (2004)

She paid his hotel bill for one more week, without telling him — and took the train.

He had promised not to stay in Paris longer than another week. He took her to the station. He gave her a look that was grateful and somehow sad. He said he would write 'about it all'. She just nodded.

He got onto the train with her, hugged her, and she kissed him on the cheek, a little too daringly. She thought he would wave, but after getting off the train he didn't look back, just walked quickly away down the platform. He disappeared into the crowd.

At the Gare du Nord.

79. ICE AGE / BOOK 1 (1953)

It was a damp November evening; she had run the whole way and she was tired. She waited without thinking, unafraid. She even smiled at the people she passed. It was quiet and lovely. She was properly dressed in a school skirt and a white shirt when she arrived at the Gare du Nord. Platform Two was half empty; the train had been standing at the platform for some time and almost all the passengers had embarked. She waited.

19:55. WOULD ALL PASSENGERS PLEASE BOARD THE TRAIN NOW.

The body was that of a very young woman, with no papers. The landlord's report of a missing person led the police to a flat on the rue Bonaparte, but the owner of the building could give them no detailed information about the woman who'd lived there — even the name turned out to be false.

They didn't find many personal effects in the flat. There was a school exercise book filled with writing and drawings, left in a corner beside some empty bottles and a pot of rouge. The box of possessions was deposited with the concierge, who didn't even glance through them. She'd always said the girl was mad and should have been put away in an asylum, before ...

80. ME (2005)

I will be on a plane soon; it won't be long now.

You are gone, wiped from the horizon. That tiny, distant speck has been obliterated.

It has come to an end. And it doesn't feel like the end at all; not like the ending I sensed all this time, when the end had not yet come.

These thoughts gallop around my head. For some reason, a song — 'Juja' — suddenly comes to mind. It's about people who can become Jujas, for whom you can be a Juja. A person worth loving, and whose love for you is worth even more. All at once, I have a desperate urge to listen to that song.

And then I think about Juja, with whom I could battle through every alcoholic night to the bitter end. I think about all the Jujas in the world, who were there when I cried out; all the Jujas who made me dream, all the Jujas who warmed my hands and who were prepared to cry my tears for me. All the Jujas who were lamps lighting every street I walked down.

Jujas ... that was what I called them. It was a word from a song in which a woman idolised her Juja, sang his praises. For a long time I didn't know what the word meant ...

I think about my Juja, who stitched my heart back together after countless wars. Think of my Juja, in whose arms I could rage like an angry bull. I think of another Juja, who gave me this song and the name along with it, when I was ill. And another who could tell me jokes at dawn with his feet up. A Juja who could answer all my questions, by asking me for the answers.

I think of them and feel guilty. I'm angry with myself, but it will pass. I can repair my mistakes, become a Juja for someone again.

And at once I feel like I'm waking up.

The next day I take a taxi to the airport. It drives away. The airport is crowded. I stand outside before checking in my luggage — I have a lot of time to kill. I sit in a café.

A young girl takes a seat next to me.

She's wearing one of these oversized backpacker rucksacks, which frighten me a little: I always have the sense that these rucksacks know better than you do yourself what your trip will be like; they insist it will be as free and easy as possible, forgetting that they themselves look anything but free and easy.

She is holding a guidebook, a guidebook for Paris. I can't help but smile. The girl is reading in English, and I find it hard to place her.

Eventually she looks at me, turns away from the guidebook, and asks me where I'm going.

And I say: 'Home.' And I smile at the strangeness of the word.

She shakes my hand.

'Going to Paris?' I ask.

'Yes,' she says. She's looking for something. 'My grandmother — her name was Fanny too, like me — she knew this woman in the fifties, in Paris …' And she tells me the following story: